Schedule two

ALSO BY GAYLORD DOLD

BAY OF SORROWS

THE WORLD BEAT

RUDE BOYS

A PENNY FOR THE OLD GUY

DISHEVELED CITY

MUSCLE AND BLOOD

COLD CASH

SNAKE EYES

HOT SUMMER

Schedule two

Gaylord Dold

St. Martin's Press
🙢 New York

SCHEDULE TWO. Copyright © 1996 by Gaylord Dold. All rights reserved. Printed in the United States of America. No part of this book may be used or reproduced in any manner whatsoever without written permission except in the case of brief quotations embodied in critical articles or reviews. For information, address St. Martin's Press, 175 Fifth Avenue, New York, N.Y. 10010.

Book design by Ellen R. Sasahara

Library of Congress Cataloging-in-Publication Data

Dold, Gaylord.
    Schedule two / by Gaylord Dold.
        p.   cm.
    ISBN 0-312-14730-9
    I. Title.
    PS3554.O436S34   1996
    813'.54—dc20   96-22418
                                                                CIP

First Edition: September 1996

10 9 8 7 6 5 4 3 2 1

The most profound relationships between
men are based on violence.

Jean-Paul Sartre
Matériaux Autobiographiques

Schedule two

Title 49, Section 841 of the United States Code prohibits the manufacture, possession and sale of certain controlled substances. The most dangerous and addictive of these drugs are listed in Schedule Two of the Act.

Schedule II

(1) Opium and opiate, and any salt, compound, derivative, or preparation of opium or opiate.

(2) Any salt, compound, derivative, or preparation thereof which is chemically equivalent or identical with any of the substances referred to in clause (1), except that these substances shall not include the isoquinoline alkaloids of opium.

(3) Opium poppy and poppy straw.

(4) Coca leaves and any salt, compound, derivative, or preparation of coca leaves, and any salt, compound, derivative, or preparation thereof which is chemically equivalent or identical with any of these substances, except that the substances shall not include decocainized coca leaves or extraction of coca leaves, which extractions do not contain cocaine or ecgonine.

Phase One

This is John Zito, in characteristic mock irony, saying, "Color these fuckers dead." Emphasis on *dead*.

Grace Wu waits in shadow, in a black curve that cuts away from tunnels made by the headlights of squad cars, which have been parked to create a halo effect. She regards the scene with detachment, a way she has of freeing herself from the tag ends and codes of her kind, and still be a part of what's going down. Also, she does not desire to become a focus for John Zito, because she knows John Zito abhors her, wouldn't want her around.

A light mist falls, slicking down the back of John Zito's leather topcoat as he holds his arms close to his chest and leans into the Browning-Ferris dumpster in order to see the victims in the glare of a flashlight held by an officer named Wilson. Leave it to John Zito not to soil his beautiful black leather topcoat while looking at two dead guys, not to get his hands dirty. Grace Wu has already sneaked a look at the dead Koreans who are, right now, face down in the dumpster. She has seen the patches of bare skin at the base of their skulls, gray burned areas that look like miniature blast sites. She can't see their faces, not that it matters.

Two squad cars are in the street, half up on the curb, with their headlights aimed at the dumpster, stars escaping from the lights themselves, while steam streams up from their hoods. It is as if something had caught fire there and had been put out, and now only smoke remains. It is eerie as hell.

Now Zito backs away and says something to Wilson, who leaves the scene and returns to one of the squad cars. Inside the car, two officers are huddled, having a talk. Grace Wu can't hear what they're saying, but she's sure it is something fascinating, surreal. Elsewhere, across the street, two winos are standing, observing, talking together. One of the winos drops a paper bag to the pavement and something inside shatters. It makes a discernible *pop* and the winos laugh. Later the winos will tire and go away, but just when this will happen is uncertain. They are people whose lives aren't governed by necessity. They do things when they find themselves in motion. Grace Wu understands this, because she has been in Hunter's Point a lot lately, driving her taxi around, looking for scores, buying and selling drugs, and trying to make contact.

A derelict named Paulie sits in one of the squad cars too, looking scared and lonely in the backseat. Paulie had been up on Army Street panhandling all day, getting a hot meal at the soup kitchen, and he had wandered back down to Hunter's Point, his own turf, and when it got dark he crawled inside the dumpster where he had been living for six months, if that's what you'd call it. The dumpster is on Evans Avenue near India Basin, behind a paint store which has been out of business for six months.

Paulie has made himself a crib in one corner of the metal bin composed of plywood boxes for furniture, some sheeting of rolled newsprint, and a ragged sleeping bag. When he got inside his crib tonight he saw the Koreans and thought he'd been aced. In his mind he was already negotiating with the two guys for space, not something he wanted to do. When Paulie finally spoke to the two guys, after several anxious moments of thought and silence, they didn't answer back, and Paulie thought they were in a stupor. He looked for their wine hurriedly, but didn't find it. It was dark, and he couldn't see well. Then the mist started and he didn't want to leave the dumpster, so he stayed. Pretty soon, Paulie saw the blotches of blood on the backs of their heads. He jumped out of the dumpster and headed for the Quick Trip at the foot of Evans where the avenue went uphill into tenements.

Right now Paulie thinks he's involved. His whole life is devoted to noninvolvement, and he's scared and upset. Before this, Grace Wu had calmed Paulie down, and got him back in the squad car. All Paulie wanted to know was when the cops were going to get the Koreans out of his dumpster. He says it's his place and he wants it back, *pronto*.

Why am I here? Grace Wu wonders—but she knows. She is here because a heavyset rookie named Stevens got a call from the Quick Trip and Stevens didn't want to be down in Hunter's Point alone, ever. So Stevens rolled down to the Quick Trip and talked to Paulie and made him sit on the curb, and then radioed Grace Wu, whom he'd seen on the freeway moments before. Grace had been taking her taxi home to Geary Boulevard to get some sleep. She heard Stevens on the radio, and when she got down to Evans Avenue she saw Stevens talking to Paulie out in front of the convenience store, the two of them standing in the glaze of fluorescent light, with Paulie looking like he might start to cry at any moment and Stevens glancing nervously around as if the gangs might come out of the night and take him away, vampire-style. She circled her taxi and came up an alley so she couldn't be seen from the street, and parked. You would have thought that Stevens was a little kid who'd just seen Santa Claus, he was that happy to see somebody, anybody, so long as it wasn't a vampire from Hunter's Point.

When Stevens had called her, she had been on I-280 heading straight toward the City. The Transamerica Tower was to her left, the Embarcadero at three o'clock in pilot talk. The glow of the office towers downtown was sheening through the mist and down by the waterfront there was an orange clock that she could almost read, eleven something, time to go home. Just then Stevens came over her police channel asking if she could come down to Hunter's Point. He said he might need backup and Grace translated this as meaning he was scared and wanted to call backup, but didn't want to go through downtown's Hall of Justice, which would take maybe five or ten minutes longer. Grace could imagine Stevens, his skin alive with snakes as he stood on Evans Avenue in the blank night, there in a jungle of graffiti and broken glass.

She turned off the freeway and negotiated surface streets to the Army Street Terminal and across the Islais Creek Channel bridge, then to Third where it crossed Evans. The streetlights glowed orange and there was nobody on the sidewalks. Far away, she could see the red cherry of Stevens's squad car. His headlights cut through the dark five blocks away. She parked in an alley off Fairfax and walked back two blocks. With her luck, the taxi she was driving would be stripped when she got back, but she wanted to see what Stevens had gotten himself into, if it was anything he could handle.

"What are you doing calling me?" she asked Stevens. He was standing beside the passenger door of the squad car, just outside the Quick Trip. Paulie had crouched down on his haunches and was making baby noises, little sucky goo-goo nonsense.

Stevens said, "I saw you going by on 280. I thought it would be faster. You never know."

The premises, the codes, the contexts, Stevens was ignoring them all. Grace was undercover and Stevens shouldn't have called. It was a stupid business.

"What's going on?" Grace asked.

"This is Paulie," Stevens replied.

Inside the Quick Trip a Filipino clerk was looking at the cops through the window. He had on a hair net and he looked frightened. "Hi Paulie," Grace said.

"Paulie found two dead guys in his dumpster," Stevens said. He gestured in the direction of the dumpster, across the street to the paint store.

Paulie had begun to tug at Grace Wu's pant cuff. The guy was wearing two indescribably filthy coats, one inside the other, an outer army surplus unit, a pair of ragged corduroy pants, and tennis shoes. Grace thought he looked young, maybe twenty-seven or -eight, with light blond hair pulled into a ponytail. He was missing teeth and there were sores on his face. Grace couldn't figure how somebody could fall through the cracks that fast, but she knew it happened all the time. Paulie had been swallowed up seriously and entirely, surfacing inside a dumpster. It was dangerous down here, for derelicts and everybody, life expectancy maybe a year at most. It hadn't been long ago that some kids had been going around doing a Clockwork Orange on homeless men in the Basin. She'd heard about half a dozen who'd been set afire as they slept.

"You'd better pull the squad over to the dumpster and set the headlights on it," Grace said. "Look like you know what you're doing. Get Paulie in the backseat and give him a lollipop, will you?" Stevens put Paulie inside the car and pulled it across the street. Grace Wu walked over. She stood there and tried to talk to Paulie.

"They call you Paulie?" she asked. He said yes. "You find those guys?" she asked. Grace Wu had already taken a quick look at the dead Koreans, and come back.

Paulie agreed that he'd found two guys in his dumpster. He went on a run about his wine and when could he get it out of the dumpster. He wondered if the cops were going to keep it and drink it themselves. Grace told him she didn't know, that it wasn't up to her, but that she was sure the cops weren't going to drink his wine. Paulie said he had two liters. He told Grace he'd been living in the dumpster for six months, ever since he'd come across from the East Bay where there were too many street kids on Telegraph, causing the panhandling to get out of whack. It was colder on the City side, but fewer mouths to feed, less competition. Nobody had been around his dumpster in all that time, and now it looked like he was fucked for sure.

That was when a light gray Caprice pulled up and stopped. Grace Wu saw John Zito inside. She could tell it was him by his black leather topcoat. She hides in the shadows and she hears John Zito saying, "Color these fuckers dead," in his deadpan gleeful way. Emphasis on *dead.*

Just then Zito jumps away from the dumpster as if the metal had burned his skin. Stevens leans into his squad car and comforts Paulie, who is whining loudly. Two winos across the street are looking on. One of them breaks a wine bottle, probably intentionally. Everything in Hunter's Point is a test, like being on red alert. The paper sack breaks, making a muffled explosion, neat and tidy.

"The fuck are you doing here, Grace," Zito says, as if he had eyes in the back of his head.

This action is part of Zito's personal style. With everyone he achieves a distance while still having his hands all over them. Grace Wu understands where she fits in with John Zito's universe, even though she is an undercover cop. She is still a woman, and an Asian, and something in this state of affairs drives John Zito crazy. Grace Wu has never quite rationalized her own position. It's racial and political and it infects everything. "Well, Grace," Zito says, louder, so he can be heard by Wilson, and probably Stevens.

Grace wonders how she can answer when she's facing Zito's back. It rankles, oh yes. Now Stevens sends her a terrified SOS glance, begging her by telepathy not to suck him into Zito's circle of hell.

"I was going across 280 and saw Stevens pull in here," she lies. "I thought I might help."

"Somebody sees you here, your operation is fucked. You can take that risk?"

"I'm out of here," Grace says. Stevens looks away, his method of saying thanks.

"I'll chew your butt later," Zito says. There is a salacious tone in his voice. Grace knows this but there is nothing to be done. She doesn't think she'll do an Anita Hill right here on Evans Avenue. Truly, John Zito possesses an entire arsenal of character put-ons, double entendres, private jokes, metaphorical butt-patts, and inside stories, all of which consist of statements made in front of Grace Wu utilizing the false premise that she doesn't understand, when everybody knows she does, even a moron would understand. This is a form of exclusion that Zito practices for sport, the way some men shoot skeet.

"Some interesting dead guys," Grace says.

Grace thinks about what she saw in the dumpster. Paulie had made it almost cozy, with a lean-to on one side, some sprinklings of plastic packing, and gray tarp sheeting for a roof, crates and plywood for furniture. It stinks inside the dumpster, but not from garbage, mostly from paint and varnish. Grace remembers the two bottles of fruit wine. She has seen the Koreans lying side by side, their hands and feet bound with baling wire. They were clothed in Asian hip-hop, black Reeboks and tight pants. One of them was wearing a Cubs warm-up jacket worth maybe two hundred dollars. Both wore gold neck chains. In the dark they looked natural and warm. They looked like dolls. There were even tight pink holes in the back of their heads so you could hang them from your rearview mirror. There was a whiff of Polo, a glint of Rolex. Both had short haircuts and looked clean, well-heeled. Grace couldn't tell if they had been tortured. Grace noticed that Paulie had some crushed pop cans collected in a mesh sack. A capitalist she thought, one of the points of light apparently.

"You seen them?" Zito asks Grace, before she has taken two steps.

"Yeah, thanks," Grace says. Grace tells Zito that her taxi is parked in an alley off Fairfax, nobody will see her. Zito gives her a false compliment, another of his articles of personal attack.

"The fuck you think these Chinese are doing over here in Hunter's Point?" Zito asks. Finally he looks at Grace Wu. They are head on, face to face. Zito has the sleek look of a raven. The nose is sharp, the eyes black. His face is a weapon. "Huh?" he says.

"They're Koreans," Grace says.

"Korean," Zito says. "The fuck's the difference."

Grace shrugs. "To you or to me?" She says this without intonation. But she wonders if she has an accent. She wonders about her moon face, so much unlike Zito's.

Zito laughs. Wilson laughs along with him. Long ago Stevens has abandoned the scene for the anonymity of the near background. He is as invisible as the crackle of the police radios. Grace can see the City through the mist, like a cloud. In her mind she swims toward it, arms pumping.

"To the state of California," Zito says.

"It's something to think about," Grace replies. This means nothing, one of Grace's tricks.

"You think a black gang killed them?" Zito says. "You think this is a little drug war?"

Grace knows it isn't that. She thinks the Koreans were killed somewhere else and dropped off in Paulie's dumpster. "It's something to think about," she says.

"Go on, get out of here," Zito says. Grace Wu has been dismissed.

She drives her taxi back along I-280 into the City. She'll catch I-80 at Harrison and go home that way. There is some traffic off the Bay Bridge, but not much.

Color Grace Wu tired, emphasis on *weary*.

2

It is a cold summer night in San Francisco. Grace Wu has been on the street for ten hours. In that time she has made fifteen deals worth, total, about eight thousand dollars, and she has made one useful contact. A contact is someone in the business above the ounce level, a person on the street who is close to the pounds and kilos, which isn't exactly wholesale yet, but nearly. Contacts are walking possibilities, and the more contacts Grace Wu makes, the more she is a known quantity with a reputation. Grace must grow into a wholesaler. That is the reason she is on the street, to deal and grow.

Grace Wu interacts with everybody. Right now she is involved on a low level with a black woman named Renee, who sells small rocks of crack in the Panhandle. Renee looks ten years old, but she might be forty-five, and is probably somewhere in between. Grace has known Renee for about two weeks, and the two have done one deal. From the very first, Renee seemed to understand that Grace was not a taxi driver, or at least not *just* a taxi driver, but something else entirely. They first met when Grace was ordering a deli sandwich and Renee was hanging around outside the café. When Grace walked out the door with her corned beef, the two looked at one another and a rhythm commenced. Renee had no innate fear of selling crack right on the street, but retailers rarely do. Grace made eye contact and they did a deal right there in front of the deli on Clement Street.

In her two years of doing this kind of thing, Grace has developed an effortless cool that rubs off on people, especially people like Renee. Part of it is that people in the business don't expect an Asian woman to be in the trade. And, of course, no dealer expects to be busted. If Grace busted Renee, she'd probably be on the street in five hours, and even if Renee went down, she would get probation. So there is little deterrent for Renee, and she can afford to have happy encounters with people like Grace.

After they deal, they talk a little, like girls shopping. Renee is an Air Force kid. She was born in Thailand and came to the Bay Area after her mother and father were divorced. She sells to stay close to her white angel, which is cocaine. Renee looks like she might starve to death at any moment. But she is also beautiful in a deathly kind of way.

It's funny, but it often takes Grace hours of thought to reconstruct her two years selling dope, all the deals. During her first six months on the job, Grace bought and sold small quantities of rock cocaine, known as crack, then branched into powder coke, even some hallucinogens, claiming to her friends that she was buying acid to turn the money into coke. Once Grace gained a foothold on the street, she started buying in larger quantities with department and DEA money, always working under John Zito of SFPD and Elgin Lightfoot of the DEA. Zito would give her money and she would buy dope. Sometimes they'd give her dope, and she'd sell it. Now she's selling powder coke on the street in large quantities, which is a dangerous deal, because you don't know whose turf you're stepping on. It is something new for Grace, something worrisome but part of the script. When you step on someone's turf, you can get dusted. This is a risk Grace is voluntarily taking, because it is now her job, although she doesn't know how it got that way, how she got to be a narc. But it happened and here she is.

One of the first things that happened with her newly found script was that she sold a pound of cocaine to a guy named Clemente Moreno. It wasn't scary for Grace exactly, because Moreno was easygoing and he didn't carry a gun. She met Moreno one morning during rush hour, in a park across from the Mission Dolores. Moreno was a pudgy man with a round happy face. Grace carried her pound of coke in a paper sack as if it were her lunch and Moreno walked up to her smiling smoothly. That meant it was going to be an easy deal, like lunch at McDonald's. The grass in the park was green and the sky was blue, and all the time Grace thought about Moreno and the coke. Grace had worried that Moreno would be tough and ignorant, take the coke, but it didn't happen. Moreno treated her like a little sister, all smiles. To her surprise, Grace got eight thousand dollars for some pretty good coke. Grace knew that Moreno would step on the coke with speed and freeze, Methedrine and some Novocaine, then bulk it up with mannite, and have maybe a pound and a half, which he would sell in grams and ounces for twice eight thousand dollars. All of a sudden Grace was really in the business. The whole deal was a song. Moreno smelled like reefer and ale and he was relaxed. Grace handed over the sack and Moreno handed over the money and Grace counted it right there, while the pigeons flew overhead. This may be enough to get Grace mentioned in the right circles, closer and closer to a source. Moreno has a sweet laugh and he uses it. Grace could hear it all the way back to her cab, which was parked by Mission Dolores.

But now it is late and Grace drives down to Land's End. There is a parking place overlooking the Sutro Baths. Grace cuts the engine and sits quietly, listening to the sea lions barking. Down in the dark the animals are there, but Grace can't see them. Their bodies are obscured, but their deep guttural grunts keep coming up out of the ocean where there is a dark hole and the waves are battering the concrete buttresses. It is windy out here by the beach, which makes it seem colder than it is. Grace listens to the sea lions for five minutes, and then walks downhill to the Cliff House and gets a seat at the bar with her back to the plate glass window all the tourists talk about. Somewhere outside is Seal Rock, and way out, Japan.

Elgin Lightfoot is at the bar too. He looks at Grace and flicks recognition her way. Unlike John Zito, Elgin Lightfoot is a human being. And he is a large man, nearly two hundred and fifty pounds, but there are no fat parts, just a barrel chest and strong legs. His face is dangerous and kind both. He is not a man you'd push around. Something in his look creates tension, but he has a good smile when he feels like producing it. His hair is long and black and disheveled, but nicely so. When Grace sits down, she is still tight from her ten hours and she thinks about buying a pack of cigarettes and recommencing her habit. But the moment passes quickly and she is back in the present, away from her bloodstream and its needs. She looks around the Cliff House, its subdued browns, candles flickering on the tables. Surprisingly, it is not crowded on Friday night. Only two or three tables are filled, right by the window. Elgin is eating a plate of boiled shrimp with horseradish sauce.

"So, you got it done with Moreno, huh?" Elgin says.

The bartender is washing glasses behind the bar. He pauses and takes an order from Grace. A minute later he brings Grace a neat vodka with ice and a lemon wedge. Grace takes a sip of the vodka and feels the click inside her head that is part of alcohol's message. It is delicious and ice cold.

"It wasn't a problem," Grace says.

"And here we are on the Pacific Rim," Lightfoot says, making small talk. His talent is management, not coercion. This is another way he is unlike John Zito. "This is going to make John feel proud." Elgin always refers to Zito as John. "No shit, Grace, you're doing great," Elgin says. "Did I ever tell you that?"

"Every time I see you," Grace says.

She likes Elgin Lightfoot as much as she dislikes John Zito. Sometimes she wonders about Elgin's private life, but they never talk about it. Grace knows that Elgin knows everything there is to know about her. That is part of management, the nut. But it would be nice, Grace thinks, if she knew something, anything, about Elgin Lightfoot. It would be nice to know if he was married and had kids. She wonders how he got started working for the DEA out of Los Angeles. But nothing ever comes over Elgin's line. Every few weeks he flies out of LAX and meets Grace somewhere in the Bay Area. He keeps records of everything she is doing, how much money she is spending, what kinds of drugs she is buying, and from whom. Grace imagines that he sends those reports to someone at DEA in Los Angeles, and that they wind up, eventually, at the Department of Justice in Washington. At the end of the line is a bureaucrat, but Elgin is the head of the line, not a bureaucrat. He is a line manager, but she likes him. That's important to her. "I don't mind telling you I was scared a little," she tells him.

Elgin nods and looks away, checking out Cliff House. Sometimes they meet in Chinatown in San Francisco, and sometimes they meet in Oakland at a Mexican restaurant called Rosa's. But this is the first time for Cliff House. Grace takes it as a kind of joke, meeting where there are always tourists looking for seals.

"I spoke to John today," Elgin says. "I told him I was gearing you up for the big time. You're ready. You know it's going to happen, so I'm not telling you anything you don't know already."

"I know, Elgin," Grace says.

"Stay with Moreno."

"That's easy for now," Grace says.

"But I want something bigger in the East Bay," Elgin says.

"How much are we talking about, Elgin?"

Elgin waits until the bartender serves another customer at the end of the bar. The foghorns sound far away, and then nearby. Grace feels unreal. She feels that way a lot of times. She is playing a part that is not her, but she must be getting good at it, she is fooling many people. She likes roles. It requires her to fool herself.

"We just want you to become necessary to Moreno," Elgin says.

"One or two buys a week?"

"Whatever you think is best. You do business on any level with Moreno and he'll get used to it. He'll like it. Maybe you can arrange some bigger sales, and make him go higher on his food chain. Say six weeks from now we try to buy twenty pounds from him. Instead of selling to him, we want to buy, and he gets these stars in his eyes, and he climbs up the wall looking for coke. When that happens, he takes you in as his partner. He smells our money, Grace, and he takes you in."

"I think I know how it works," Grace says.

"Hey, I'm not patronizing you, Grace," Elgin says. "If I lay it all out for you, it's because I want it to work."

"Do you have anything more on Moreno?" Grace asks.

"His hometown is Morelia. We've plugged everybody in that town for information on him. He's a *nada* there, Grace. He buys his shit from some Los Angeles people on Wilcox Boulevard. From there the pipeline goes to Panama. You want to vacation sometime in Panama, you let me know. I can get you a room with a view." Elgin smiles, letting Grace see it for once. "Seriously, Grace," Elgin says quietly, "I can get you a million dollars when you need it. You can hurt somebody with that kind of money." Elgin peels a shrimp and douses it with horseradish and eats it. Someone has fed the jukebox, and an old Limelighters tune is playing. The tune is from another time, another place, something that used to be here, but isn't anymore.

Grace takes a spiral notebook from her shoulder bag and lays it on the counter in front of her drink. She says nothing, but goes to the ladies' room and washes her face and waits. Elgin will pick up the notebook and put it in his suit coat pocket, then take it to Los Angeles and enter it on the computer. Each night when she goes home, Grace writes down everything that happens to her during the day when she is doing deals. She has written down the details of her deal with Clemente Moreno. She's written down her meeting with Renee, and who's new on the Fell Street block where the Panhandle runs into the Park. She has also written about a new guy, someone big in the East Bay named Kyungmoon Nho, a heroin connection. Now, she dries her face and thinks about Elgin again. She knows they will spend only a few more minutes together, then her thread to someone real will be broken.

Grace steals a glance in the mirror. She is alone in the bathroom and she can hear the foghorns. She frowns and pouts, trying to look more or less Chinese, as if she could will her appearance to be another way, this, then that. Deciding she likes her face, she splashes some more water on it. She goes back to the bar where Elgin has finished his shrimp. He looks ready to go.

"There's a guy named Kyungmoon Nho," Grace says. Elgin shows an immediate interest. "He's East Bay. I met him out in the street, believe it or not."

"Cultivate him like a rose, Grace," Elgin says. "I'm real serious about that."

"He's big."

"Huge," Elgin says. "I can't say much more."

"I'll do what I can," Grace replies.

Elgin is quiet. He has had his cue to leave, but he hasn't done it yet. "How's your head, Grace?" he asks.

Grace ponders the truth. For the moment an answer escapes her, but then it comes to her that she hasn't a clue. "My head is good, Elgin," she says. "By the way," she continues, "two Korean dealers were killed, dumped at Hunter's Point."

"I heard," Elgin says.

"Tell Zito it wasn't the black gangs. He thinks there's a war, but there isn't."

"Who did it?"

"I'll work on that one," Grace says.

Then Elgin is gone. He drops a ten-dollar bill on the bar and hurries out the door. Grace is in the middle of a sentence but it trails off. Grace realizes that it was something personal, now gone forever.

a nother Saturday in a succession of Saturdays, a life full of Saturdays. Grace Wu is on the roof of her building on Geary Boulevard, where she rents a one-bedroom apartment, second floor front. The landlords are newly landed Russian emigrants named Piltka, who adopt an abused and hangdog way in their actions. Their son is a lawyer in the financial district. The Piltkas claim to be very protective of Grace, indeed of all their tenants, whom they refer to as family. Actually, the Piltkas come inside Grace's apartment when she isn't there and look around the place, even leaving overt evidence that they've been inside, perhaps to increase their power and mystery. Grace knows they open her mailbox downstairs with their key, and examine her mail. It isn't as if Grace has been singled out for such treatment. All of the tenants are in the same boat. Grace wonders if the Piltkas spend their days and nights worrying about tenants, the rent, whether existence is such a struggle for them that they constantly snoop through their own heads, or if this is something left over from the old country. Nonetheless, Grace maintains good relations with them because she requires an absolutely spotless personal and private life. There can be no moving, looking for apartments, readjustments. Grace must be inert. She must pass through the screens of life without leaving a telltale trace.

In order to do this, Grace pays the rent early, sometimes as much as a week in advance of the due date. Even though the rent is six hundred dollars a month, somewhat high, she never complains. She has lived in the apartment for two years, and the rent has been raised every six months, twenty dollars at a time. She doesn't complain or question the motives of her landlords, who watch her come and go from their office on the ground floor, facing Geary Boulevard. Of course, there is nothing of interest in her mail either, just a letter every month from her mother, the regular bills. Mrs. Piltka smiles at Grace and Grace returns the smile, all with meaningless ease.

When Grace went undercover she knew she would have to live a characterless life, at least for a while. Her success in doing this surprised her at first, but now she realizes that she could have rented almost any apartment or small house on the Avenues, in the Sunset, or along Clement Street, and could have achieved the same result. She is not the only person in this area who lives anonymously. Her apartment is narrow and somewhat dark, with its windows on the east. She opens the door to a long hallway. Her bedroom is to the right facing Geary Boulevard, with two windows on the south, but no light, given the positioning of the building itself. The bedroom is noisy all the time, or at least until about two o'clock in the morning when the buses stop going by every twenty minutes. There are drunks on the street at all hours and cars going and coming too. A fish and chips joint is located two doors down from her building. Its patrons are Canadian and Australian sailors who drink strong Foster's beer and play darts, and begin to sing about two o'clock in the morning on weekends. By the City's standards, there is not a lot of crime along Geary, way out in the Avenues, but that is just window dressing. Crime is everywhere, and everybody knows it.

Grace's living room is small and square, with beige carpeting of nameless design. A single window in the shotgun kitchen looks out on the fire escape, letting in only a little afternoon light. It doesn't matter, this problem with the light and the noise, because Grace isn't home much. She is usually out driving her taxi and making drug deals. Grace does a little cooking, but she is usually too tired to bother. It is from the kitchen window that Grace gets up to the roof. She climbs through it, onto the fire escape, and there she is.

Grace is feeding her rabbits. She keeps them in three connected wire cages next to the landing. This is a concession the Piltkas have made to Grace Wu, probably because Grace is early with the rent, and makes no trouble about their diurnal visits to her apartment when she is gone. The rabbits are male harlequins who can live outside year round because of the mild weather. There is a plywood roof over the cages, which slopes enough to keep off the rain, which falls mainly during the winter months but sometimes continues into early- and mid-spring. This morning the rabbits are nosing their cages hungrily, anticipating Grace. Their food consists of bits of carrots and cabbage, some lemon rinds and leftover tomato peelings and cores.

One afternoon, just after Grace went undercover, she was driving around the Sacramento delta. It was a lark, a way to see something different, and she decided to visit two or three semi-ghost towns that had once been inhabited by the descendants of Chinese laborers who had worked on the Central and Southern Pacific railroads before the turn of the century. The towns had been centers of real Chinese culture in California. But now they were nearly deserted, no longer centers of anything. Most of the people who lived there were old, existing on Social Security or welfare, and their small savings accounts.

In one of the towns Grace went to an estate sale and saw the rabbits. She bought them on impulse from an old Chinese widow whose husband had been dead for about a month. The rabbits came with their cages and the plywood roof, and Grace paid fifty dollars for all of it. Grace got her brother Greg to help her transport the rabbits to San Francisco, and up onto the roof. She put aluminum cooking pans underneath the cages to catch the rabbit shit, and every Saturday Grace disposes of it in a dumpster behind the apartment building.

Grace opens the cages one by one and places bits of carrot under the rabbits' noses. They each nuzzle her hand and chew the food. From a can, she pours fresh water into porcelain dog bowls, then locks the cages. Someday she expects to come onto the roof and find the rabbits stolen. She has prepared herself mentally for this eventuality by refusing to give the rabbits names. Then, perhaps, nobody will ever find out about them. She has lived in the City long enough to know that loss is what urban life is about, but she still hopes. Who knows, she has had the rabbits for two years now, and they're still around. This is a good streak, she thinks, considering her luck with pets as a child. Before she started running away from home and getting into trouble, Grace had owned some dogs and cats that were always getting killed or lost. After she became an adolescent, her life was too, as they say, unstructured to have pets. Now the rabbits lend an appearance of structure, maybe that's what they do.

This morning Grace is wearing bluejeans and a blue woolen sweater. Her karate clothes are downstairs in a gym bag, her *gee* and brown belt. When Grace finishes with the rabbits, she sits down on an avocado crate and studies the Bay Area skyline in all directions. Early in the morning the sky is breathtakingly clear to the horizon, and a fresh breeze is blowing off the ocean. Grace can't see a single cloud in the sky, even over the East Bay hills where there are usually a few piling up even in summer. Since the big fires a few years ago, there are bare patches of brown in the Oakland and Berkeley hills where the trees burned away, and all the grass too. There are blank spots in the picture where big houses have burned down and have not been rebuilt because of insurance problems and delays. All that's left in those spots are charred foundations and a few chimneys. Grace knows personally five or six drug dealers from Oakland and Berkeley who had expensive houses completely destroyed by fire, but haven't rebuilt because they didn't have insurance. They are coke dealers who pay cash and don't buy insurance. Pretty soon they'll build up their stashes again, and move over to Sausalito, let all the other people hassle with lawyers and insurance companies.

Looking around, Grace can see the tip of the Golden Gate Bridge. As usual in summer there is a mass of white fog over the entrance to the bay that stretches in as far as Angel Island and Alcatraz. As the day wears on, the fog will retreat slightly, back out onto the cold surface of the ocean, but when night comes it will come back onto the Avenues as mist, sometimes covering the streets so that visibility drops to nearly zero. Marin County is over there too, far away and green, and Grace can trace with her eye its curves, and the gray peak of Tamalpais. Just now a jet streaks over, making noise.

Grace's mother and father live in Los Angeles. They moved there six or seven years ago, to Encino out in the Valley. Grace is third generation. Her parents were raised in Hong Kong, their parents in nearby Canton. Her paternal grandfather is still alive, and Grace's parents receive an occasional letter from him. The old man is eighty years old. Grace has read some of his letters because she can read Chinese. Still, Grace is a Californian, born at San Francisco General Hospital, and raised on Washington Street near Chinatown. Early on she thought she was losing her cultural identity, becoming, by definition, a Californian, no longer wholly Chinese. It is this mongrelism that has gotten her offtrack, away from herself. The odd thing is that she thinks she has a lot of *wu-li*, or inner organic power, and she knows she has a feeling for the Tao. The rabbits are Tao. Her relationship with the Piltkas is Tao. Being an undercover narcotics cop is strictly California.

Grace's father is a modestly successful importer of a variety of small items like chess computers, calculators, some fashion items, and tools. He is a hard small chattery man with a bad temper and a penchant for gambling. He spends a lot of time with his Chinese cronies, and knows members of the gangs, tongs, and associations, though he was never connected in any business way to these people. Now that he is older, and living in Encino, he spends less time gambling and hanging out with his friends, but it is what he would do if he could.

He paid little attention to Grace when she was a child. Nor did he care about her brother Greg. In this regard he was a Chinese father whose ideals had been corrupted. By the time Grace was fifteen, she was alienated and angry, and she began to get into trouble. Nothing serious happened to Grace. She missed some school, and stayed out at night. In her culture, this was a major problem. Grace calls her mother from time to time and they talk. Grace does not talk to her father. They never mention brother Greg, who has a heroin habit and isn't much seen.

Even after all the negative stuff, Grace and her mother have a kind of relationship. Her mother studied to be a dancer at school in Hong Kong, in the classical tradition, but later married mostly to get to the United States. Grace and her mother share *wu-li*, an artistic nature, and an even temperament, so different from Grace's father. Grace admires her mother's inner strength, but she doesn't admire her silence. Grace's mother admires Grace's outspokenness, even though it frightens her, and isn't Chinese. Finally, joining the police force was something that neither of Grace's parents understood at all. If they knew what Grace really did they would both be completely shocked and disillusioned by their daughter. Grace's work is never mentioned.

After feeding the rabbits, Grace goes downstairs and drives across the Bay Bridge to her dojo in Oakland. She has studied karate for two years, ever since she went undercover. It has a special place in her life. It is not an obsession, but it does dominate her physical being. She never leaves the discipline behind. She has come to believe that karate is not about self-defense, nor about self-denial, even though defense is an important byproduct of the many hours of practice and work. In fact, karate is not about violence at all. Grace is subtly amused when she hears her fellow students talk about their nightly jogs around Lake Merritt in Oakland, hoping that they will be attacked by muggers or thieves, who will, in turn, get their asses kicked for their trouble. But for Grace, Japanese karate, *shoto-kan,* is too essential to waste with fantasy. It is not a transcendent discipline, but it is the next best thing. It teaches you to stay on the ground and go right through an object, a target. It teaches you to see a point and strike six inches beyond. Grace enjoys the utter exhaustion that her workouts bring, the sense of well-being which follows, and the emptiness that is a concomitant of both. It is better than heroin, even though heroin was very good.

Grace is in the dojo for two hours. Then she showers and drives up Telegraph and has a bowl of soup and a sandwich at the Bateau Ivre. She sits in the window of the trendy lunch spot and watches the street people of Berkeley march up and down, panhandling and begging, selling grass, tranquilizers, Quaaludes. It was on Telegraph Avenue, about six months ago, that she first ran into Kyungmoon Nho while she was cruising downtown Oakland, right around Jack London Square. She knew the Square was beginning to get a reputation as a major heroin buyers' hangout. It was late in the evening and in the middle of the week, and Grace was parked down the street from the Tribune building. Grace had just sold some powder coke when Kyungmoon Nho, the Korean big-timer, got in the back of her cab. He was slightly built, wearing a black cowboy hat with silver and turquoise buckles on the brim.

"You just gonna drive around, OK," Nho had said.

Grace drove a triangle up Telegraph, down Webster and over to College, and then back down Telegraph again while they talked. Nho told Grace he knew she was dealing coke on Telegraph, and that it was all right with him because it wasn't his product. He adopted an amused, slightly superior air, probably because Grace was a woman, a strange kind of dealer. A long time passed with nothing happening, when all of the sudden Grace saw her chance passing and asked Kyungmoon Nho if he needed somebody to run some heroin around the City.

Nho touched his chin. "You a cop?" he asked.

They were downtown again, crowds on the sidewalk. Grace thought for a minute. "I'm no cop," she said.

"You don't smell like a cop," Nho said. He had gotten out of the cab and was standing on the sidewalk. "But then maybe all that good pussy smell cover it up."

4

IRE SEASON IN CALIFORNIA say the headlines of the San Francisco *Chronicle*, though, in fact, fires are raging throughout the western United States. John Zito, with his forehead pressed against the glass of the patio doors, sweating, can see the Sunday paper reflected, spread out on the carpet where he must have thrown it yesterday. Most of the major fires are in southern California where development and drought lead to inevitable chaparral burns, which take down houses and commercial structures, skip over freeways, threaten everything in their path. But there are fires elsewhere, woodland burns in the Sierra foothills near Sonora and Chico, top fires in Mendocino County where the fire crews can't reach them to make a perimeter, two thousand acres, five thousand acres, smaller ones here and there all over the place. One fire is burning up behind I-80 where the Bay Area suburbs have covered the grassland with condominiums, townhouses, shopping centers, and strip malls. All those tanning salons up in smoke. No rain for years, everybody talking about water. From where John Zito is standing with his head against the patio glass, he can see down the sloping backyard of his San Rafael home, across the north bay, all the way to the hills north of Berkeley, beyond which there is layered purple and gray smoke from a six-hundred-acre fire.

John Zito has a terrible hangover, one of the worst ever. His eyes are swollen and his lips are parched, and he feels dry down to the bone even though he drank two Diet Pepsis when he got out of bed. The patio he is looking at is a flagged area that leans down into an expanse of wild rose and ice plant. There is another suburban house down there. He can see its roof through the trees. There are hundreds of houses like these poised on the hillsides of San Rafael, above Sausalito and San Quentin, and a black asphalt road winds up and down through the hills, connecting all the houses to a road at the bottom of the hill, which connects eventually to the freeway and the Golden Gate Bridge, maybe six miles away as the crow flies. In the backyard there is a young lemon tree full of unripe green fruit. A hummingbird feeder hangs empty on the eave. Whitecaps bump in San Rafael Bay and there are sailboats on the water.

Zito takes a long shower. As the water runs off his head, down his body, he tries to remember back to the time before he got drunk and stoned, to last night, before he started drinking in earnest. What he wants to do is picture his wife, Lenore, in some locus of real life, before she left. When he got out of bed this morning and went into the kitchen, there were dozens of San Miguel bottles on the countertop, and an open bottle of Glenlivet that was half empty, or half full. He gets an image. He kicks out at Lenore, maybe punches her in the temple or the jaw. For a moment, wiping hot water out of his eyes, a wave of guilt suffocates his mind. These are emotions triggered by what he can't remember, as much as by what he can. There is no anguish here, only self-loathing and anger.

Thirty minutes later Zito is dressed in a suit. Standing in the kitchen he is in place in a quiet suburban scene, his reflection captured in the window glass. He is so detached from this environment that it might as well be a museum. He's someone who's paid admission to witness his own life. A dry white light bathes the tile, the porcelain surfaces. The appliances seem to glow and growl.

Zito is certain that Lenore won't be coming back, not unless it's with a sheriff's deputy and some legal process. He opens the door which leads from the kitchen to their three-car garage and makes certain that her Lincoln is gone, and it is. Nausea is making it hard for him to concentrate. He takes two Valium, washing the capsules down with Glenlivet, straight from the bottle. There is a reason he is detached. The house belongs lock, stock, and barrel to his wife, really her father. Zito owns his clothes and his weapons, but the rest belongs to her. When she wants it back she is going to come and get it and there is nothing Zito can do to stop her, nothing he would want to do right now. It is going to happen, he is sure. It would be just like her to have photographs made of her bruises, and send them to his boss.

Zito vomits hard into the kitchen sink. The vomit is a viscid liquid colored brown, some of it splashing on the cuff of his clean white shirt. Leaning over the sink, with his head supported in his hands, Zito gets rid of the nausea. But now he is plagued by anxiety and anger both, the twin towers of his existence. When he feels steady enough, he goes into the bathroom and cleans out his blow, what Methedrine he has, and puts it in a paper bag, just in case Lenore comes home while he is in San Francisco today. Before he leaves for the City, Zito takes three Tylenol and drinks some milk.

It takes forty minutes to get across the Golden Gate Bridge, downtown, and to park in the city parking garage. He has an office in the Hall of Justice, and when Zito finally makes it he sees some traces of Elgin Lightfoot. It is well after nine o'clock, and John Zito is late. He sits down in the air conditioning. The room is cold and mechanical, even though it can't be more than sixty-five degrees outside.

When Lightfoot comes in, he is well dressed in a gray western-cut suit and a string tie. Zito doesn't bother to explain why he is late, but he does try to look busy and harried in order to make Lightfoot think something has caused this minor fuck-up. In this way, Zito avoids announcing a lie. For Zito, it is better to live a lie than to confess to one. Actually, life has been going this way for Zito as much as five years now. Trying to maintain, Zito just manages to get by. At times, he realizes that his lined and sweaty face must be giving his lifestyle away, but he hopes that in this evil environment it will pass. Everybody looks pale and flaccid in the artificial light of the Hall of Justice. Zito has passed his illnesses off as emotional stress, the line-of-duty thing. It is the premise that Zito hopes will go on excusing his lateness, and all the other shit he is doing.

"You want some coffee?" Zito says.

Both men are sitting with the door closed. They are alone and it is quiet. Lightfoot declines the coffee. He has been up since four o'clock, having taken the early PSA flight from LAX. He's had his coffee.

"I'm bringing you some gold, John," Lightfoot announces.

"But first—" Zito is sick, nauseated. He is finding it hard to concentrate. His mind is assailed by the bitch Lenore, and by her rich father. He knows they are going to clean him out, financially and emotionally. He imagines that he will wind up in a fleabag room on Sutter. He doesn't particularly like the house in San Rafael, but it is worth about four hundred thousand dollars and he likes that.

"But first I want to talk about Grace Wu," Lightfoot says, taking the lead. "I think her two years on the street is about to pay off. She's met someone in the East Bay who I think is very close to the source. She's a quiet lady, John, but I think she's right on to Hong Kong, a heartbeat away."

Zito nods, touching his forehead. There is a film of sweat lying on his skin and he wonders if Lightfoot can see it. Zito can feel the Tylenol, it is making him sick. "Grace is all right," he mumbles. "I don't have any complaints about her."

"She's underutilized, John," Lightfoot says.

"Meaning?" Zito asks.

"Meaning, we need more bang for the buck with her. I know down deep you don't want her doing any big busts. I know you'd like her to stick to small-time dealers and their suppliers, but just now I think she's so close she's hot. You can feel her getting there. You can feel her, John." Now Lightfoot wishes he had asked for coffee. It would give him something to do with his hands, a way to fill these silences between sentence exchanges. He doesn't like John Zito, and it isn't anything personal. Maybe someday Zito's heart rate will kick up, and he'll become a mensch. For now, Lightfoot wishes he was a more enthusiastic cop. But these transformations are things Lightfoot hardly believes in. He deals solely with the present tense. "Meaning I think a lot of Grace. I think she can handle this fucker in the East Bay."

"You talking personally, or do you have something else in mind?" Zito smiles salaciously. There is a fly inside his head. It is licking his eyeballs. "You fucking her, Elgin?" Zito jokes.

Lightfoot sighs and closes his eyes. He envisions his apartment off Venice Boulevard in Santa Monica, where he has lived for the better part of five years. In his reverie he has two cats in his lap and he is watching a Lakers game on TV. The good old days with Magic streaking down the lane, off to Worthy, score. The apartment is quiet except for a jet careening over to the airport, not an unpleasant urban sound. The cats are sleeping, purring. Chick Hearn is extolling the virtues of Magic. Lightfoot says, "Bang for the buck, yeah I get it, John. Very funny." There is no animosity in his voice. He has to work with Zito and tolerance and management are the keys. In his life, he works with hundreds of Zitos, and worse. "So, what do you say? You with me on this one, John?"

"Drive me someplace, let me out," Zito says. "She's my cop, but you want to utilize her, you tell me when, where, and how, then we'll see."

Lightfoot has the facts and figures in a notebook. The notebook is one of ten he takes care of personally. It is his portfolio, and Grace Wu is the only woman. The DEA investment in her amounts to about a hundred thousand dollars in two years, give or take a few thousand. DEA picks up a share of her salary and does part of her training. They bring Grace down to Los Angeles, they send her to Washington. Then they push her out of the nest and start her career in the drug business. Only now Lightfoot knows that Grace is on to something real. He likes her getting close to Clemente Moreno, but he's enthusiastic about her approach to Kyungmoon Nho. This last name has drawn interest as far as D.C., which is a long way. It is this interest that Lightfoot wishes to exploit. He knows that Grace Wu has a past, drug user, runaway, and that her brother is in the land of nod most of the time. But it isn't her past he cares about, it's her future. Elgin knows she is smart, and has good street sense. The way he thinks about it, her past is a plus on the street. Add the pluses and minuses, and you get a plus with Grace. This is what Light-foot tells Zito, who appears to listen.

"Let's invest in her," Lightfoot says.

"How much?" Zito asks.

"Up to a million."

Zito is surprised, you might say shocked. "You want to let her fly to this Korean with that kind of money?"

Lightfoot says hell yes. It depends on how the situation develops, but Grace Wu has locked on to both Clemente Moreno and Kyungmoon Nho. "I want your permission. I want your enthusiastic approval, John," Lightfoot says. "I'd like to share all my intelligence on Nho with her, but I can't do it unless you sign off on this thing. And I can't let her get close to Nho without my help."

Zito has mixed feelings. The million would make his budget look very good, and he could use the publicity if there was a big East Bay bust. On the other hand, he doesn't trust Grace Wu because she's a woman, and women are bad luck. Before he can fix on what he wants to say to Lightfoot, his mind wanders, miles away. In the inventory of his own possibility, Zito sees nothing. He owes seventeen thousand dollars on his new Jeep Cherokee, four eighty-five a month. His savings account at Crocker Bank is dead empty. Both the Visa and Gold Discover cards are maxed out, and he's getting deeper every day at eighteen percent annualized. Lenore was his safety net. He resents her for it, but that's the way it was. They had a good year together before he found out she was a bitch.

"I want reports," Zito says.

"Good, good," Lightfoot says. "You'll get a folder with a plan and a budget. Grace will work hard on this, John, I'm telling you she's got what it takes. Try to lighten up on her for now. She'll be busy. Anytime you have any questions, you call me down in Los Angeles, OK?"

"She's still my officer," Zito says.

"And our money."

"And I thought it was the taxpayers' money," Zito says.

Lightfoot touches his string tie. Now he is feeling pretty good, having just gotten back from a short vacation. Sometimes when he goes home to Montana, it depresses him and he comes back feeling worse than if he'd never gone. But this time in Kalispell, even though it was cool, he played a lot of basketball with some kids on the reservation, and he spent some quality time with his sister and her son, whose husband finally disappeared for good. The apple trees had been in fruit and he took his sister and her boy on a picnic in the hills. They enjoyed themselves for a whole day before he took them back to the trailer. They made some fried chicken and sat up watching TV together. Lightfoot knows that his sister drinks too much, and that sometimes she neglects her son, but this time it was fine. There is some resentment, but leaving the reservation is a two-edged sword.

The two men rise and shake hands. Zito's palm is wet and he makes the gesture quickly. After Lightfoot leaves, Zito takes a Valium and sits back down. He looks at the clock. In an hour, he can go to a bar on California Street and have a drink and call home, see if Lenore is there.

his afternoon Kyungmoon Nho is overwhelmed with pride. A bright three o'clock sun is shining on his brand-new Lexus LS400, for which he paid forty thousand dollars in cash to a car dealer in San Jose, counting the money out to the surprised sales manager in crisp, one-hundred-dollar bills. This automobile is fully equipped, leather electric seats, tinted windows, a fax machine, in-situ telephone, and four thousand dollars worth of sound, so much sound you could blow out your ears if you wanted. When Nho drives around the East Bay, surveying the scene, sometimes he turns on the fax and lets it warm up, especially at night, because the fax makes a nice hum, its red go-lights making a nice counterpoint to the space-age gauge faces in dark green.

There are thirty suits hanging in the closet of the house he owns in El Cerrito, high up in the hills at the end of a semi-private drive. From Nho's front yard he can see the entire Bay Area, a spectacular view of the golds and reds of the Golden Gate sunsets. Sometimes Nho stands outside and smokes a number and imagines Korea, thousands of miles across the Pacific, a cold bump of land with snow. He has come a long way, both literally and figuratively. This is his American Dream come true.

But what Nho is most proud of among his many expensive possessions is his six dozen pairs of shoes, arranged according to color and style, right under the suits in his walk-in closet. This is what he thinks about as he drives the Lexus up into the hills on a glorious day in the East Bay, his shoes. When he finally reaches the house in El Cerrito he shuts down the Lexus. The car operates like a jet, he imagines, making smooth hushed noises, operating, interfacing, rather than running.

The El Cerrito house is surrounded by eucalyptus groves and lemon trees, fields of untended California poppies. When Nho shuts down the Lexus there is no internal sound. He pivots his left leg from behind the steering wheel and allows the sun to soak down on his Moroccan slip-ons, which cost him two hundred and forty dollars, cash, at a leather import shop in the Piedmont. They are beautiful shoes. As he walks in these slip-ons, Nho feels as though he were flying, they are that soft and image-increasing, enhancing his self-esteem in ways too numerous to detail. After a moment's hesitation, looking down at his shoes, Nho remembers what it is about the shoes that engages him, those days in Korea when he was too poor to own a single pair of shoes, and went about town with bare feet, even in the cold. His feet were constantly cold in Seoul. This will never happen again, he thinks. He is free in the land of opportunity and justice.

Even in Seoul Nho used to dream about shoes. Born in an enormous shanty town on the outskirts of the capital, before the economic miracle, as they say, Kyungmoon Nho was a street kid, an urchin who shined shoes first, then dreamed of owning his own pair. It didn't take long to get out. Pretty soon he was an independent businessman, kidnapping shop girls and laundresses, runaways, and students who'd had too much to drink on Saturday night. He would bundle them into his minivan and drive them around the slums of Seoul while two *gahmpeh* thugs kept watch over them in the back of the van.

It was a simple business. They would see a woman late at night, alone or with a friend in a secluded area, and they would swoop down and surround her and force her into the back of the van. One of the *gahmpeh* would bind the woman. It took almost no effort to locate a Korean businessman or Japanese tourist who would pay for an evening with the woman. Kyungmoon Nho would stand outside the minivan while the woman was being used, imagining what was going on, looking inside, all for a cash price, up front. It was a good business with very little risk. The women were always poor, thus without power. If any students were kidnapped, Nho relied upon prevailing attitudes to cover his behavior, attitudes that dismissed the woman's pleas, which owed much to the culture's *she deserved it* sensibility. In this way, Kyungmoon Nho graduated into the drug-smuggling trade, then into guns, and eventually into the United States of America by way of Hong Kong, where the prevailing attitudes and sensibilities were really gonzo, where there were so many guns and drugs it was almost too easy.

Nho is wearing gray linen pants, with a thin see-through shirt made of black silk that is as thin as the kid leather of his Moroccan shoes. He likes the soft feel of his shirt. He likes hearing himself move when he walks, the sensation of creating a wake, like being inside a cloud.

Nho locks the car and walks up the flagstone path and sees the front door to his house in El Cerrito open and the guy named Kip standing behind it in semidarkness. Nho prides himself, too, on his eye for detail. He has, he believes, a snakelike ability to envelope everything, wrap himself around it. He believes that it is this talent, his acts of careful preparation and mental acuity that have brought him all the way across the Pacific Rim, from the slums of Seoul to the heights of the San Pablo ridge, where he can look down on six million people, most of them Caucasian or black. Before going inside the house, standing so high above the Bay Area, he thinks how fortunate it is that so many among these six million are interested in guns and drugs. This is a good and happy life, better than kidnapping shop girls.

Besides Kip, there are three men in the living room of the house. The room itself is a large walk-through to the back, including a dining area. It is full of cigarette smoke. Korean pop music is playing on high power. Kip, a small, lithe Korean, turns down the music. The Glock tucked into his jeans is the only weapon visible. The other Koreans are sitting on a sofa drinking bottled beer, picking at little paper cups of kimchi and spiced shrimp. As soon as Nho enters the room, the two Koreans eating and drinking begin to clean up their mess, put out their cigarettes, haul their bottles and paper cups to the kitchen. Kip goes around emptying ashtrays. The drapes in the back of the room are opened and diffuse light enters the room, illuminating its simple furniture, the light gray carpet, the wood fixtures Nho has painted in black and gold leaf. Ten minutes later a taxi pulls up in the circular drive and a Korean named Keok Kim comes inside the house. He notices the faint aroma of marijuana in the room and his eyes take a moment to adjust to the dusty faint light of the table lamps, a definite contrast to the high blue California afternoon light. Keok Kim is over from Hong Kong. Everybody defers to him because this is the order of things. Nho doesn't like it, but it is worth it for the money he is making.

They speak in Korean.

"You had a good trip, I hope?" Nho asks.

"Bad stupid movies," Mr. Kim says. "Eddie Murphy all the way." All the men laugh together politely.

Things are safe here. There is no telephone in the house. Kip remains inside the house most of the time, except when he drives down to the Oakland flats on errands, or when he goes somewhere as a bodyguard to Nho. Kip takes care of the grounds, keeping the grass mowed, the hibiscus trimmed. None of the men in the room have proper immigration documents, except for Mr. Kim who carries a British passport (Hong Kong) and a B visa good for twenty entries into the United States over the next three years. Mr. Kim's I-94 is in proper order. Unlike the other men, he is documented, a national in good standing.

"Please give my regards to the gentlemen in Hong Kong," Nho says. Mr. Kim politely acknowledges this bit of the drama. Nho lights a cigarette and places it in one of the clean ashtrays where it smolders. Directly thereafter, the two wholesalers on the couch light up. All of the men in the room are less than five and a half feet tall. But unlike the others, Mr. Kim is extremely well built inside his blue business suit and white dress shirt. He looks like a gymnast or swimmer, or a judo artist. His hair is black, gray around the edges.

"What are your numbers?" Mr. Kim asks, opening the business session.

"Fifty-five a week," Nho answers. Nho nods and Kip puts on a record, Korean classic *gayagum* music. This music remains in the background at all times. Neither Nho nor Kip would dare play any of the schmaltzy Korean pop-schlock they really enjoy while Mr. Kim is in the El Cerrito house. "It goes up and down," Nho continues, "but we're making good progress."

Mr. Kim nods, obviously expressing pleasure.

Nho requests that Kip get the money for Mr. Kim. A brief hiatus of silence develops, which is polite, while Kip leaves the room to retrieve the money that is kept in a locked safe in the back bedroom. Very soon Kip returns holding a metal briefcase, which he places on the teak coffee table in front of Mr. Kim. There is nearly three hundred thousand dollars inside, which is the net profit of six weeks of work for Kyungmoon Nho, and for the two men who are currently employed wholesaling heroin in the East Bay, the men who were eating kimchi and drinking beer. Kip unlocks the briefcase and opens the top, swiveling it around so that Mr. Kim can see what's inside. Mr. Kim nods once and Kip closes the briefcase with a metallic snap. Mr. Kim does not touch the money. This too is part of the order of things.

It is understood here that five percent of this money is going into a special Swiss account for Kyungmoon Nho, and that another ten percent is being invested for him by independent financial advisers in Hong Kong. Mr. Nho probably owns stock in the market, and has shares in restaurants, bars, and casinos. The two men who work for Nho wholesaling heroin in the East Bay receive cash up front and off the top of the product, but they receive no share of the net, nor do they have financial advisers or Swiss bank accounts. Of course, each of them hopes to break into middle management, but that day is not yet come.

On the coffee table in front of Nho there is a bound account book. Nho hands the book to Kip, who hands the book to Mr. Kim, who requires ten minutes to examine the coded figures inside, which represent the six weeks' worth of business. The entries are in Korean script and epigrams, not a combination for someone on the outside to decipher. When Mr. Kim is finished with the accounts, he takes out a handkerchief and wipes the book clean. Later, when Mr. Kim is gone, Kip will take the book back to the safe and lock it up again.

Nho sends Kip for beer. The men make small talk, mostly about women and America. While he makes this small talk, Nho is secretly aching to understand the inner workings of the mind of a man like Mr. Kim. He yearns to know where the heroin comes into the country, though he thinks it is probably at LAX, SFO, and the like, all on Korean boats and airplanes, hidden in car bodies, shipments of flowers, cooking oil, plastics, electronics. But he is dying to know the details. He wishes to wrap himself like a snake around this inner process. Nho will give this money to Mr. Kim, but he will not understand how it is laundered either, another mystery being kept from him. As part of the small talk, Nho tells Mr. Kim where he can go in San Francisco to get a massage from Vietnamese whores, some of them quite young and pretty. This seems to please Mr. Kim, who expresses delight. Kip returns with beer, a bottle and glass for Mr. Kim, two bottles for the dealers. Likewise, this is the order of things.

"When we crossing the bridge?" Mr. Kim asks in English, just to show his proficiency.

"I have already taken the first step of the journey," Nho replies.

"I think I read about this in the newspapers," Mr. Kim says slyly.

Nho is pleased that the "cat is out of the bag," especially in this backhand way. It obviates the necessity of telling Mr. Kim that he and Kip have murdered two rival wholesalers in San Francisco, and dumped their bodies in a trash bin in Hunter's Point to make it look like the blacks did it. These dealers were members of a competing Hong Kong association and were not amenable to changing their allegiances. Nho mentions that the operation was very efficient and Mr. Kim smiles knowingly. Everybody in the room understands that it was Kyungmoon Nho who took off these drug dealers who would not listen to reason, and dumped their bodies at Hunter's Point. It is a coup d'état of sorts, with as yet unknown consequences. It was Kip who pulled the trigger, of course. But Kip has *gaibatsu* blood. Murder is the sort of thing that doesn't bother Kip at all, and he does not expect to move up in the organization. This sets him apart, and makes him extraordinarily useful.

"We have a vacuum now, but we going to fill it," Nho says expertly.

Mr. Kim glances at his watch, an expensive Swiss timepiece. Nho realizes that he must hurry now, because Mr. Kim never stays in the El Cerrito house more than thirty minutes. He comes for his money and a look at the account books, then goes. He arrives by cab, then Kip drives him down to the Claremont Hotel in Berkeley and drops him off, drives away. "You have a plan for taking our business across the bridge to San Francisco?" Kim asks.

"I'm working on some people," Nho says.

Mr. Kim raises an eyebrow, expecting an answer more fully developed. In his heart of hearts, Kyungmoon Nho would like to wholesale in San Francisco himself, take another five or ten percent, up his cut from a million a year, to two million a year. But he doesn't have the guts to say it. "I met a woman last week, but I don't know."

"A woman," Mr. Kim says skeptically.

"She been selling coke in San Francisco."

"But a woman," Mr. Kim says.

"I know, never mind," Nho says.

"You sure this woman isn't a cop?" Mr. Kim says.

"Don't worry. I'll watch her for a couple of weeks. I got some other guys in mind for the wholesale trade over there. This woman won't get close to us."

"What's her name?"

"Grace Wu," Nho says.

Mr. Kim is disturbed by what Kyungmoon Nho is telling him. He thinks about vocalizing his displeasure at the idea that a woman is getting inside their circle, even a little. But he doesn't because he thinks he has made his point. And, already, he is thinking about his evening in San Francisco. He will have dinner alone at the Top of the Mark, then take a cab to Broadway or Koreatown, to bars where he knows women are for sale.

"How you run into this woman?" Mr. Kim says.

"She's been working the street over here," Nho says. He is anxious to correct his mistake in bringing the woman into this conversation. "She buys and sells on Telegraph Avenue."

"What's her product, you say?"

"Cocaine."

"You think she have a boss?"

"She just a trader," Nho says, trying to minimize the damage, even though he knows nothing about Grace Wu's connections to her stuff.

"I don't want her," Mr. Kim says. "We stay with Korean boys. We have a position to protect and we do it with our own people, people we understand." Mr. Kim smiles. "People just like you, my friend."

"Don't worry," Nho says, "there won't be any more business with this woman. I find you some people in San Francisco the next time you return to the States."

"She might be a cop," Mr. Kim repeats.

"I gotta test for her." Nho laughs.

Mr. Kim rises, straightens his tie. There is a half bottle of beer left. Tonight Mr. Kim will drink Chivas Regal, but when he isn't on business.

Kyungmoon Nho and the other men stand quickly, only a heartbeat behind Mr. Kim. Nho walks up to Mr. Kim and the two men shake hands, Nho remaining just behind the man's left shoulder. Kip goes out the front door and starts the Lexus, which makes a cat-purr noise on idle. Nho escorts Mr. Kim to the door and watches him walk down the flagstone steps and get inside the Lexus. He disappears behind the smoky glass and the car glides down the circular drive and onto the private street amid the flowering oleanders and hibiscus. Nho is not privy to Mr. Kim's arrivals, only his departures. He watches the Lexus fade into the far background of green.

"Maybe she pass the test, maybe not," Kyungmoon Nho whispers to himself. A wave of resentment passes through his physical body. In his mind he is saying, Fuck you, you asshole.

Fuck this fifteen percent shit, I do the work, I take the risk, you take eighty-five percent back to Hong Kong. Right now, Kyung-moon Nho is picturing Grace Wu. He sees the shop clerks and laundresses he used to kidnap, their frightened eyes, the screams of pain and humiliation. While he stands on the porch, his penis grows hard. His dick is pressed against the linen fabric of his pants. If this works out, he is going to fuck Grace Wu but good.

It is now just after three-thirty in the afternoon. Nho takes a number from his pocket and lights it and tests the cool sweet smoke, taking it down into his lungs where it settles. He is staring at the sun, straight ahead, due west. Miles away on the flats he can see Golden Gate Fields and he decides that he will drive down and catch the last few races on the card. His shoes are like wings.

nited Airlines flight 1627, SFO-LAX, dips sharply and reveals the silver teeth of Century City to Grace Wu, who is sitting in seat 20F, near the rear of the aircraft. This plane is full of commuters on business. At that exact moment Kyungmoon Nho shifts position and reveals his own Moroccan shoes to himself, pushing them out of the silver Lexus where a spot of sunlight can kiss the kidskin. Of course, Grace Wu is far away from Nho, in the air above Los Angeles, which she sees when she places her forehead against the porthole window and looks down at a forty-five-degree angle, L.A. burning through the smog. The condensed gases above the city form a pillow that pushes against the summer fog along the coast, fog that hovers two miles out in a solid layer all the way to the Channel Islands lying far off in the distance. The plane continues to bank and Grace's vision is obscured. She can see neither the ocean nor Century City.

She remembers that she has forgotten to feed her rabbits. Drinking the last of her diet cola, she feels a sudden coldness at the center of her being. It is a message coming across her wires telling her that she is into something very dangerous, a trip she is taking away from one kind of being into another. She tries to locate the feeling in her body. She places it in her upper stomach, just below the heart, which Japanese karate teaches is the center of spirituality. In her head, she performs an imaginary *kata*, one of *shoto-kan*'s ritual dances in order to calm herself. The manufactured air inside the airplane, its closeness and lack of freshness, all combine to make Grace Wu feel claustrophobic, out of control.

Down on the ground she doesn't need to go to the luggage carousel. She hasn't checked anything. All she carries is a large shoulder bag with two changes of clothes. She has her purse, which contains two hundred dollars in cash, her American Express and Visa cards, her checkbook and cosmetics. The concourse of L.A. International is crowded with the comings and goings of thousands of people, all dreamlike and intense. The colors inside are damped-down pastels. Everyone seems exhausted by the competition for space and light, like plants with too little food and water. Billboards are everywhere. Commerce is the byword.

She rents a medium-size car from Dollar and drives east through Inglewood and South Gate until she hits the Santa Ana freeway. The traffic is bumper to bumper and moving, which means that she is in a flow along with thousands and thousands of pounds of metal surrounding her, each of the vehicles attached to the one ahead and behind it by a thin thread of reaction time and emotional detachment. At any time, Grace feels that the string could break, and these cars, Grace in one of them, will hurtle like missiles in many directions, skewering passersby, passengers, and drivers alike. The sky exhibits a drab dark brown cast. There are no clouds beyond a few scattered cumulus on the horizon. This driving at seventy miles an hour, bumper to bumper, takes nerve. There is no context hereabouts, just miles and miles of apartment buildings, shopping malls, rows of palm trees, and dusty oleanders, all baking under the weight of heat. Everything looks tired and busy. The human beings Grace sees are behind the wheels of their automobiles, engaged in work. Now Grace is in Downey, Norwalk, Buena Park. What exists never shifts focus. There is an aircraft factory, a huge Sears warehouse. Concrete covers everything and anything. The Puente Hills loom up north, and beyond that are the San Gabriels, seen in a haze.

When she gets to Anaheim Grace parks in the lot of a May Company store that looks like a nuclear power plant. Walking amid the acres of cars, she feels the enormity of the moment, its clear and present danger. Here she has been riding around the streets of San Francisco for two years earning a reputation as a buyer and seller of cocaine. It is a way of being she can handle. There is a certain respect that she is due, and she has even managed three or four small-time busts. But now she is on to something different, and she thinks the stakes have gone up. Strangely, although she has an ideal image of Kyungmoon Nho in her head, a small guy with a wispy mustache and linen slacks, she can develop no real fear of him in a personal way. What she is afraid of is more subtle and complex than anything with a human face. It is a distant prospect which frightens Grace Wu, which makes her wish that she weren't in L.A. at all, but somewhere in the Sacramento delta.

In the basement of the May Company, Grace wanders around the sporting goods department. It is cool and hushed in the underground and a few clerks stand around doing nothing. Customers pause over consumer items, but most are just browsing, cutting out part of the day. Grace is about to sit down when she sees Elgin Lightfoot beside the elevators across the hall. He is wearing a plaid shortsleeve shirt and gray slacks. He looks calm and dressed down, not at all the way he usually looks when he meets her in the Bay Area. His belly is getting bigger, and there is some gray in his long black hair, but he looks good for a man in this business.

They exchange smiles and Grace follows Elgin up the stairs and outside to the parking lot. Elgin gets in a gray Chevrolet and drives circles, then comes back and picks Grace up by the bus stop in front of the building.

"I'm glad to see you, Grace," he says as Grace gets inside the car. They are on a surface street going some direction, Grace doesn't know which. This is Anaheim. It has no feel. "You have a good flight?" Elgin asks.

Grace nods, not saying much. She isn't sure why she's in Los Angeles, and this too is part of her anxiety. After a while she tells Elgin she had a good flight, such that it was. Two hours at the airport, an hour in the air, an hour driving to Anaheim. Elgin laughs. They are in California, sharing an understanding of travel. They are part of the West Coast concept and talk about Honolulu and Seattle as if those faraway cities were part of their own backyard, as if they could fly in and have lunch anytime. The West Coast is an experience, they say.

The drive ends ambiguously. They pass under a set of concrete supports and are beneath a stucco office building built on stilts. A row of oleander separates them from the street. Grace can't see a freeway and she can't see the mountains. They are buried inside Anaheim. Elgin rounds the Chevrolet, opens the door for Grace, and escorts her to an elevator, which deposits them on the third floor of the four-story building. The hallways are littered with gray fluorescent light. The walls are gray with blue piping and the carpet is worn. On all the doors are plastic name trays with convertible name plates. There are thousands of these kinds of offices in Southland, holding thousands of firms, partnerships, joint ventures, a whole gamut of capitalist experience. Like ant colonies, these ventures are constantly busy, and when one dies, another comes into being, takes up the load.

Elgin opens a door, and they enter a small suite of rooms full of space-age electronics, computers, televisions, data banks, black space-age computer files. The windows, wraparound, are smoky, and opaque. A man in a wheelchair wears earphones, head in hands, listening to something inaudible.

Elgin pours Grace a cup of coffee. They sit across from one another at a conference table in the middle of the room. Sunshine glances off the smoked glass. The sound of traffic reaches them, but it is muffled.

"You've never been down here," Elgin says. "This is the central bank. It's where we collect all that stuff you write down in your notebooks."

Grace gestures at the man in the wheelchair. He is a communications officer, an electronics and explosives expert, someone who maintains the wires that go everywhere and anywhere to their agents all over California and the Pacific Rim. He tends the webs for all the spiders.

Grace doesn't touch her coffee. "I'm impressed," she says.

"Everything you've worked for in the past two years comes down to today," Elgin says. "You've been out on the street mixing it up with the little people, and that's all right. But the person and the moment are about to come together."

"That's now," Grace says. "The moment is now."

"The moment is now, the person is you."

"Clemente Moreno?" Grace says.

"I don't think so, Grace," Elgin answers. The man in the wheelchair is rewinding tapes. Reels whirr in the background. "Clemente is a trader, and a good-size one. We think he gets his stuff on Wilcox right here in L.A. I mean we could bust him and his suppliers, and it would be a nice headline. In two days another guy from Morelia would enter the scene. We can take Clemente Moreno down someday, I don't mind. But he's one of the mushrooms in the basement."

"So, why am I here?"

"Kyungmoon Nho," Elgin says.

All of Grace's fears coalesce. "He told me he works heroin," Grace says. Her fear of this drug is enormous. Now she realizes what is behind her dread. She thinks about her brother Greg, an addict. She thinks about the time she herself spent kicking. Just hearing the word spoken is enough to make her sweat.

"Once he showed up in your notes, I started working on him. He's a hard little son of a bitch to crack, but I've got some pictures and notes. That's why you're here, Grace. I want you to see everything before you get going."

"I've been with him already," Grace says.

"Yes, I read about him. He's a treat." Elgin takes a drink of coffee. "I want you to get close to him. Do business with him."

"He has wholesalers in Oakland. He warned me off that trade already."

"I'm not talking about Oakland," Elgin says.

"You think he needs somebody in the City?"

"Hey, remember last month in Hunter's Point?" Elgin says. "John Zito finds these two Korean drug dealers dead in a dumpster on Evans Avenue? John probably thinks those two guys were offed by black gangs. But I have information on these guys. They were wholesalers for a Korean association in San Francisco who brought in small quantities of heroin. They were just getting started. I think Kyungmoon works for an association in

Hong Kong too, that didn't want competition in the Bay Area. I think your friend put a hole in the back of their heads and dumped them in Hunter's Point. Right now I think Nho is looking for someone in San Francisco, and it might as well be you."

"You think I could do it?" Grace asks.

"You think you could?"

Before Grace can answer, the man in the wheelchair wheels over and says something to Elgin. Grace is introduced to the guy, who looks like Jerry Garcia, only thin. The lights are dimmed, and for an hour Grace watches videotape of the house in El Cerrito, another apartment in Oakland, Kyungmoon Nho out on the street, Telegraph, Broadway, College Avenue where the SLA kidnapped Patty Hearst. The tape is grainy and diffuse, but intelligible. A Lexus emerges left frame, ascends a circular drive, side-shot, with sunshine falling on the silver metal surfaces. Nho opens the door and goes inside. These shots are taken from far away. While the tapes run, Elgin briefs Grace on everybody he knows, the Oakland wholesalers, the houseboy they rarely see.

"I don't know names," Elgin says. "The houseboy carries a gun. Nho has two wholesalers in Oakland, no names, no papers on anybody. Once every six weeks or so, a guy named Kim comes over from Hong Kong and probably takes money away from the house in El Cerrito. I don't know this for sure. And I don't know how the product gets inside the country, or what Kim does with the money when he leaves El Cerrito. He comes and goes, he's hard to follow. He stays in hotels and sees some shows on Broadway. Other than that, I don't know much. But I do know we're close to the real thing here. One stage away from the heroin pipeline and their laundromat, bing, bing, bing."

Finally the tape is cut, the lights come up. The man in the wheelchair commences to rewind, back in his control panel world. Grace has been watching, making mental notes. She wonders how she can get started, and she acknowledges this by asking Elgin directly. Elgin goes to one of the file cabinets and returns with one hundred thousand dollars in cash, all hundreds. They make two nice green stacks, with rubber bands.

"This is your start, why you're down here."

"What does Zito say about this?"

"I told him you were underutilized," Elgin says. He shrugs honestly. "It's OK with him. Besides, he's busy beating up his wife on weekends."

Grace doesn't want to hear more about John Zito. They work out the details of her reporting schedule. Grace is given the address of Nho's apartment in Oakland, in the Lake Merritt area. Evidently, Nho isn't a heavy user, but he does blow some smoke now and then. Elgin thinks she can spend a hundred thousand dollars with Nho, and then ask for a job. It might work. Grace agrees that it is worth a chance.

At seven o'clock in the evening, Grace and Elgin are back on the streets. The traffic has thinned, but it is still crazy out there. Low above the ocean is the sun, looking like a spot of blood. Grace bothers to ask Elgin about himself, and he tells her he is from Kalispell, Montana, or at least the reservation. He left the reservation to go to Vietnam, came back and went into the drug business on the government side. Out of the blue he tells Grace that both his parents are dead, that his only sister lives in a trailer on the reservation and has a drinking problem. Elgin surprises himself, talking this way, as it is the most personal conversation he has had in years. He chalks it up to being lonely tonight, far from home, like everybody in L.A. At any rate, when he stops talking he senses a mutual embarrassment. Grace takes up the slack, telling Elgin that her folks live over in Encino—gesturing north to the Valley. Her voice is flat and emotionless and Elgin doesn't follow it anywhere.

They are near the Santa Ana freeway entrance when Elgin says, "That's Disneyland over there." He smiles. "You ever been to Disneyland?"

Grace is amused and happy too. She is at a place in her life which seems both dangerous and right, full of *wu-li*. "No, I've never been," she says.

"Why don't we go over there and have dinner," Elgin says. He is looking at the traffic, and an empty field being readied for construction. "There are some restaurants on Main Street, my treat."

7

These days John Zito runs on a rich mixture of vodka and cocaine. *Blanco y blanco,* as the Colombians might say, and some mornings *tinto y blanco,* coffee and coke, the quicker picker-upper.

Since five o'clock in the morning he has been trying to locate his wife, who he thinks checked into a hospital somewhere in the Bay Area. Now that he has some distance from the original event, he thinks he probably broke her jaw. At the very least he sees it as trauma-room action, which is why he has been on the telephone for two hours in a desperate attempt to track her down and do some damage control. It is no use, he knows, to try to telephone her father at his estate in Burlingame. Lenore's entire family hates him. Or perhaps it is a more distinct kind of contempt, a superiority of breeding—that's what John Zito thinks, anyway. The truth is that Lenore's father is a partner in Pillsbury, Madison, and Sutro, which gives him a long golden look from his corner office, all the way down to Palo Alto. He is legal counsel to the Board of Supervisors, and has run campaigns for two Democratic mayoral candidates, both of them winners. This produces huge suck. And it is this suck that has John Zito beside himself with worry, because the old man said he'd take Zito off if anything bad happened to Lenore.

Zito has been staying at the house in San Rafael. There is nothing to eat in the refrigerator. The place is filthy, and all weekend Zito has been watching TV, pacing up and back in front of the picture window that looks down on Sausalito and the San Rafael bay. This early in the morning even, there are sail-boats near Angel Island, bumping through a heavy sea.

On Saturday, Zito drank a fifth of Stoli, then went to the liquor store and bought two more fifths, and started them on Saturday night, pausing to snort cocaine as he went along. Pretty soon he had lost the distinction between the alcohol and the cocaine. His head would go blank for minutes at a time. He was running on white noise, getting loaded time and time again, until it got to be nearly dawn and he began to telephone the hospitals, one by one. The next morning he was so sick he had to drink a glass of vodka just to steady his hands, and get to the shower. All day long he kept hearing voices. He yells into the telephone, his voice slurred. He finishes a second bottle of vodka. He has had, total, a couple of hours of sleep all weekend, doing the cocaine because it keeps him awake, and the vodka because it keeps him angry and unaware. What now matters is that inside his own conception of himself, he makes sense. There is nothing else.

At eight o'clock in the morning, two things happen. A duty nurse at the Peralta Hospital in Oakland tells him that his wife had been admitted. Beyond that, she couldn't say anything about her condition or exact room. Her visitors were severely restricted. Reading between the lines, Zito knows what she means, but he takes a shower and puts on some clean clothes and calls the Hall of Justice to tell the captain that he's going to be late to work, if he comes in at all. He was trying to put on a tie, when the doorbell rang. When Zito answered it he was confronted by three Marin County sheriff's officers. This was the second thing that happened.

The officers were looking slightly belligerent. They apologized in their own way, and went to work. They had brought along a local locksmith. Zito was served with a summons and complaint in a divorce action, a temporary order requiring him to get out of the San Rafael house, and a restraining order. Zito stared at the papers, barely able to read because of the cocaine haze. He knew he was going to have to leave. Maybe he could come back later. While the locksmith works, Zito packs a bag with some dress shirts, ties, socks, and shoes. He cleans up the cocaine and puts a full bottle of Stoli in his suitcase.

Zito stands and looks at the San Rafael house, cool and shrouded. His clothes are in the car. The locksmith is patiently drilling out the front door. Before Zito can get inside the car, an officer hands him some more legal papers, this time a domestic violence charge in Marin County Court. Now Zito is angry. He feels himself being turned and cuffed, hearing his rights read. Pretty soon Zito settles down and the officers allow him to follow their car down to the courthouse where they book him and he posts bond, five hundred dollars. Zito walks through the blue tunnels of the Marin County offices. He is tracked by security cameras, metal detectors, officers with guns. Zito remembers the old days when they had Angela Davis inside and he worked a special duty in Marin County, all the shit coming down outside the jail with protesters and terrorists. Now it is different and Zito is a defendant and nobody gives him deference. Behind this Zito can feel the hand of Lenore's father, all the way from Burlingame. This angers and humiliates him beyond measure.

Zito is caught in traffic on the Golden Gate. A news helicopter flies over, reporting back. Cars are pouring out of Marin County and onto the bridge, wedging themselves into neat lanes, hardly moving. A fresh breeze is blowing off the ocean and Zito can feel the bridge move gently underneath his Cherokee. He feels sick and emaciated. He knows he hasn't eaten properly in days. His hands shake as he grips the wheel, and he can smell himself. In a burst of energy, he does a quick reckoning. He has nothing in the bank. His credit cards are maxed, and his coke habit is about an ounce a week, maybe three thousand dollars, unless he can find a cheap deal. He isn't in line for any community property and he's stuck on the bridge.

Now he thinks: How did I get here? His reality is a steady incline down. He has always had a vodka habit, but never thought much about it. He drifted into diet pills, and then white-cross amphetamine, just to get going in the morning. He was kick-starting himself, but the kick didn't last very long. The only thing that would get rid of his headaches was vodka, and so on.

Once upon a time, it wasn't hard to steal cocaine down at the Hall of Justice, you just went down to one of the property lockers, or made a bust, and there you were. The world crawls with cocaine, dealers, wholesalers, an ounce of dust just an arm's length away. The basement of the Hall of Justice is filled with cocaine and nobody knows exactly how much is down there in the first place. But now it's locked up and guarded. Zito is proud that he hasn't sold any of the stuff, just used and used. Zito knows that it's in the nature of a habit to grow, which is the same as saying that it's getting worse, but it isn't something you notice while it's happening. This whole business has a light, feathery position in his head. Even now, he thinks it must be happening to someone else. He doesn't know it, but this is denial, pure and simple.

The traffic jam breaks at nine-thirty. It takes him half an hour to get across the peninsula and onto the slow approach to the Bay Bridge, which runs smoothly in midmorning. In another half hour he finds a parking place and goes up to the fifth floor of the hospital. These are all private rooms, and there is no noise. The halls smell of iodine and flowers, and you can barely see in the dark. Zito walks around until he finds a room with two large men standing on either side of the door. Their arms are folded and they wait, looking at Zito as if he were nothing. Now Zito can feel the suck of Lenore's father. A well of emptiness opens in his head and he falls all the way to Burlingame. For a brief moment, Zito fantasizes taking these two guys on right here in the hospital, breaking into his wife's room and killing her with his bare hands. He is having an episode. He is not in phase with reality, as the psychologist would say. Fortunately, he phases back in, and goes away without saying a word.

Zito sits in his Jeep looking at the eucalyptus trees. This is a medical plaza and there are clinics, doctors' offices, and laboratories. There are some nurses and techs out for an early lunch in the sunshine. Zito thinks that it is about ten degrees warmer on this side of the bay, and he thinks about finding a place to live over here. He rolls down the window and ponders cocaine. He'd like a line now. He wonders if he has the guts to sell coke.

He realizes that for five years he has been doing coke and vodka without giving it a second thought. *Fucking bitch,* he says to himself, thinking about Lenore. *Goddamn fucking bitch.*

Zito decides to skip work today. It won't be any secret at the Hall of Justice that he's been arrested and booked in Marin County on a charge of beating his wife. But he can't see any of the guys taking it seriously. It's just another domestic beef, which most of the officers regard as a raw deal for the man. Now, if Zito can get his affairs in order and rent a place to live, he can survive. One day won't make a difference if you're trying to outswim a huge undertow like this.

Zito is back on the Bay Bridge when he takes a drink of vodka. Something warm and soft enters his bloodstream and he slows down finally. When he gets to the City he drives down Sixteenth Street until he can see Mission Dolores. He crosses Guerrero and sees some homegirls and his head is so unclear that he makes a comment in Spanish to them, something obscene. He parks on Camp Street and walks up Dolores Terrace until he is above the mission and can look down at it with the park in the rear. The air is salty and fresh, the way it always is in summer in San Francisco. Hustlers work the streets around here, and more homegirls walk up and down the sidewalks. Vodka is running Zito's own engine now, and the sweat on his body feels cool in the breeze. He feels like he is glowing from inside, and it feels good. He thinks of himself as an electric wire, ready to burn somebody.

Thirty minutes later he finally sees Clemente Moreno. He knows Moreno from the files. It is because of some reports written by Grace Wu that he's come up here to the Mission Dolores. Zito is inspired. He puts on his black leather topcoat and some sunglasses and angles toward Moreno who is walking up Church Street. Moreno is a short man with a round happy face and one finger missing from his left hand. For a moment, Moreno stops, as if he has recognized Zito right in front of him about ten paces away. They are in the shadow of some royal palms and Moreno isn't smiling anymore. He keeps walking and Zito does an about-face, walks alongside for maybe fifteen steps.

"Do I know you, man?" Moreno asks.

Zito opens his coat and shows Moreno a badge. Moreno begins to walk, but Zito slows him with a hand on the shoulder. Moreno is cool and sits down on a bus stop bench where some little girls are playing, waiting for their ride. Zito stands beside Moreno. He can't remember what he is doing here. Everything seems to be in slow motion. Moreno is wearing a cowboy shirt and a leather vest and a fedora hat which accentuates his fat face.

"So, what's the deal, man?" Moreno says.

"I've been reading up on you," Zito says.

"You can read?" Moreno says.

"Oh, it's easy," Zito replies.

"The fuck man, you been drinking early, huh?" Moreno says. "That old shit you can't smell vodka, officer, it isn't true."

This burns Zito, who is trying to maintain. "There's a list downtown and you're on it," he says. "You're pretty far down the list, but you're moving up."

Moreno rolls his eyes and looks away. He can't believe this shit is happening. "You got nothing, man," he says, worried now. Moreno is normally a happy soul, easygoing. But now he is tense and unsure.

"Anytime I say the word, you go down. It's all in the book, names, dates, amounts. We even got pictures of you doing business."

"This is bullshit," Moreno says. He wants to leave, but he is afraid. Moreno utters something in Spanish that Zito can't understand. A bus comes and the little girls get on it. The two men are left alone, in clear cold sunshine. Above them is the Mission Dolores, a white cube in the light. "You're playing a game," Moreno says.

"The taxi driver you deal with," Zito says. "She's a narc. She works for me. She can open the door to ten years in Quentin for you. It's that simple."

"Shit," Moreno says. He had been certain of the woman. He even liked her. She was pretty and easy to deal with.

"I'm going to be your partner," Zito says.

"Sure, I know," Moreno answers. "It's like I always needed

a partner, you know? This is the happiest day of my life."

"Say half an ounce of cocaine a week, and five hundred cash."

"I can't do that, man, you know that."

"Let's give it a try."

"Let me think it over, man, I got to have some time."

They agree to meet the next day, same place. Moreno sits for a while and then gets up to leave. Zito tells him that he expects half an ounce and five hundred cash, after that it will be cowboys and Indians. Moreno will be the Indian.

race sees the girl Renee sitting under a monkey-puzzle
tree on Euclid Avenue. This is just around the corner
from Clement Street. On this windy Monday, Grace is
selling drugs and driving around the Bay Area. She has been
doing this for weeks while she waits to make contact with
Kyungmoon Nho.

Renee is wearing a floppy hat and a velour sweatsuit. She is
lost in thought, smoking a cigarette and squatting on the curb.
The sweatsuit is too large for her. But it is not the Renee that
Grace is used to seeing, a hip-hop girl with a nice smile and a
good word for everybody. This is another, more somber Renee,
who looks like she is short the rent.

Grace pulls to a stop and the two women exchange fifteen
minutes of small talk before Renee realizes that Grace is not
going to buy any crack today, that Grace is just killing time. It is
the lunch hour, and Grace eats a piroshki that tastes warmed
over. Renee finishes another cigarette. She smiles. Grace knows
that Renee will be busted someday. It's in the scheme of things
for Renee to go downtown, have her photo taken. But she is just
another small-time crackhead-dealer. Maybe one day she will
disappear from the scene. Maybe she will OD, or she will run off
with a dealer, or some fuzzhead will blow her away. That will
be it for Renee.

Grace does four hours on the street after lunch. She turns a
deal with Clemente Moreno for two ounces of cocaine. When
they meet at the Mission Dolores, Grace finds that Moreno has

lost his bounce. His usual sense of humor is gone, replaced by a world-weariness that Grace has never seen before. Perhaps he is worried about business, she thinks. It happens to drug dealers. But the deal goes down in front of the church with the wind blowing hard now, food wrappers and newspapers tumbling down the streets, school kids screaming in the playground. Grace tries to talk to Clemente, but he is silent. He has on a new outfit, a white suit and a panama hat. Grace can envision him in seventies gear, Day-Glo pants, a broad painted tie and platform shoes. Now his face is pinched and he sits idly on a bus stop bench as if he is waiting for a bus, but she knows he isn't. Someday she will bust Clemente Moreno, but that time is not now. Until then, Clemente Moreno will ride around town in his lowrider Impala and be happy.

About five o'clock in the afternoon Grace takes a break at Coolbrith Park in North Beach. She parks her taxi on the Vallejo hill and climbs to a public restroom. The traffic at this time of day is terrible around Columbus and Broadway. People are coming to the Beach to have a drink after work. When Grace gets back to her taxi there is a young man leaning on the door. He looks inside the cab and Grace thinks he is casing it, waiting to steal something. She isn't worried because she always takes her cigar box full of money with her when she leaves the car. The young man has a graceful face. He looks like a young Mel Gibson, before success. He is the Road Warrior, hair grimy, gray raincoat, off-brand tennis shoes. When Grace arrives he backs away to show that he is not a thief.

Grace gets in the taxi. She has cocaine in the trunk, about two ounces now with Moreno's. There is some cash in there too.

The young man leans down. "Hi, there," he says.

Grace says, "Need a taxi?" She is annoyed by this event. She needs to get over to Oakland tonight to cruise around and look for Kyungmoon Nho, as she does every night. She did not want a rush hour fare.

Without permission, the young man opens the door and sits in the passenger seat. This is not permitted, it is against company policy. Grace hesitates to say anything about it because it seems so innocent. Many people are on the sidewalk surrounding them. There is traffic in the street. She is not afraid. "Can you run me over to Berkeley?" the young man asks. A faint odor emanates from his body. It is neither pleasant nor unpleasant. "I'd really like it if you could run me over to Berkeley."

"I'm not licensed there, sorry," Grace says.

"Well, you know," the young man replies. Grace does not know.

"Come on, haul ass out of here," Grace says.

The young man produces a twenty-dollar bill. He places it on the cigar box, face up. The bill is much handled, wrinkled with one torn edge. It is a bill that has been in the economy for a long time. "Surely for a twenty you could run me across," the young man pleads.

"I'm a taxi driver," Grace says. "That's all I do. This isn't the circus." Grace does not express anger. After all this is North Beach. She is used to freaks and addicts, all sorts of people.

"Hey, no joke," the young man says. "You don't know how much I hate the C bus to Oakland."

Grace turns off the overhead light. She takes the twenty-dollar bill and puts it in her cigar box and starts the engine. It takes about five minutes to get into the flow of traffic, but finally there is a break and Grace makes the circle back toward the Bay Bridge, ten miles an hour. The young man relaxes as Grace finds the flow and fits into it, through the Financial District and across the Embarcadero. The streets are torn up, but they are always torn up. She tells herself everything is OK, that she was going to Oakland anyway. Really, she doesn't know what's going to happen. It could be an easy twenty dollars and it could be something else. While she drives, she thinks about the men in her dojo who go out at night and jog around Lake Merritt just to see if a mugger will jump out of the oleanders. They take risks in order to use their karate in a situation. Grace is concerned that her present behavior is like that. It is more than a passing thought that she is getting used to the idea of a present danger. She realizes that she may be enjoying herself in a subliminal way. If that's the case, some of the subliminal pleasure is lapping over now.

They are bumper to bumper, five miles an hour. Off to the left is Treasure Island. Its offices and quarters are already in shadow and there are lights twinkling on and off, off and on, amid the dense chaparral that covers the rocks. The young man has been quiet until now, but all at once he unbuttons the plastic raincoat. Quickly he folds down the top of the sweats he is wearing and reveals himself to Grace, who looks once and then looks away. His body is white, without hair. When she looks again, she sees that his penis is hard. Her heart beats quickly as the young man begins to masturbate, slowly at first, working his penis up and down in rhythms unknown to Grace. He closes his eyes and smiles. He tries to watch Grace, but it is too much, and he closes his eyes again.

"Oh come on," Grace says.

The young man arches back. He works his pelvis into an inverted position and struggles against whatever it is inside him. Men and women in other cars are so close, Grace is certain they can see what is happening to her. She doesn't want to look at the young man, but nevertheless she glances at him once or twice. He catches her eye, and smiles. Grace curses under her breath. The traffic continues to crawl across the bridge and they pass Treasure Island and are out over open water. To the south tankers and cargo vessels plow up to Alameda and San Leandro. Jets streak away from SFO. The young man lifts his left arm as if he is orchestrating something, silent music. He strokes himself harder and begins to moan. His eyes are mechanical objects, opening and closing. Bubbles of spit appear on his lips.

When they reach the end of the bridge the lanes widen and the traffic thins. Grace has her window down and she turns on the radio and listens to the news. She can see the Fiftieth Street exit when the man emits a groan and leans forward. His sweatpants are down around his ankles now. He heaves sideways and spits his sperm onto the cigar box.

Grace gets off at Fiftieth Street and stops the cab. Telegraph traffic whizzes by only three blocks up. The young man is looking smug now. Grace takes out a Smith & Wesson, which she carries tucked behind her left hip. She points the revolver at the young man whose eyes go wide as saucers.

"Clean up your mess," Grace says.

"OK, OK," the man says. He is scared to death. His hands tremble as he pulls up the sweats and buttons his raincoat. Grace holds the revolver still, aimed at his stomach. With his right hand the young man wipes the sperm from the cigar box. He looks to Grace for approval. She nods and the young man asks if he can get out of the cab, while already in the act of doing so. In a flash, he is gone, running toward Telegraph.

It is a beautiful evening and Grace is both angry and relieved. She wishes that she had stopped on the Bay Bridge and forced the young man out in the middle of traffic, maybe with his pants down. She can see him standing there in the middle of six lanes of jammed traffic, three miles over the bay, with his pecker on hard. She enjoys her fantasy for a moment, and then realizes that it is possible that she was a willing participant in this charade. It is as if she had jogged around Lake Merritt, and was surprised when a mugger jumped out of the bushes.

She drives downtown looking for Kyungmoon Nho. She cruises past Chinatown and Jack London Square. For weeks she has failed to hook up with him and she is anxious for it to finally happen. She worries that he may be out of the business, replaced by someone else and that she will have to start all over again. She is on her third time around Chinatown when she thinks she sees Nho walking into Jack London Square. He is on the opposite side of the street and it is just getting dusk. There are many people on the sidewalks, going to and from restaurants and bars. He wears a white silk shirt and black slacks. She drives around the block and comes up behind him, passes, and then parks so he can walk right past the taxi.

Kyungmoon Nho is happy. He has eaten some prawns and he drank some beer. He is on his way uptown to Grand Avenue to watch hard-core films. If anything is bothering him it is the fact that he hasn't found anyone in the City to wholesale his product. He has been searching for weeks, ever since the last visit of Mr. Kim. What he wants is someone he can control, who is afraid of him, and won't object if Nho skims product, cuts in on the profit on the street. As always, Kyungmoon Nho is regretful of the fifteen percent, and he harbors a resentment of Mr. Kim, whose manner is annoyingly haughty. Mr. Kim will be back in about four weeks, and Kyungmoon Nho must have something set up before then. After all, he and Kip have committed two murders just to get to here.

Nho sees the taxi and he sees Grace inside. All of a sudden he feels a surge of power. He had almost forgotten about Grace Wu, the dealer from the City. He gets in the back of the taxi.

"You not been around," Nho says. "You still selling small shit over in the City?"

Grace is having a profound moment of doubt. She can see the face of the Korean in the rearview mirror. He seems relaxed and satisfied. "You want to take a drive?" she asks.

They pull away. Nho tells Grace he is going to see the hard-core on Grand Avenue. He describes some of the action in an effort to make Grace feel uneasy and to establish a definite sexual superiority before undertaking business. Grace thinks about the young man. She drives around Lake Merritt on a metaphorical jog.

"So, what you want to do?" Nho asks. Before dark, there are real joggers around the lake. "You want to sell some of my product? You want to go into that business?"

"What do you have?" Grace asks.

"Finest H," Nho says. "Pure stuff from Hong Kong. I going to guarantee you you can step on this all night, and you still make a profit. People not going to know the difference, they be so high. That what you want? You want to sell some H?" Nho smiles into the rearview mirror. He admires himself and looks away.

"One hundred thousand dollars," Grace says.

Nho nods and ponders. "You got that kind of fucking money?" he says.

"I've got it," Grace says.

"Ten ounces good stuff," Nho says. "That two more ounces than you deserve, but this introductory offer." He laughs, more to himself than anything else. "I do this because you new to the business. I show you what a good guy I am." They are south of the lake and Nho tells Grace he wants to be let out at the next stop. They are on the Grand Avenue side where the streets go uphill to huge white houses surrounded by trees. On the other side are the porn theaters all lit up by yellow neon. The last of the sun strikes the plate glass of the houses. A thin layer of smog covers the hills. "So, you be outside the Paramount Theater next Friday, seven o'clock. I come by and pick you up and we drive around. You not gonna be sorry you did this."

Grace stops the cab in a bus zone. Nho leaves and walks up Grand Avenue to the theaters. Grace buys carryout at a place she knows in Chinatown and takes it across the bridge with her. When she thinks about the young man, he hardly seems to exist. She wants to eat her lo mein and get some sleep.

9

lemente Moreno is up early, watching cartoons on cable TV. His normal sleep patterns are unsettled, and now he is awake in front of the wide-screen Sony television on which Yosemite Sam is cavorting in brilliant color. His apartment is a one-bedroom walk-up flat on Guerrero Street at Alvarado in the Mission. This is his dream come true. In the living room there is too much furniture. It is the same in the bedroom. Right now, Clemente Moreno has the windows thrown open in the front room so that he can see the street and all the people below, though there aren't many so early in the morning. He is tired now, tired all the time since John Zito got on his case. He is used to sleeping until eleven o'clock every morning, getting out of bed and drinking coffee, maybe smoking a joint of mild grass, letting the day surround him. This morning he has a hangover from tequila, which gives him cottonmouth. The screen produces a glow. The cartoon backgrounds are static and empty, the characters' movements programmatic, situations uncomplicated and violent.

This kind of thing suits Moreno. He likes the uncomplicated life. This is why the situation with John Zito and Grace Wu has so troubled him. He has been thinking about what to do for days, weeks, and nothing has come to mind. Never in his wildest dreams did he imagine that he'd be doing business with an undercover narc. In the past few weeks, he has begun to drink more than he is used to drinking. This thing is consuming him, making him crazy, and cutting into his profit.

In the bedroom his girlfriend Paz is getting dressed. They have lived together for six months. Moreno is starting to like Paz more and more, although she is simpleminded and probably only fifteen years old. Paz comes from a border town in Chihuahua State named Agua Prieta, which is across from Douglas, Arizona. Paz ran away from home when she was thirteen when her uncle began to abuse her. He would beat her, and force her to perform fellatio when she was at home alone, her mother and sisters out on the streets trying to sell belts to the tourists, what few there were. Paz crossed the border with a group of others fleeing Mexico and landed in Half Moon Bay picking artichokes. She wound up panhandling and begging on the streets of the Mission, and one thing led to another. She found herself cooking and cleaning for Clemente Moreno, and finally in his bed.

She is part Apache, and her skin is copper-colored. She has the skinny limbs of a child. Her breasts are small with large brown aureoles that excite Moreno. Paz does what Clemente asks of her. She thinks he is not a bad person. He does not beat her, and he praises her when she does well. Paz thinks she could do a lot worse in the Mission District. She misses her mother in Mexico, but not the heat and squalor.

Clemente Moreno is a self-made man. When he was seventeen years old he was cutting brush, digging cactus, and stringing fence on a rancho outside of Morelia. The time came when he was recruited as a mule for a small syndicate of smugglers, and told to run a pound of cocaine across the border, up to Denver. The dealers gave Moreno two hundred dollars and the name of a man in El Paso who would drive him to Denver. Moreno had never been outside his hometown. The prospect of money and adventure excited him. His involvement made him proud. It was as if he had won the lottery. Of course, from the standpoint of the drug dealers, Moreno was taking all the considerable risks for very little of the profit.

However, when Moreno crossed the Rio Grande just south of El Paso, the Border Patrol discovered the group of immigrants he was running with and everybody scattered. Moreno wandered in the desert outside El Paso for a day, and then was able to catch a freight train moving north. He rode in a boxcar all day and all night, and part of the next day and night, until he realized that he was in the plains, and not the mountains. He saw some lights out on the horizon, and jumped off the train.

He was in Garden City, Kansas. It so happened that many Mexicans had gone to Garden City to work in the beef-processing trade, and Clemente made friends, found a place to stay after only a day on the street, and got a job stacking carcasses and draining cow blood. He didn't realize that he was doing dangerous work. Pretty soon, he forgot about the men in Morelia. Instead, he envisioned himself as a businessman and entrepreneur. He abandoned the idea of going to Denver, and turning over his pound of coke. Instead, he drifted on to the Bay Area, partly because the destination appealed to his imagination, and because he had an uncle in Portola Valley. Already, he thought of the cocaine as his own. He sold some of it and purchased a car, then sold some more, and he was on his way. He was in business. His trade became small and safe and lucrative, and he made contacts in the barrios of Los Angeles. Once a month he would drive to Wilcox Avenue, called Crack Alley, and buy a pound, and turn it in San Francisco. His closets were full of clothes. He owned an Impala, low-rider. The girl Paz cooked his meals and slept with him. Now John Zito and Grace Wu were fucking up his good thing.

Moreno has a breakfast of fried eggs and peppers, two cups of strong black coffee. He feels strong and well, finally over his hangover. His belly is full, and normally he would have a happy heart. Yet he is surrounded by bad vibes. Everytime he sees John Zito, the man appears nervous and fractious. It looks to Moreno as if Zito is using narcotics himself, and that he is drinking too much. When he comes to meet Moreno, his skin looks yellow. He smells of sweat and he is nervous and demanding like his mind is clicking on and off, a neon weapon. Zito is making Moreno's life miserable, a life that was once carefree. It is the kind of situation that can't last. Zito will explode, everything will go to shit. Moreno's mind is toying with the idea of murder as a way out of his current problems. It runs counter to his basic nature, but his life is settled and Zito has threatened to destroy everything. Moreno is not afraid of violence. He is alive to its possibility.

Moreno dresses and goes down to the street and walks a few blocks over to the Mission Dolores. It is Friday and morning mass is being said inside the cathedral. Moreno believes in God. But he also believes in fate and destiny. These are, he believes also, two sides of the same coin.

Going to meet John Zito, Moreno has dressed in slacks and a cowboy shirt. He is wearing Tony Lama boots made of lizardskin. In the pocket of his slacks he has a .22-caliber automatic pistol. Naturally, he is not going to shoot John Zito while the man sits on a bus stop bench in front of the Mission Dolores, but Moreno wants to get used to the idea that it could happen. He wants to feel the weight of the gun, its mass. If he carries it, perhaps he will use it. He and John Zito and Grace Wu are sharing a destiny now, faces on one side of a coin.

As Moreno approaches the bench, Zito looks up and appears startled. The day is warm, but Zito is wearing his black leather coat.

"You got it," Zito says.

Moreno hands Zito a vial. It is only six grams. Moreno says it is all he can spare this week. A game is being played now, Moreno bringing some coke, Zito pressing him for more. Every time they meet, this is all they talk about. Moreno opens his right hand and reveals two hundred-dollar bills. Zito takes the bills and stuffs them into his coat pocket. It is clear he is angry. "This is all I can get you now," Moreno says. "You're ruining my deal. I have my expenses, you know."

"Is this a joke?" Zito says.

"You wait," Moreno says. "You doing OK, huh?"

"I read your file," Zito says. "I told you. You're doing pounds, maybe fifteen thousand a month. The fuck you think I'm doing here?"

"Take it easy," Moreno says.

"You're into me three weeks at three hundred dollars a week short. You owe me a thousand already. You're shorting me on the coke too. I'm going to pull your string."

"You got to be patient. My other customers have the same needs you got."

"That's it," Zito says. He gets up and looks around the streets. The sun is angled in, giving everything a whitewashed look.

"Hey look, man," Moreno pleads. He takes two more hundred-dollar bills and hands them to Zito. Moreno was holding out, but he can't any longer. "You know I was saving this out for essentials."

Zito stands still and clutches the money. He is late for a business meeting at the Hall of Justice, one of many meetings he has been late for, or missed altogether. His own problems are getting worse and worse. Not only has he been thrown out of the San Rafael house, but he's been scheduled for arraignment in Marin County on the domestic violence beef. He knows that he is being recommended for counseling at work, partly because he secretly reads the personnel files compiled by his captain. In addition, he has received notice from the bank on his Jeep. His coke habit is worse too. He's tried calling and writing to Lenore, but he can't make contact. This time he thinks she has finally snapped out of his orbit and back into her father's. It is possible that he's going to be on probation from his job. This is the shit that is knotting him up in balls of anger. In reality, he believes that his desperation is entirely justified. He believes that he is a victim.

Zito takes five or six steps away from the bus stop. Pigeons scatter around him. "One more time," he says to Moreno.

Moreno relaxes. He knows that he has bought another week. It is possible he can do this indefinitely, or at least until he can decide what to do. But Moreno knows the psychology of addiction. He knows that addiction has no tolerance, that it understands only fulfillment. He knows he must eliminate the addiction in order to kill the need.

Zito drives downtown to the Hall of Justice. Once he gets to his office, he can see the traces of Elgin Lightfoot, his coffee cup and his file folders. Zito knows this meeting is about Grace Wu, and he isn't prepared. He hasn't read her reports in weeks, nor those of any of his other operatives. The whole matter of his budget and his busts has taken a back seat to Lenore and the mess she is making of his life. When Lightfoot comes back to the office, he is looking rested and laid back.

"It's a pleasure," Zito says, as Lightfoot sits down. Lightfoot is carrying a briefcase. He places it on the floor between his legs.

"You have time to talk about Grace?" Lightfoot says. Lightfoot is relieved that Zito hasn't made another of his Indian jokes, which are tiresome and facile. Besides, Lightfoot never knows how to respond.

"I'm at your disposal," Zito says.

For weeks, Lightfoot has been compiling his dossier on Kyungmoon Nho. He has digested it, and it is here for Zito. There isn't much. It is hard to watch the house in El Cerrito because it is high up on the crest of a hill and on a semiprivate drive. On one side of the house is a wall of oleander, and on the crest of the hill, behind the house, is a waterworks and a small reservoir surrounded by barbed wire and chain link. In fact, all these weeks of work have produced only some tape and a few well-chosen photographs. Lightfoot wishes he had more.

"I'd like to put Grace on the Korean guy from El Cerrito," Lightfoot says. He pushes two file folders toward Zito. He has been briefing the man, although he's left out the deal for one hundred thousand, which comes down tonight. Now there is nothing to hide. Zito glances over the materials.

"You have to be shitting me," he says.

"This has approval, all the way to D.C.," Lightfoot says.

"And you want me to bless this thing?" Zito says.

"You don't have to be gung-ho, John," Lightfoot says. "I'm not asking that."

"Then what are you asking?"

"Just let her take a crack at this guy."

Zito thinks. "It's her funeral," he says.

Lightfoot breathes deeply. He drinks some coffee and looks at Zito. "I wish you wouldn't say that kind of shit, John. I really do."

"Sure, yeah," Zito says. "I didn't mean it like that."

"John, we've got a million budget on this. Kyungmoon Nho is directly connected to a heroin pipeline to Hong Kong. Money is laundered on this deal. That's why it's special. If we bust this group, we've fucked up an entire operation. Grace is ready to go."

"Fine with me, then," Zito says. "I'll read the file. I'll back her, that what you want?"

Lightfoot opens the briefcase and puts it on the desk. "There's nine hundred thousand," he says. "Give me a receipt. Put this in the safe in your basement. I can count on you for this, John?"

"Leave it here, Elgin," Zito says. Zito begins to write out a receipt.

"Grace goes out tonight. She'll give us a complete rundown when it's over."

They talk for another few minutes, polishing the details of this important operation. To Lightfoot, Zito seems upset and distracted. Lightfoot has heard rumors about the man's domestic violence charge in Marin County. But looking at him, he thinks there might be more to it than that. He supposes this could happen to any cop, anywhere, anytime. Finally, the two men shake hands and Lightfoot goes.

Elgin Lightfoot has taken a room at the downtown Hilton. It is a bad room at the back, small and cold. He is driving a rented car, which he takes out to the far end of Golden Gate Park. At the zoo, he spends an hour watching the animals. He feels for the bears and lions in their cages. He worries about Grace Wu. Ever since they had dinner together at Disneyland he's been thinking about her. They had a good time and ended up staying late and going on some rides together and, later, walking around Adventureland. They probably have something in common, it turns out.

Elgin is at loose ends. He is waiting out the night.

10

hat Grace Wu sees when she steps onto the roof of her apartment building this morning is an unexpected shock. The wire of the rabbits' cage has been snipped open and the rabbits are gone. What remains are some bits of carrot and cabbage, the water bowls, aluminum tubs full of rabbit shit. In the many days of tension that Grace Wu has lived through in anticipation of tonight, this is the one event that had eluded the radar of her early warning system.

She climbs over the parapet and stands quietly looking at the empty cages while anger and despair sweep over her. She realizes that she has always known this would happen. The City seems to pulverize every joy, but each day when she fed the rabbits she felt a renewed hope that for once she would cheat fate. Now, as she looks at the cages, an ocean breeze comes off the bay. She remembers the Chinese widow in the delta who sold her the rabbits two years ago. She remembers the rustle of the wind through the tules that stood in the marshes behind the old woman's house, and the graceful smile on the old woman's face. Grace takes a deep breath, and pours out the water in the rabbits' bowls, disposes of the cabbage and carrot. The way she feels now she will not try again with rabbits. Her secret place has been discovered, spoiled.

Earlier in the morning, Grace drove across the Bay Bridge and spent two hours in the dojo. At this session the sensei has only a few students, and he is surprised to see Grace, who usually attends in the evenings, or on Saturday when she is free. He believes that Grace is one of his best pupils. She has ability, and she understands the purpose of the discipline, which is not to break boards or bones, but to tone the spirit.

During the first twenty minutes, Grace remains on her knees, breathing and meditating, maintaining silence. Nothing hinders Grace in her thoughts, which glide toward an empty coolness. She is free of anxiety. She can feel her muscles and their connection to the ligaments. It is as though her body has become an anatomical model. When the silence is over, the sensei announces that he has been asked to act as bodyguard to Joan Baez at a concert at Mills College, and he invites his students to join him at a party afterward. There will be wine and cheese, and a chance to meet Baez, maybe.

The students perform their katas for an hour, under the guidance of the sensei. Along with the other students, Grace flows around the wood-paneled room on an oaken floor that has been sanded and worn smooth. She performs a series of front and back kicks, yakazukis, complicated blocking motions and aggressive strides. This is a formalized kind of dance, intended to bring the student to a place of involuntary obeisance to the form. Thereafter comes a tortuous period, which lasts nearly an hour, in which the students do pushups on their knuckles, and walk back and forth across the length of the room with another student on their back. In this way, individual pain is subsumed in the group consciousness. Grace feels her lungs heaving. She is tired in all her muscles and joints; she thinks she will pass out. When this period is over, the students punch and kick posts wrapped in tatami, breaking down the cartilage in their hands and feet. At the end of the session is personal combat. Grace is paired with one of the Lake Merritt joggers, a huge black belt who outweighs her by fifty pounds. When she drives back across the bay, exhausted and clear, she finds that her rabbits have been stolen.

Grace has taken the day off from the cab company. She does some shopping along Clement Street. She buys fruit and vegetables, and she visits one or two bookstores to browse. In the late afternoon she tries to nap, but she can't sleep because she is thinking about the night. In her mind, she practices a kata. She can see herself performing actions and managing her reality. She lies on her bed in the semidarkness, listening to the traffic on Geary, the ceaseless roar of cars and buses. At some point, Kyungmoon Nho passes through Grace like a ghost. Grace has already faced him in the mirror of her soul, and he has disappeared like the wind. For a long time she lies still in the orange light and thinks about her parents in Encino, and then about her brother Greg, whom she hasn't seen in months and months. It is nearly six o'clock when she gets up and goes into the kitchen for a soda. She has a desire to call Elgin Lightfoot just to talk. Instead, she dresses in jeans and a sweater and goes downstairs.

The City is spiderwebbed with light. It has been a warm September day, but now it is chilly. Grace can see Berkeley across the bay. The Bay Bridge is backlit by orange lamps, and inevitably, on Friday night, the traffic is thick and moving slowly. Just short of the approach to the bridge, a trailer truck has had a flat tire, and Grace sits in the unmoving traffic for twenty minutes. For a time, she thinks that she might be late for her meeting with Kyungmoon Nho, that her chance to deal with him will vanish. This is a relief in a way. But then she realizes that it isn't true. She will have to do this. Her palms are sweaty against the steering wheel.

She gets off the freeway at Grove-Shafter and heads for Telegraph Avenue. She passes the dojo, where an evening class has begun. Her hands and feet are sore from her morning session, but she is happy with her body. Right now it is the thing she trusts most in this life, and she believes that it can get her through something terrible, if that time ever comes. Her stomach, the center of her spiritual life, is hardened and toned, ready.

The traffic creeps down Telegraph, Friday crunch. Along here, the street life is varied and lush. All kinds of people are out tonight, drug dealers, bums, panhandlers, yuppie bond salesmen, cops, prostitutes. She passes from Berkeley into Oakland, and the scene shifts to a rougher dimension. Grace wonders how it got this way, so dirty and misspent. Some of the people who pass on the street mumble to themselves, make noises.

Grace has seen people down and bleeding in the gutter, other people walking by unconcerned, scared. It is war all the time down here.

Grace parks on Twenty-second Avenue and walks to the Paramount Theater. There is a concert or performance, because the sidewalk in front of the theater is crowded with society types dressed in suits, chiffon dresses. Grace is carrying a paper sack containing one hundred thousand dollars in hundred-dollar bills. She stops across the street from the art deco building and admires its form in the evening light. It is a beautiful old place, the last of its kind, something left over from the heyday of Oakland.

Grace is startled by the voice of Kyungmoon Nho. He has pulled up behind her in a silver Lexus. The passenger window is down and he speaks out of the dark. The other windows are up, smoked glass making it impossible to see inside. All she can see is the face of the Korean as he speaks to her in a whisper, barely audible. He has babyish features, narrow dark eyes, plump cheeks, a thin cruel mouth. His face is like the moon on a velvet background. The evening traffic streams up and down in front of the theater.

"Get in the back," Kyungmoon Nho says.

The passenger window hisses up and Grace is alone on the street, cut off from the source of Nho's voice. Sunset has produced crimson streaks on the hills above Oakland. Neon reflects from the surface of the Lexus. The car looks sinister, and it makes Grace afraid. She walks to the Lexus and taps on the window. Through it, she says that she wants to do the deal here. She says this is what they agreed to do. Nothing happens. The smoky windows remain rolled up and Grace ponders what to do. She tries to look through the front windows, but it is dark inside. Kyungmoon Nho stares straight ahead, unmoving and bleak. The Lexus begins to roll forward. Grace opens the door as it passes by, and falls inside, pulls the door shut.

A Korean sits in the seat beside her. The Lexus has picked up speed and they are going down Twenty-second Avenue at thirty miles an hour and gaining. Her chance to get out of the car is gone forever. Now Grace can't see outside and she doesn't know where they are going. The Korean beside her is impassive. Nho senses her uneasiness and tells her to relax, that they are going to a safe house to do the deal, no problem. Even with this, Grace is on her guard, trying to see the route, make a mental map of their direction in her mind. She thinks they are heading dead into East Oakland where the streets flatten out to Fruitvale Avenue, long anonymous patches of stucco houses, mini-malls, convenience stores. It is a place with no discernible contour, no context. Stucco house, apartment house, chain link fence, convenience store, bright intersection, repeat, repeat, repeat. It is pure subtextless urban blight. Next to her, the Korean breathes in and out impalpably, as if his lungs were a metronome. Grace can smell the odor of beer and kimchi on his breath, and his clothes are full of cigarette smoke. He is small, his hair jet black and scruffy. He is wearing black sweats, expensive Reeboks, a leather jacket.

"You got the money?" Nho asks finally. He is looking at Grace in the rearview mirror. Nho exchanges a few sentences with the Korean in back. Grace doesn't understand. She holds the paper sack, shows it to Nho, who nods happily.

"Where are we going?" Grace asks.

"Don't you worry, lady," Nho says.

The avenues go by relentlessly. Grace tried to see some street signs.

"I got the product for you," Nho says. "You didn't think we'd do a deal right there on the street, did you?" He laughs like a child. Grace feels her heart pound. "You going to get your product, don't worry. You going to be a big dealer on your side of the bridge."

The Lexus slows and pulls into a dark side street where there are apartment complexes up and down the block. This could be anywhere in the East Bay. They go up a drive and park in a covered garage. The two Koreans get out of the Lexus and lead Grace through a covered portico to a duplex. Nho and the other man have begun a constant conversation in Korean, punctuated by laughter.

Once inside the duplex, Grace knows she is in a bad situation. It is a small, sparely furnished place, brightly lit and smelling of disinfectant. The living room contains a secondhand couch and two folding chairs. The carpet smells of dog and cat. From where she stands, Grace can see a baggy full of white powder on the kitchen table in the next room. There is another Korean in the kitchen too, a large man wearing dress slacks and a sport coat, a gray knit shirt, and tasseled loafers. His face is square and expressionless. All the men are speaking Korean now. Grace holds out the bag of money, and Nho takes it.

"There's your H," Nho says, pointing to the baggy in the next room.

Grace walks into the kitchen. She feels like a little girl, in over her head. Still, she passes through what she has to do. She stands beside the table while the big Korean moves aside. She opens the baggy and wets her finger, then puts her finger into the powder. She runs some of the white powder on her lip, tasting it. What she tastes is baby powder, pure talcum.

Grace strikes the big Korean below his nose. She begins to cross the living room, making for the front door. In her mind, she has prepared to die, and she is surprisingly calm, her fear offset by the tremendous rush of adrenaline produced by her glands. Behind her, the big Korean has caught the sleeve of her sweater, and Nho is standing in front of the door. Grace pivots and kicks the big Korean hard in the shin and emits a piercing *ke-ih* at the same time.

There is a burst of activity and Grace is inside it. She kicks again and is surrounded by the Koreans who have created a small human hole and are burying her. The big Korean holds her around the waist and she can feel others pulling her hair, hands at her throat too. She whirls and whirls, tries to kick and punch, but her arms are being pinned, and she is slowly wrestled down to the floor. She knows that she has done some damage to the big Korean, but it has not been enough. She is being overwhelmed by three men and a terrible weight descends onto her back. Her face is pushed into the carpet, someone strikes her back and arms. There is a foot on her neck. These men are hurting her, but she feels no pain right now. In a few minutes more of struggle, Grace is quiet, lying on her stomach, the men all over her, everybody breathing heavily.

"You not going to deal product," Nho says in her ear. "You be quiet now, we let you go."

Grace struggles, relaxes. She knows she is going to lose the hundred thousand dollars. She wonders how far these men are going to take her, if she will survive. One of the Koreans strikes her hard on the back of the neck, and she fades away. When she returns to consciousness, she can hear the men laughing. They have taken down her jeans and torn away her panties, leaving her partially naked on the floor. Grace can feel warm blood draining from her nose, its iron taste in her mouth. One of the men, Nho she thinks, sits on her neck and head while another lies on her from behind. She can feel a penis enter her. She is parted and separated and burned as she continues a weak struggle. Time has a surreal quality and Grace endures it. A man ejaculates on her back, and another man takes his place, forcing himself into her anus. She is silent, wondering if they will kill her, tolerating her pain for now. If given the chance, she will try to strike out again, but she doesn't know if she can lift her arms, which have gone numb. She thinks of all the katas she has done, all the pain and exhaustion she has worked through. Finally, the big Korean mounts her from behind and he too penetrates her rump. Grace goes through a window to another side of life.

When they are finished, the men watch while Grace pulls on her jeans. She is dragged outside to the Lexus and put into the backseat. Blood has dried on her lip and her back and arms ache. She sits between two Koreans, while Nho drives the car.

Somewhere in East Oakland, the men push Grace out of the Lexus and move away. It is dark here. Most of the streetlights are out, having been shot or broken by rocks. From houses and apartments comes a dull flickering light. The air smells hot, like burned eucalyptus. The Lexus stops and Nho exits the driver's side and opens the trunk. He comes around the car, and Grace thinks he might shoot her. Instead, he is smiling, holding something in his hands. It is a wire noose onto which have been strung three bloody rabbits' heads. He places the noose around Grace's neck and leaves.

Alone, Grace begins to sob.

Phase Two

onday morning is docket call in domestic violence court, Division Six of the Marin County Superior Court. John Zito sits on a bench in back near the door. He wears a lightweight tan summer suit with a white shirt and a pale green tie. His hair is neatly trimmed and he's running on six cups of coffee and some Tylenol with codeine. Part of him wants to be noticed and part of him doesn't. It's a war between his pride and his shame, and the shame is winning. But there is deep anger too, at being in a place with all these creeps and weirdos.

When he got up this morning John Zito wanted a line so bad he prayed for one to happen. It was before dawn and his room was completely dark, and for fifteen or twenty minutes he lay silently orienting himself to what was new in his life, the shabby room, its smells and sounds. The sheets on his bed were wet from a distraught night of tossing and turning. He had a sore throat and a runny nose and his eyes were scratchy and blurry. He went to the bathroom and looked at himself and choked off the urge to do some blow, an urge so strong it placed his existence in the balance. While he was looking in the mirror, he got the impression of a man on the edge of doom. This fact he blamed on Lenore and on her father and her family, his lousy job with its long hours and low pay, and the concomitant responsibilities, which were tremendous, and on the system, which placed men like him on the line and didn't compensate them in any way. When he got dressed finally and went downstairs he found that his Jeep Cherokee was gone from its park-

ing spot outside. Taped to his mailbox was a notice from the re-
possessor.

☒

Two days after being evicted from the San Rafael house, Zito had
rented a single large room in an apartment building on Turk
Street, just a block down from the YMCA. The six-story gray
stone building shares a sameness with all the others on the block.
There is a liquor and tobacco store in the lobby where residents
gather to talk and smoke. Around the corner is an adult book-
store, where you can see dirty movies for twenty-five cents, and
on down toward the financial district are several bars and restaurants. From this building John Zito can walk the ten blocks to
the Hall of Justice where he works. He parks on the street and
tears up the tickets he accumulates. Subconsciously, he is pleased
by the nearness of the liquor store in the lobby, its congruity with
his life and needs. He remembers when he would have to drive
drunk from his house in San Rafael to a liquor store in Sausalito about five miles away, just to get his late-night booze when
everything in the house was gone. Often in the morning he
wouldn't remember driving there or back, and he was constantly
worried about being arrested and charged. Now he can walk
downstairs and buy vodka anytime he feels the need, take the
stairs back up to his room on the third floor, disappear. His existence is never noticed, which gives him a feeling of satisfaction
and comfort. Nonetheless, sometimes it frightens him that he can
coexist so easily with pensioners, drunks, widowers, drug addicts. John Zito is forty-six years old and counting. He is like a
space shuttle with a bad O-ring.

His room is high ceilinged and cold. Almost no sunlight comes
inside because the windows face a brick wall and an alley between Turk and Eddy. The single bed has an uncomfortably thin
mattress. The floor is linoleum. There is a washstand and a bathroom with a small, dirty shower. Because he is in the back of the
building, there are no real street sounds. Nonetheless, there are
subliminal and subversive sounds because the walls are thin and

there is much life in the halls. You can hear people talking, radios playing, and occasional arguments and sex.

◼X◼

With his Jeep gone for good, John Zito took a thirty-eight-dollar cab ride across the Golden Gate Bridge to the Marin County courthouse. His lawyer was waiting for him in the hallway outside the courtroom. Also there are other lawyers, prosecutors, witnesses, and defendants, all smoking and talking. Zito's lawyer is a man named Harold Biscomb, someone Zito picked out of the Yellow Pages. Biscomb has an office near the freeway in San Rafael and specializes in domestic violence and divorce cases. Zito and Biscomb have met once, briefly, in Biscomb's office in a minimall. The retainer was set at one thousand dollars against one hundred seventy-five dollars an hour and expenses, copying, gas, and process service. Biscomb is a short tough guy who is aware that domestic violence cases are mundane, almost trivial. His self-assurance translates to his clients as unconcern, but John Zito doesn't know or realize this as yet.

Still, Biscomb is aware of the tremendous political and moral suck generated in the Bay Area by Zito's wife's father, and flatly predicts a guilty verdict if they try the case to a jury. Even without the suck Biscomb believes that his client lacks a legal defense. Therefore, Biscomb has suggested a plea bargain and a negotiated probation, say about two years, along with community service and an AA program. Right now they are only as far as the docket call and the arraignment, so there is time for it all to happen. Months maybe, perhaps a year. Even so, time is not on Zito's side.

Nothing Biscomb says this morning affects Zito one way or the other. He is focused on his problems, the ones outside the world, the ones inside his bloodstream. Besides, Zito has seen these things transpire before, courtrooms, bargaining sessions, lawyers, and judges. Hence, he has little fear of a system which works slowly and inefficiently, and which is overwhelmed by the products of its own rules and procedures.

Even though he has no fear of the system, still Zito resents the numbing wrangle it represents, and he resents being made to wait three hours to enter a plea of not guilty to a black judge who mispronounces his name. He is angry at having to sit in a room full of deadbeats and crooks. So now, as he sits on the rock-hard bench, he sees fifty or sixty other men and women, most of them plainly hardcore poor, welfare mothers, glazed looks of fear and incomprehension on their faces. This is the color of dread.

The courtroom is done in gray corkboard, drop ceilinged, a quarter acre of pale light with a security camera in the wall, guards with guns in each corner and at the glass doors outside. Some of the defendants appear only on a television screen, having been in jail for more serious crimes, their voices garbled and far away. The judge speaks through a microphone clipped to her robe. At twelve-fifteen in the afternoon, Zito is outside the courthouse on a brilliant blue day. By his reckoning, he owes Biscomb five hundred and twenty-five dollars.

Once outside John Zito breaks a hard sweat. He is at the commencement of a paranoid episode. This is something that cocaine produces in regular heavy users and Zito has had one or two episodes since he struck his wife. The fear curve crests and falls, but in between his head will fill with every conceivable spook and ogre, black kachinas. As he stands in the tended gardens on county grounds, his reality begins to dovetail with his drug-induced paranoia, suspicion on suspicion. Zito has been asked by his captain to speak to the substance abuse counselor, ostensibly because the captain is concerned that Zito may have a drinking problem, man to man. Zito is scheduled to speak to the counselor once a week for the next two weeks, and then an evaluation report will be prepared for a committee of fellow officers. It is well known that the committee is sympathetic. Zito believes that he can hang together enough to answer the counselor's questions. Yet, just now, standing in the gardens above the parking lot, Zito feels his skin crawl and prickle. He remembers the bottle of Absolut in the Jeep, but the Jeep is gone, and with it the bottle of vodka. He thinks shit, why is this happening to me? All he wants now is a swig of vodka, which he often takes as he drives around. It cuts the need for coke. Still, vodka creates its own system of needs and rewards, payments for its services. This matter of abuse is very complicated for someone on the outside. But it is simple too. It is a world like any other; only it is an alternative.

Zito takes a cab across the Golden Gate again, another thirty-eight bucks. He gets out on Market Street uptown and finds a bar in the Mission where it is dark. He has a quick drink, and then two more. There are about a dozen men in the bar, drinking toward afternoon. It is dark inside and Zito sits on a stool near the front door. Finally he is nearly level zero, where his systems are in balance. There is the smell of the bar itself, which is of beer and whiskey, and the smoky exhaust smell of the street, and there is the feel of his Colt Python behind his left hip. Zito drinks and tries to decide what to do with the rest of his day.

Everyone on staff knows that he was due in court, so he has an excuse not to show up at the office. The hours crawl by. He is in a tunnel of need. When he drinks, he picks up the glass and smells the vodka and its tiny necklace of lemon, he sees its rich collocation of tones and hues. It is a reward in itself, something he can feel in his brain, his stomach. Someone puts music on the jukebox. It is a Mexican ranchero tune, a mariachi, with guitars, accordion, violin.

The music makes John Zito move. It triggers something in his memory, and so he leaves the bar and walks a mile up Guerrero Street where the people are out happily in the street, shopping, loitering. Now the vodka is working. There are three drinks, about two and a half ounces working on him, and he feels fine, he understands what he must do. He works his way up the street until he is outside the building in which Clemente Moreno lives. Up on the second floor there is a hallway with some kids playing ball. Zito finds the right door and he leans on the jamb, simultaneously pounding on the wood with the butt of his Colt. The way he feels, he gives not a care to the children in the hallway, whether they see the weapon or not. His power has come again, after failing him at the courthouse. He must ride it while it is hot, heating him from inside.

When the door opens, Zito sees the woman Paz. Behind her Clemente Moreno is pulling on a pair of white jeans. The man is barefoot and shirtless. He looks as if he has just gotten out of bed, though it is late afternoon. In reality, Moreno has been resting and smoking reefer for about an hour. He has been readying himself to make his rounds, sell some coke. But now he looks up at John Zito and tells the woman Paz in Spanish to get out of the doorway and let Zito inside.

Zito comes in and closes the door. The room is a mess, but happy nonetheless. Paz has hung drapes and put pots of geraniums on the windowsills. Paz is terrified, and emits a low moan. She has heard of mass killings involving drugs, and now she is afraid she will be shot for something Moreno has done or not done. Moreno speaks to her in Spanish, telling her to be quiet, not to worry. When Moreno studies Zito, he thinks he looks popped, probably on alcohol, which makes him dangerous and unpredictable.

"What you say, you put the thing away," Moreno says, gesturing at the gun. Moreno pulls up his jeans and stands still with his arms folded. He feels unmanned, but he must keep up appearances. Something has been brewing in his head for a long time, and now he knows if he can survive this moment, it will come to fruition. "There is no need for the gun, my friend," Moreno says gently. Paz is backing away, but is still moaning. She knows no English, but she watches Spanish-language TV, where there are always stories of families murdered, men, women, and children indiscriminately mowed down like pigs. Dealers come inside a house and begin blasting with their weapons. Paz pictures this inside her mind. She can see herself bleeding, nobody helping her.

Zito levels Moreno with the Colt. "You're shorting me," he says. "Every fucking week."

"I told you, man," Moreno says. "I'm spread so thin," gesturing with two fingers collapsing together. "I got so many expenses, you know. You got to take it easy."

Zito tips over a vase, which crashes to the floor. He scans the room, seeing a table, a couch, a television stand behind him, the geraniums. A light breeze blows through the open panes of glass, and he smells beans and bread. He flicks the barrel of the Python and moves Moreno and Paz back into the bedroom. Moreno speaks again to Paz in Spanish.

Zito nears the woman. He backhands her with the butt of the Colt. A string of blood erupts from her nose and she falls to her knees. Zito pushes her back with his shoe and she falls, nearly unconscious. Moreno kneels down and touches her softly, but she is gone. In a moment, she wakes and is shocked.

"I want everything you have," Zito says. "All the coke in the house."

"Hey man," Moreno says, opening his palms in mock supplication. "You put me out of business, you out of business too."

"Do it, just fucking do it. I don't have all day."

Moreno now knows that Zito is not going to shoot either him or Paz. He did not seriously believe that this would happen, but he did think to himself that there could be an accident of intentions, something could get out of whack, especially because Zito seems half drunk. There is that smell on his breath. His eyes are red and unfocused. Now Moreno does a quick calculation in his head. He arrives at a figure of about eight ounces of powder cocaine in his suitcase, which is in the bedroom closet on an upper shelf. There is an ounce of basuco base in a leather pouch on the nightstand near the bed behind him, paste he uses to turn on his friends and associates. He likes the basuco because you can smoke it and it isn't expensive, and the kick is easier to weather. Thinking, Moreno hates to part with the eight ounces of powder. Yet he is confident that this amount will more than satisfy Zito's current fixation, so he decides to sacrifice this to the situation. He has another pound niched in a box at the base of the toilet bowl, but it seems to him that he can risk saving this from Zito.

Moreno holds up his hands. "You seem *loco*, my friend, you

know?" He levels his hands and approaches the closet. He opens the suitcase and shows Zito the baggies. Moreno puts the eight baggies in an old McDonald's sack and hands the sack to Zito. He smiles. "You going to sell this product on the street, officer?" he says. He is risking this irony, thinking it will fail to trigger anything in Zito, who seems dulled.

"Now some cash," Zito says. "You're way behind in your payments too."

This troubles Moreno. Right now he wishes he had the nerve to jump Zito, but the man is bigger and crazy, and he has a gun. Moreno's cash is in a drawer of the nightstand. It amounts to about forty-two hundred dollars. This he takes and places on the bed beside Paz, who has gotten up and is sitting still. Her terror has reduced itself to silence. In another moment she expects to die, and so she is praying to the Virgin. Zito picks up a handful of bills and places them in his pocket.

"Seed money," Zito says.

Moreno does not understand this locution. He decides to be cooperative, meek. "I hope this don't put me out of business."

"So, get to work," Zito says. "And meet me every fucking Friday of the week."

Zito backs into the main room, followed by Moreno. Paz rises and looks fearfully from the door of the bedroom, but she comes no farther. Zito is wistful for a moment, now on the downswing of the paranoid episode. His nostalgia makes him almost sorry he hit the Mexican woman. She looks no more than a child, with big ocelot eyes and skinny arms. There is blood up and down the front of her cotton dress. It looks as if her nose is broken.

"Hey look, man," Moreno says. "There isn't anybody going to do business with me this gets around. You going to kill your goose, you go on this way."

"Shut the fuck up," Zito says. He is without resource now, free-floating. Something painful shapes in Zito's consciousness. He kicks out sideways at the big Sony TV that is on a table by the front door. His kick isn't hard, nevertheless several small dials and buttons fall on the floor. Surely, the tuning system is ruined.

Across the room, Moreno opens and closes his eyes. He is

truly mortified and offended now. This was needless, he thinks to himself. Moreno recognizes a deep affliction passing through the cop, but even so, this act hurts Moreno more than any other right now. This affliction he has been around all his life. He himself is not immune to its effects, and by his own judgment he is not surprised that the cop is here, demanding cocaine and cash. After all, the cop has an affliction and a need. Moreno understands the risks of being around such desires. Still, his TV?

"Oh man," Moreno says sadly, "what you want to do that for to my TV?"

Zito backs out of the room and closes the door. Paz begins to wail madly.

"Shut your mouth, woman," Moreno says in Spanish. "Clean up this mess. I got to go out."

Moreno bends and picks up the tuner knobs. They are made of black Bakelite and are irretrievably fractured.

12

renee holds a coke spoon in both hands. She taps a fingernail of the drug onto a hand mirror and closes her eyes. She is alone with it for a moment, and then opens her eyes and begins to cut the scoop into quarters with a single-edge razor blade, chopping and sorting the powder into smooth white lines. It is work she loves, like singing a hymn in church. Pretty soon it is clear that she is playing with the drug, getting into her play, humming "Baby Love," working the razor with precision until the lines are separated by perhaps half an inch, smooth declarative sentences of malevolence and desire. The mirror holds the lines as if each were under water while Renee sings. This is truly her baby love, her ambition, her atonement.

Grace looks on from a pallet in the corner of the room. Renee smiles and lifts her eyebrows. They are great arcs of paint applied haphazardly.

"I don't blow that crack shit," Renee announces proudly. "That shit blow your mind," she says, as if everybody didn't know it. "I seen what that shit do to your head. I sell that shit, yeah, but I ain't never gonna do that shit 'cause that shit kill you."

A few moments pass while Renee investigates her next move. She takes a metal straw from a drawer and snorts one of the lines. There is a tight delicious smile on her face when she finishes. She rubs her nose and chokes briefly, then takes another snort and puts down the mirror.

The morning light is a frosty gray coming in from two windows on the south. It is foggy outside in the Panhandle, though it is probably beautiful somewhere in the Bay Area. Grace listens to Renee: "You my white angel, you," she says. "Put your hand on me, bless me." Renee is at play, hoping that Grace is watching her performance.

Grace sits in the lotus position, watching Renee bob and weave somewhere out of range. Grace understands the focus of events. She is near to them and can feel the certitude and palpability of their nearness. As a fact, the coke is already inside Renee's brain, pushing out toward her bloodstream in curious neural streams. Everything inside Renee is firing simultaneously and fast, the drug sending messages that otherwise wouldn't be there. Renee will drift in and out of range until the effect wears off, maybe five or ten minutes, and then she will be manic for another half an hour, and then she will do her two more hits and put down the mirror. It will continue that way until something upsets the flow, until Renee has no more cocaine, or until an outside force lowers the curtain.

This is Renee's room, an old Victorian boardinghouse just near Masonic and Fell. This is the outskirts of Haight-Ashbury, and it still recalls the hippies' heyday, with rainbow paint on the houses, dirt and garbage everywhere, but cool and hip in a dangerous way. The house itself is run-down and decrepit, peeling wallpaper and exposed laths, steam heat and rats. It is chopped into rooms, some with and some without bath. In the early morning it is misty outside. By noon the mist will burn off, and the sun will be shining.

Renee resides alone. Her living room fronts Fell Street, and in back are a small bedroom and bath. The floors are scarred oak, with many cigarette and candle burns, stains, dog piss spills. Right now Renee is sitting on a stool in front of a portable bar that came from St. Vincent de Paul. There is a picture of Diana Ross on the wall behind Renee. Renee looks up at the picture of Diana and sings more "Baby Love," over and over, without the verse.

Renee stops. "They say Diana a bitch," she says. Now she is out of sequence and talking to herself, with Grace Wu a participant. For Grace Wu it is like watching an automobile accident. You are involved, but you are not. "They say she ruined the Supremes," Renee continues. "They say she went off by herself without giving nobody a second thought." Renee looks at Grace. "Shit," she says loudly and with obvious irony.

Grace looks down at Fell Street and the Panhandle across the way. Some young people are jogging by in yuppie fluorescent gear. At least two or three are leading or trailing dogs on leashes. Brittanys and Labs, of course. It is too early for people to be on their way to work, and for that reason the street is relatively free of traffic. It is quiet but there is no quietude. There is an impending rush that will happen around seven-thirty or eight. Until then everybody is waiting for the alarm to ring, including Grace Wu.

"You know what I think?" Renee asks. Grace says nothing as there is no real need. "Diana, she not a bad old chick, you ask me. She done good, real good." Renee smiles to herself, eyes now closed again. "They say that same old shit about every woman makes something out of herself. *She no good, she a bitch.* You see some woman doing good, you watch. They gonna call her a bitch, eventually. Woman do good, they call her a bitch." Renee is cooking now, manic and running, eyes bright and glazed. She is an ice storm happening to herself. A real ice storm inside her head. She can barely sit still on her stool and she lights a menthol cigarette and takes deep consecutive drags on it until it is half gone. The smoke rises slowly. "You see *Lady Sings the Blues*?" Renee asks Grace.

"I saw it on TV," Grace says.

"That pretty good, you think?"

Grace agrees. For the first time in three days Grace feels practically well physically. She is not together mentally, but her back and neck are better. She turns and rests her head on the windowsill so that she can feel the cool mist on her cheek. This soothes her. She must consider what to do. She cannot continue to hide this way. And she worries terribly about Elgin, who she knows is checked into the downtown Hilton and probably waiting for her to call. It is conceivable that Elgin has pulled the plug on this whole operation and is looking for her everywhere. She wonders about John Zito too, whether he has heard that Grace has failed to report the results of her meeting with Kyungmoon Nho. But Grace is hurt and confused and can't explain to herself why she has not contacted her superiors. Something personal has happened to her, and it has created a lacuna in her will. For a moment Grace sees her reflection in the glass of the window.

There is a gray bruise under her right eye where the Koreans bounced her face on the floor. Her neck is stiff where they took turns sitting on the back of her head. All she remembers is everything, and it is terrible. She recalls each smell and thrust. She remembers the drive to the duplex, and she remembers being alone in East Oakland after Nho drove away in his Lexus. For a long time she sat silently with the necklace of rabbits' heads around her neck because she was too shocked and humiliated even to move, even to get rid of those heads around her neck. While she sat that way she thought that she could feel bruises developing on her spine where they had beaten her, hot numb patches between her shoulder blades that she couldn't touch. East Oakland was all around her, and it was a coffin of nothingness. She was lost inside a city. It took her half an hour to stop trembling and come to her senses.

Finally she took off the rabbits' head necklace. It was evening and almost fully dark with a bright orange moon rising in the east. In time she walked to the nearest convenience store and called a cab. She rode across Oakland to where her car was parked down the street from the Paramount Theater. It took her another half hour to get across the Bay Bridge. She went to Clement Street and got a cup of chocolate at a café she knew, sitting alone in the bright light, afraid to go home. Her sweater was torn and her right eye was swelling. She knew that the waitress was looking at her and she was ashamed. Still, she couldn't say how long she sat in the café, ordering one cup of chocolate after another. In all that time, though, she would have periods of lucidity, followed by periods of confusion, a roller coaster of panic and calm. She would begin to cry and stop herself. She hallucinated the faces of the Koreans. She imagined she smelled the cat piss in the carpet as they pushed her face into it. She descended into the smell itself, became one with it. More than anything she wanted a hot bath, the comfort of strangers.

Renee came into the café while Grace was crying. Renee saw Grace and came right over without saying anything. She looked as if she had been hustling all day.

"Say, girl," Renee said. "What happened?"

"I'm OK," Grace said.

"You look OK," Renee said. She slid into the booth and sat down across from Grace. "Me, I be Queen Sheba."

Grace tried to smile. "No really, I'm OK," she said. "It's just been a hard night." Grace was grateful for Renee. Strangely, she didn't want her to leave, but she didn't want to talk much either.

"You got the man trouble," Renee said. "I seen that shit before, it all over you, honey. He done ripped your pretty sweater too."

"It's that obvious?" Grace asked, knowing.

"Shit girl, *tell me,*" Renee said. "I fussed with them mens my whole life. When they get down they get down. They stupid fuckers too, you know?"

Grace laughed a little.

"You know why mens give a name to their dicks?" Renee asked Grace.

"I don't know, why?"

"That so a stranger don't do all their thinking," Renee said.

Now Grace laughed for real. "The men I know can call it Pee Wee," she said.

Now Renee laughed. "Say honey, you need a place to stay?" Renee asked.

Grace looks back from the window. She is grateful to Renee. Here she has found a refuge, even though it is pretty terrible. For Grace this room has traces of something that is fundamental, something familiar. Grace has been here for three days, mostly on her own while Renee leaves to do business, comes back with a pizza and soft drinks. They have eaten together and talked a lot. Grace has taken five or six hot baths. For some reason she thinks she could take five or six more, but the feeling is passing.

"As soon as it's light," Grace says, "I think I'll try to go home."

"You welcome to stay, girl," Renee says. Renee is coming down and Grace wonders if she'll do the two lines right away or wait. "You know you welcome to stay, honey."

"Thank you, Renee. Someday I'll pay you back."

"Ain't no payback, girl," Renee says. "They been times I could use some place to go. Back then I wasn't smart enough to know it. But I know it now."

"You have a man, Renee?" Grace asks. It is the one thing they haven't discussed.

"No man now, honey," Renee muses. She lights another cigarette. "I ain't got no back teeth and I'm nearly worn out. All I need is a man." Renee thinks. "My husband is dead," she says.

"I'm sorry, Renee," Grace says.

"All my men dead and gone," Renee says.

"Dead?" Grace says, truly surprised.

"Some dead, some gone," Renee laughs. "Shit!" she adds.

Grace must go. She has no bags, just a purse and the clothes she is wearing. Her car is outside, parked along the Panhandle, probably ticketed. "You got married young, huh?" Grace says.

Instead of speaking, Renee does another line. She uses the straw to suck up the cocaine. The lines disappear into her nose, into her blood, her brain. Renee is in the land of nod and her eyes close and she rocks on the stool. " 'Oooooo, ooooohhhh, baby love, my baby love,' " she sings. Renee is at one with a vision of herself, somewhere. Grace knows that for Renee there is nothing better than this moment. It is absolute. There is a Zero in the air and Renee is floating inside it. The cigarette smolders in her fingers. While she sings, Renee stares at the picture of Diana Ross on the wall. "They say that girl broke up the Supremes," Renee says. "They call her bitch. But you know any woman do good they gonna call her bitch. *Any* woman. Shit!"

"You know, I think you're right," Grace says. Perhaps Renee hears, perhaps not.

"Was I married young?" Renee asks herself. "I had me two babies in high school," she says. "Grew up in the Western Addition. I didn't get married, but it was the same thing to me."

"Where are your kids?"

"One he dead," Renee says without emotion. "The other he run off long time ago. That man who got me pregnant turned out to be a fool. He run off and got killed too."

Grace is standing, waiting for the moment to arrive when she can leave. She looks at Renee, her sad bulging thyroid eyes. Grace has seen her eat two slices of pizza in three days and drink dozens of diet sodas, snort coke, smoke menthol cigarettes, nothing else. The woman has an ageless old face, like a baby, a Somalian child. She has occasionally wandered the room in a semblance of confusion. There are no electronics, she has told Grace, because they would be stolen immediately. Renee has fallen into selling small quantities of crack because her last boyfriend was in the business and got killed and when he died she inherited his gig. She makes a little, snorts a little, makes a little, nothing greedy or dangerous. It was stable cake.

Grace gathers herself and approaches the door to leave. She knows that she will never bust Renee or cooperate with anyone who tries. Grace knows how bad drugs are, especially crack, but this is different. This is complicated stuff and Grace is not in any position to judge. She can only act.

In the few minutes she has been standing, waiting for Renee to come down from her third and fourth lines, Grace has decided what she will do. She will go over to Clement Street and telephone Elgin Lightfoot. She hopes that he is still in San Francisco. She thinks that it will be early enough to catch him at his hotel. Elgin isn't going to be happy with her, nor is he going to be happy that she has lost the hundred thousand government dollars. But right now she knows she needed exactly three days in hiding, her healing and praying space. Maybe Elgin will understand.

"What about you, girl?" Renee asks, out of context. "You got some good man who don't beat you?"

"No man," Grace says.

"Not married?"

"Not married," Grace replies. "Too busy and fucked up."

"Don't you worry," Renee says. "You too busy for a man, they gonna call you a bitch."

Grace opens the door to go. It looks as if Grace will be followed at least partway down the hall by Renee. Somewhere there are babies crying and radios playing.

"I don't know, Renee," Grace says. "Without you, I don't know."

"Don't worry, honey," Renee says.

"Maybe you'll find that good man," Grace says in parting.

"Shit, it ain't gonna happen for me," Renee says.

"Still, maybe."

"No," Renee says. "I got the HIV."

Grace touches Renee on the shoulder. She is stunned and brokenhearted about how things make sense, and don't. When she gets down to Fell Street the mist is burning off. It is going to be beautiful in the Bay Area.

The morning is busy on Guerrero Street. The sun shines brightly, there is a fresh breeze off the Bay, and there is the smell of fresh bread and coffee in the air. It is a morning to be happy, with young girls, schoolchildren, and tradesmen coming and going. The Mission District has the feel of a barrio, the sun just now climbing over the white walls of the church with its lace filigree of oleander and poinciana.

But Clemente Moreno is not happy, and walks quickly without enjoyment. He is dressed in white jeans and a tank top. He is wearing his dirty tennis shoes, and no belt. It is not how he desires to appear, especially because there are so many young women and girls he wishes he could impress.

On a normal morning he would glance at each of them as they went by, making eye contact and fixing them with his personality and holding them in his gaze like deer in the road as a large automobile with shining headlights draws near. Without the immediate presence of his self-esteem, Clemente Moreno feels humiliation and anger. These are the twin components of his unhappiness. It is the reason that he is unable to discover these women with his eyes and explore them, the reason there is an atmosphere of tension and doubt in his demeanor. It is shameful what John Zito has done to Clemente Moreno. This shame has plunged inside Moreno and he wishes he could eliminate it. But in order to expel his shame, Moreno must acquire new face, something that will soothe his conscience and erase the fate that has befallen him. He is precisely unmanned. This is the reason he has spoken as he did to the woman Paz, because she has seen his shame. He is angry with her for good reason, but as he walks farther south into the Mission, he decides he will do something to forgive himself for being cross with her. But for now he has other, more pressing, business.

Moreno is seeking the man called El Tiburon, the shark. Moreno knows that he may not find this man today, but that eventually he will if he keeps looking in all the correct places. El Tiburon will appear, he will be stumbled upon and come to life. It is just that this man does not have a schedule like another man. He answers to no particular call, even though he is known to frequent certain bars and restaurants and to drive a beautiful cherry red Impala. Moreno does not know where the man lives, to the extent that he does not know if Tiburon lives on this side of the bay or not, if he could live in San Jose or Santa Clara, or in some other town along the water. Moreno does know that Tiburon conducts some business here in the Mission District, and is often seen having coffee or tortillas here and there along Guerrero, or beside the mission. Because it is just now late afternoon, there is a chance he may see the man. The thing that has been fermenting inside Moreno's head is now fully brewed. It is a necessary thing, even if it is evil.

Moreno crosses Twenty-first Street, then Twenty-fourth Street, marching uphill with purpose. This is an area of shops and restaurants, laundromats and outdoor markets, which sell fruits and vegetables, woven goods and grain. There are panhandlers here, just as there are panhandlers all over the City now, and homeless beggars too, although fewer of these than in the Tenderloin. Spanish is spoken. When Moreno closes his eyes at a street corner before he crosses with the light, he can almost imagine that he is back in Morelia, although it is neither so hot nor so dusty, nor is the air so sanguine and dry. What is important is not this imaginary event, but the real event that has pushed its way into his life and taken it over. For this Moreno has nothing to compare with it, nothing experiential. But he is not without a fundamental understanding of what the experience might mean and entail, after all. He is a man.

Before crossing the border at El Paso, before the change in his fate, Moreno had spent the better part of his young life chopping cactus and digging irrigation ditches on estancias and ranchos. He has no education, although he can read and write small bits of language. Nevertheless, he is proud that none of this has stopped him from succeeding in America, from making money and owning a car and from assuming a position of some importance in the street, for the street is where a man receives his life's blood. Yet his experience with violence is strictly limited. There was the time when he was sleeping beneath the porch of a workers cabin on a rancho when he was awakened by the sound of two men fighting. This sound was utterly unmistakable and dense, and when he had adjusted his eyes to the dim starlight he could see that one of the men had been stabbed in the stomach and had staggered outside the cabin and onto the wooden veranda and was about to collapse in the dust. There was much blood and a terrible gurgling toilet sound in the stabbed man's throat. Moreno remembers exactly the terrible event, with the blood soaking into the sandy moonlit soil, which in the day is bone white. Moreno can remember the man's anguished cries, his prayers near the end, just as the life was going out of him, and his vicious personal curse against the murderer. It was then that the name of God had been invoked, as blood sank into the soil.

And another time Moreno was part of a work crew far out in the barren arroyo countryside sawing fence posts when a gang of *judicales*, led by a single uniformed *federale* arrived in two Buicks and took away one of the other men. This man, who had been working on mesquite with a saw, turned in horror when he saw the police, but in the expanse of desert and rock there was nowhere to run. Six of these officials, carrying rifles and clubs, grabbed the worker and beat him. This was a sight that Moreno has never forgotten. These were sounds that would always haunt him, of broken bones. In this way Moreno was taught that violence was both serious and fundamental.

Moreno proceeds to Army Street, then backtracks to Valencia and goes the way he came, one block over. Valencia Street is quieter than Guerrero, although there are still many shops and stores. The sky is a lovely shade of blue and seems to single him out, making him wish more than ever that he was not wearing white jeans and a tank top. The women on Valencia walk in pairs or fours, arm in arm, never alone, and he wishes he could look at them and embarrass them in fun. He thinks that his life has been a fine thing, a thing like a good watch or leather belt, something with shape and form and craftsmanship, at least until this John Zito came along. And then when Moreno arrives at Hill Street he sees the Shark.

The Shark is seeking a break in traffic so that he can cross the street. Standing still with his long arms hanging loose and his thin but long mustache arcing across his upper lip, he is the essence of freedom. He looks as though he has no care in the world. He is thin, like a stiletto, and his face is thin along with that, and his left eye is at the edge of a dark blue scar that inches along his left cheek, ending at the corner of his mouth. He wears a white guayabara and clingy black pants. He is the kind of man you can look closely at and never catch a hint of his emotion. It is said that he is clairvoyant, that he has enormous sexual powers and appetites, and that he has killed two men. This creates a tremendous persona for the Shark, and one he carries well.

In truth, Moreno has spoken with Tiburon on several informal occasions, in bars and cantinas. Once he sat and drank with the man for thirty minutes during a street festival when both of them were out and enjoying the day. Moreno remembers that the Shark is very factual. He is not a showman, even though he has a cold stare that holds you fixed. At times what he says makes no direct sense, only there is an underlying texture of meaning and intent that bewitches. Moreno knows that the Shark does not lose his center when women are present. If anything, he does not seem to notice them at all.

Moreno approaches before the traffic breaks. "Hey, *señor*," he says.

Tiburon is from Mexicali. It is there that he is said to have murdered a policeman. Tiburon nods but does not speak. It is obvious that Moreno is welcome to continue.

"Hey, I wish to speak with you on business," Moreno says in Spanish. "Strictly man to man," he adds.

"All right," Tiburon replies.

"You want to have a drink?" Moreno asks, gesturing behind him to a bar on the corner. It is called El Patio, and every Saturday and Sunday there is live music. The walls are pink stucco, the windows small circles of dark.

"I don't mind," Tiburon says.

Moreno precedes the other to the door and opens it while the other enters. Moreno will defer until their relationship is on a different basis. But for now this is the way he feels he can advance his own interests, even if it hurts his pride to do so. The formality of his feeling will guide him to the proper proportion.

Inside the two men sit in a booth in back. There are only a few people drinking beer at the bar. One or two are gringos, but the rest are locals. Moreno orders a beer and Tiburon a glass of orange juice.

When the drinks come Tiburon says, "So, what is it you want now?"

"This is business," Moreno says.

"So, that's good," Tiburon replies. "I'm a businessman." He drinks some of his juice and places the glass on the table.

"I have great trouble," Moreno says.

"You come to me?"

"This trouble is large. It is so large I cannot handle it alone, even though I wish to do so. I need a service and I am willing to pay well."

"This is a good thing," Tiburon says. His mustache has captured some of the pulp. The bones in his feral face seem to send messages.

"Such things are hard to speak about," Moreno says. In their traditional way, these men will coerce the truth from a situation. In addition, it is impolite to be direct with someone you hardly know. "I am involved with a woman who is the source of great anxiety to me. If she continues to live, she will destroy everything I have worked for all my life. Therefore, she must not continue to live."

Tiburon continues to stare. "A woman," he says, an implication of disapproval.

"This woman is a whore and a dog," Moreno says. He uses the word *puta* in such a way that he clearly means cunt, not prostitute.

"This woman is police, no?" Tiburon says, smiling and touching his mustache.

"I sold to her," Moreno admits.

"And she has your balls in her sack," Tiburon says. In Spanish this is very derogatory to Moreno. In essence, the whole conversation turns on this moment. For Moreno must now transform his disadvantage into leverage.

"No, it is not so simple," Moreno says. "There is a big police lieutenant named Zito who has me by the balls." Moreno leans over the table and whispers nastily, "This fucking police is now on my payroll, you understand? And if I do not pay he is going to hand me to the puta."

"This puta is a narca," Tiburon concludes.

Moreno shrugs, which is enough.

"Your trouble is indeed large," Tiburon says. The waitress returns to the booth. She is a plump girl, perhaps twenty years old, serving illegally. Neither man wishes anything more to drink and she leaves. "And what is it you want with me?" Tiburon says.

"In the normal case, I take care of these two myself," Moreno lies. "But I must kill these two police at nearly the same time. One without the other is no good." Moreno takes a drink of beer and wipes his mouth. "These two must arrive in hell holding hands."

This amuses Tiburon, tickles his fancy. "You know where these two live?"

"Yes, of course," Moreno lies. He knows where John Zito lives, but he must find Grace Wu. "That is not a problem," he continues after a moment. In the war of formalities he is definitely holding his own. "I kill the puta happily," he says. "I will fuck the puta after she is dead with a smile on my face. I will drag her body into the street for the dogs to eat." As a part of the performance, Moreno heaves out his chest. "You kill this other police for me and I make you rich."

Tiburon taps his juice glass on the table, then again, and makes a circle with it, around and around. He licks his mustache. Not once have his eyes left Moreno's eyes. It is unnerving to Moreno to see such concentration. But Moreno is proud of his speech. He thinks it worthy. He thinks it has set the right tone.

"How rich?" Tiburon asks.

"Half a pound of blanco," Moreno says.

"I'm not a fucking salesman," Tiburon says in slang.

"Then I turn the blanco into cash for you. Fifteen or sixteen thousand American. Whatever I can get in Los Angeles in the next week. The way this big lieutenant is going I don't have much time. His eyes are red and his head is light."

Tiburon listens to the spheres. They are talking to him now, convincing him that this business has distinct possibilities. While he listens, Moreno explains that Zito has a house in the hills of San Rafael. The address is easy to locate and the man goes across the bridge every day. The home is quiet and secluded, surrounded by trees with a steep driveway that goes down between shoulders of earth and vines of ice plant. Moreno says he will locate the puta and kill her whenever they are ready. In this way, both of the police will enter hell holding hands. He will deliver half of the money to Tiburon now, and half when the job is done.

Tiburon shrugs implacably. "So turn the blanco," he says by way of agreement. "You have the money you tell the woman named Gloria at the bar. She will let me know. Then I will meet you here when you say." Now Tiburon finishes his juice, precisely at the moment of truth. He smiles. "And we kill these fucking police," he says.

Moreno walks with Tiburon to the door, an equal now. The Shark opens the door and Moreno follows him outside and into the beautiful evening sunlight on Valencia Street. Moreno knows that he must wait while Tiburon goes away. But already his confidence is better, his pride has partially returned.

When Tiburon is gone, Moreno hurries back to Guerrero Street to his apartment. He finds that Paz has cleaned the broken vase from the floor and has mopped up the blood. He sees her standing in the middle of the room. She is afraid of him and moves away, back into the bedroom.

Moreno goes to the bedroom where Paz huddles like an animal. She is sitting on the bed, hands folded as neatly as a napkin. Her long red dress is made of thin cotton and Moreno can see through it. Quickly, he takes off his pants and lifts her dress and fucks her from behind.

In this way she is forgiven for witnessing his shame.

onday morning Elgin Lightfoot wakes at three-thirty, four-fifteen, five-twenty, by then worn out. He abandons the effort to sleep and lies awake looking at the spackled ceiling of his $98.50 room, plus city, state, and entertainment tax. This is his third night in the room, which is two more nights than he had intended to spend, a fact which is making it difficult for him to keep from notifying DEA in Los Angeles.

The room is at the end of a hallway at the back of a building in downtown San Francisco and its view is of an alley and a brick wall. All night an ice machine outside his door chugs. It has become a meeting place for drunks who wander the hall making noise at all hours. The maid comes and cleans at eleven, putting down new sheets, bars of soap, a sanitizer on the toilet, and a chocolate heart on the bed pillow with a card inviting him to evaluate the service. Twice he has ordered room service breakfasts in order to stay beside the phone, a twelve-fifty choice, plus tip, for coffee, bran flakes, some half and half. However, there is a complimentary copy of the morning *Chronicle* outside his door at eight, but as yet there is no article in it mentioning the murder of an Asian woman, five six, black hair, dark complexioned. Nothing at all.

Elgin has had recurring dreams. In one he is in country like the Glacier National Park, high pine hills, mountains far away, the heavy silence of deep snowfall. The sky is slate gray, as they say, and there are crows screaming as they fly in random formations. Elgin holds a heavy ax in his hands, walking through the trackless pines. Finally, he reaches a mountain lake and walks out onto the solid ice with the ax raised, and proceeds to chop a hole in the ice, near the middle of the perfectly circular lake. He has no fishing equipment or other implements, just the ax. It is cold. He can see his breath. The silence is deafening. When he manages to break through the ice, a dog's head appears, snarling and vicious, teeth bared and bloody. In a slow transmogrification, the dog's head becomes the head of Elgin's long-lost father, which is frozen blue in an attitude approximating that of the dog. Elgin wakes in a sweat and stares at the spackled ceiling.

But this morning at seven o'clock, having lain awake for nearly two hours, the meaning of the dream becomes clear to Elgin. He concludes that the surface of the lake is his psyche. He reasons that the ax is his ego, and the ice his past. The snarling dog's head, and the emergent head of his father, represent his id. Coupled with his present worry over the fate of Grace Wu, the dream is a cautionary tale of loss and transfiguration, and Elgin wonders what his ancestors would have made of such a vivid dream as they sat around their campfires at night, worrying over the symbology and etiology of their visions. Such dreams, Elgin knows, were challenges to the individual intuition. Such things were considered omens of the clan, spiritual alarms. But in America in the late twentieth century, such events are annoyances, impediments to rationality, causes for concern. These dreams are calling Elgin home.

He does his stretching exercises, designed to lessen the influence over his knee of an old shrapnel wound. Some mornings it requires over thirty minutes for him to properly loosen up, to eliminate his slight natural limping gait. In the cold or the rain, his knee often tightens immediately. After any exercise, the knee is always a problem. He takes a shower. He is toweling off when the telephone rings.

Elgin has run out of hope for Grace. From his hotel room he was able to reach John Zito late Friday night, but the man was mumbling and drunk. Nevertheless, it was clear that he had not heard from Grace Wu. All day Saturday and Sunday Elgin made efforts to contact Zito again, but failed. He didn't dare phone Grace at her apartment, if she was there, and so he drove around and around it, and then up and down Clement Street where she did her deals, but she wasn't there either. Likewise, he didn't dare surveil the El Cerrito house, or Kyungmoon Nho's apartment in Oakland, for fear that he would be spotted and his usefulness at DEA ended. So he spent his days waiting beside the telephone, trying to remain calm and confident. He is a manager with nothing to manage. He suffered a recurrent dream. He ate expensive and inferior room service food.

When the phone rings, he expects disaster.

"It's me. Grace." Elgin listens intently. There is no background depth. Just empty space.

Elgin sits down on the bed. He has been coming his long hair. "Where are you?" he asks.

Grace says she is in a coffee shop on Clement Street. She hastens to reassure Elgin that she is OK, although the operation is in difficulty.

"Just say *shut up* if someone is there with you," Elgin says.

"It isn't like that, Elgin," Grace says. "It really isn't. I'm OK, all the way."

Elgin is evaluating, managing. He looks at the electric clock on the nightstand. Here it is nine o'clock Monday morning and his agent is two days late reporting. He is relieved and concerned. To his trained ear the voice of Grace Wu reveals a distanced quality, something transcendental and opaque that is hard to calculate. She sounds like a diver who has been down too long and come up too fast. When he finally plugs in all his experience and skill, he has to admit to himself that he is without a clue as to Grace's present predicament. This worries him, as much as if Grace were lying on a stretcher in the Life Watch helicopter.

"Then we need to talk, *now,*" Elgin says. "If you're alone we need to talk." Elgin is not convinced. He has not suspended his disbelief yet.

"I know you're concerned," Grace says.

"That's putting it mildly."

"I don't want to go home," Grace says.

Grace says she will drive her taxi over to the Geary Boulevard apartment, but that she'll just sit outside. "If that's OK," she adds. Elgin agrees to meet her there while she goes up the stairs and gets some clothes. What is happening is fuzzy to Elgin, but he goes along. He has no choice.

In thirty minutes he is dressed and on his way across town. He parks in a bus zone in front of the apartment and sees two people watching him from their real estate office. Grace stands outside the front door, waiting. She is dressed in jeans, but her sweater is torn at the sleeve. Mr. and Mrs. Piltka stand in the window of their office as mute observers, eyes swiveling on reptilian stalks. Grace steps over to the vehicle and tells Elgin that she's going upstairs to shower and change clothes. He says he will pull around the corner and wait for her on Fifteenth Avenue. Nothing happens between them at this time. Elgin notices her diffident mood, and he sees her disfigurement.

Grace goes upstairs and is forced to enter her bathroom and take off her clothes. The sight of herself naked is sickening. Quickly she takes a shower and washes her hair and applies conditioner. She soaps herself and scrubs her body with a loofah. Once again, as she emerges from the shower, she is forced to see her body naked. It is like an alien being. It is as if something has come from outer space and is accusing her mutely. For a moment she wishes to break the mirror, thus shattering her sickness. But her anger subsides. She dries her hair and combs it out until it falls right. She is not going to tie it back today. With meticulous care she applies lipstick and eyeliner and spends ten minutes picking out a plain gray pleated skirt and a dark blue cashmere sweater that she hasn't worn in years. She puts on pantyhose with dark blue pumps that match her sweater. When she finishes dressing she feels like crying, but doesn't. She has destroyed the alien, but it is still there beneath the skin. She goes out of the apartment and locks the door, testing it twice. Downstairs, Elgin is waiting for her, smiling as she gets inside the car.

"I'd like to go somewhere fresh and clean," Grace says.

Elgin starts the motor and nods. He is driving a rented Buick that smells of artificial leather spray. Something has happened to Grace, he thinks. Something has happened, something is happening, something is going to happen. As Elgin pulls away from the curb, Grace leans over and turns on the FM radio. Classical music comes from the speakers. It is lush music, too lush for Elgin, but soothing. Grace watches the streets. There are fancy and not so fancy restaurants, used-book shops, boutiques. There is danger in them being together, but Elgin has dismissed this from his mind. He rides the fog that is Grace Wu. He circles through the Presidio and heads across the Golden Gate, from which you can see the white mist lying three miles out in the Pacific Ocean. Sailboats are spinning around Angel Island. From this far away, the Oakland Hills are abstract and lovely. They are like the forms of Cézanne.

Elgin goes north on 101 past Mill Valley. The traffic is moderate at first, then thins as they leave the suburbs. San Pablo Bay lies to the east. On their left, the mountains of the coastal range appear. The grassy hills alongside the freeway are drought brown. They drive in virtual silence except for the classical music. The Mobil Oil refineries and storage facilities appear. There are dozens of massive tanks crowded along the edge of the water. Each has been painted in a different pastel hue, sherbert orange, lime, rose. Tankers nestle up to them, offloading, loading, like bees at flowers. When they reach the road to Sonoma, Elgin cuts north into the countryside that has been clawed to death by development. Townhouses and condos rise up in clusters, housing tracts, minimalls cut out of the hills. Ten miles later they are in wine country and Grace Wu tells Elgin everything that happened to her in the duplex apartment in the East Bay. She tells Elgin that she was sodomized and beaten. Her words are like a sound track to the highway. She speaks as if she were a tape recording. Elgin keeps track of everything, the road, the speech, the classical music. His mind is running clear and strong. They go through vineyards turning orange and gold. There are wineries and villages.

In Sonoma Elgin parks on the city square. He goes into a bakery and buys French bread, Greek olives, a fresh block of camembert, a small salami. He has no idea if these things match. There is a winery on the edge of town and Elgin purchases a bottle of cabernet and drives to a park. Elgin leads Grace to a picnic table under a dusty sycamore tree.

"This is as fresh and clean as I know," Elgin says. "Around here," he adds.

Grace breaks the bread. Elgin pours two cups of wine and he drinks some of his. In the meantime, Grace has made two sandwiches and is busily eating. She realizes that she is hungry. In three days she has eaten only a few slices of pizza and had some diet sodas.

"I'm sorry about the operation," Grace says.

"Yeah," Elgin says. "It isn't important now."

Elgin tries not to notice the tears in Grace's eyes. He looks away and back nervously.

"I don't know the rules anymore, Elgin," Grace says. "What good am I supposed to be doing? I'm out on the street selling drugs. The product I turn winds up in junior highs." Grace touches her own face. "I'm not saying I feel sorry for myself," she continues. "But what does the DEA Handbook say?"

This irony flutters between the two of them. It is quiet in the park. "The Handbook doesn't recognize individuals, Grace," Elgin says. "It's all statistics, body counts." Elgin tastes his wine. It is dusky, like crushed apples. "There's only you and me, Grace," he says.

"Me and you, you and me, me and you," Grace says. She is teetering on something important.

"Zito is out," Elgin says. "Even Clemente Moreno is out. It really is you and me."

It is midafternoon in a city park in Sonoma, California. The cottonwoods are clicking in a dry breeze and the sun is dappling the dry grass. It is almost hot in the shade, but not quite, and thus comfortable.

"So what are my options?" Grace says.

"Sure, we have those," Elgin replies. "For one thing, you can play it straight and file a criminal complaint in Contra Costa County. Bring these guys up on kidnapping and sodomy and all that. The county gets a search warrant and we have these guys for guns and drugs."

"And some defense lawyer does an Anita Hill on me?" Grace says. "Zito puts me on meter maid detail along Market Street."

"OK, here's another option. We use what we have now on Nho and his wholesalers. It's enough to hit him hard. Sure, we lose Mr. Kim and his money. But it's a federal rap and you maintain your integrity as an agent."

"I lose my stinger and die for the DEA."

"You're through in undercover, but that's part of the option," Elgin says.

They spend some time eating olives and drinking wine. Elgin thinks about his dream again, this time from a new perspective. He hears the ax bite against ice. He sees the snow in the trees. Something heavy coagulates in the cold air. And just then Elgin realizes that the snow symbolizes cocaine. It is snowing in his world and there are no rules. Like Grace, he is far away from his home and his roots. Sitting here in a park in Sonoma, California, Elgin can smell the soil and the bark of the cottonwood trees. He can feel the substance of the wind. But there is something else too, a different feeling. When he looks at Grace Wu, he feels something for her too. She is as real and substantial as the smell of the dust.

"Would you do something for me, Elgin?" Grace asks.

"Sure, if I can."

"See if you can locate my brother. He's been in and out of halfway houses and programs in San Jose. See if you can find him for me. I haven't heard from him in six months. I'd do it myself, but I don't want to involve my parents. It scares me right now."

"I'll punch him in," Elgin says.

Grace thinks about her life now. She is quiet, pondering its imponderability. She realizes too that there are no rules. Everything is a matter of tactics. Now she is part of the body count. She is a statistic, as dry as ink.

"I don't want my usefulness to end," Grace says.

Elgin sighs. He is admiring the sound of the wind in the cottonwoods, which is like the rustle of paper. He thinks about the ideal and the real, the ice and what is underneath. "Give me some time," he tells Grace. "Maybe I'll come up with something."

"No matter what," Grace says. "I want you to promise me one thing."

"You name it."

"Don't ever bust Renee," Grace says. "She's in my notes."

"I know about her."

"She's dying, Elgin," Grace says by way of explanation. "And there are other reasons besides."

"I can do that."

Now Grace is sleepy from the wine. She is exhausted from her ordeal. Flies dance on the bread crusts. Elgin is wondering where all of this is going. His management skills are of no use to him.

"There's another option," Grace says.

"I don't know," Elgin says.

"I could do what a drug dealer would do," Grace says. "You know what I mean?"

15

his is John Zito, sterile lab rat. "YOU THERE, LIEU-
TENANT?" Zito listens to the beeper, its faint electrical
pulse in his ear. He thinks it is morning, but can't be sure.
The shade is drawn over the single window in the back of his
room. It is a pumpkin-colored rectangle. It is a dish of paint. On
a table beside Zito is a water glass half full of vodka. Zito tastes
the vodka and listens some more. "WE GOT A CARAVAN, WE
GOT A CARAVAN DOWN ON LOMBARD BY THE BIG SAFE-
WAY. CAN YOU GET DOWN HERE?"

For a week John Zito has been receiving messages from afar.
His brain is a computer on the blink. It prints out symbols in
bizarre fonts. He has tried not drinking, but it makes him crazy.
In his ambivalence he snorts cocaine. The alcohol calms him, the
coke roars in his head. He is in a race with reality. The record-
ings in his brain are scratchy. What he hears on the beeper he
thinks is real. But then again?

Emotion number one for Zito is anger. He keeps replaying the
first meeting with his impairment officer.

"So, you have a problem with alcohol?" the officer said. She's
a woman, naturally. The two of them are in a corner room at
the Hall of Justice. Right away, Zito sized the woman up, a dyke
with a degree from San Francisco State. He sat down across from
the woman, prepared to do his time. The desk is a clutter of file
folders. He felt divided off, but still there. These women, he
thought, they're all liaison persons, file clerks, meter maids, and
now impairment officers.

"Relax," the woman said. "Let's just talk about alcohol."

"My fucking problem is you," Zito said.

"You're very angry, John," she said.

"Let me ask you something," he replied. "You ever get shot at by two blacks in a jewelry store?"

The woman was wearing a navy blue suit. She glanced inside a manila envelope. "It says here you broke your wife's jaw. You've had all your sick leave. Your car has been repossessed."

Traffic on the expressway outside went by in cold lock step. Zito was in a controlled fucking rage. This woman was raping him right there on the second floor.

"Sometimes it helps to talk," the woman said.

"Fine," Zito said. "So talk."

The woman said, "No, Lieutenant. There's a thing called denial, maybe you've heard of it." And for Zito, there were indignities and there were indignities, but this was something special. It was more special than domestic violence court, more special than divorce court, more special even than finding a note taped to the mailbox telling you your car has been repossessed. It was a jungle of shit.

"CARAVAN, LIEUTENANT, WE GOT A CARAVAN STOPPED DOWN ON LOMBARD BY THE BIG SAFEWAY. CAN YOU GET DOWN HERE?"

Zito speaks into the beeper. He goes to the bathroom and confronts the white noise of a shower. He remains in the bathroom for a long time after his shower. He thinks about how unclean he has become. One of his recollections of Lenore is her devotion to hygiene, all her bottles and tubes committed to the subject. In a way, he is glad that he is away from her because now he is free to be dirty and to snort coke. He always considered it unmanly to have to sneak away from the San Rafael house to get a drink, or to try to hide his drunkenness when he came home late. While peering into the mirror, he realizes that he does not look well. His nose is runny all the time. He is surprised that the impairment officer didn't ask him about it, but secretly he believes that she ignored this symptom in order to lure him into a secure and confidential relationship.

Zito manages to get into a suit and tie. He's driving his departmental car across town. He's driving it all the time, which is against regulations, but so far nobody has called him on it. When he gets to the top of Russian Hill, he becomes slightly paranoid because of the great drop in elevation to the bottom of Bay Street. Making it to Lombard, he turns left in heavy traffic and goes six blocks until he can see flashing lights, squad cars, and a roadblock. A green BMW is sideways against the curb. Zito maneuvers around the roadblock, parks in the Safeway lot, and walks back to the scene. His head is pounding but he thinks he can handle it. He sees a man face down in the street. Half a block away, an EMS crew is talking to some cops. The street corners are full of onlookers and there is a news crew filming already. Live at five and all that jive, another happy news hour for KSFO.

The uniformed officer who approaches Zito has been studying the BMW. It is a stripped-down model with tinted glass all around. One of its tires is flat. The officer introduces himself and walks away, waiting.

Zito goes over to a detective on his squad. The man is an old-timer who doesn't know about Zito's problems, or at least doesn't care. They speak, but aren't friends. In fact, John Zito has few real friends on the force anymore. "What a mess," the detective says.

"Who got shot?" Zito asks.

"Black dude in the BMW. He was alone."

"We have any liability problems?"

The detective grins. "Not this time, John."

"And the EMS?" Zito asks. The moment is wearing on him. The sky is blue. There is an aroma of peppermint in the air.

"Rookie named Stevens got winged," the detective says. "He was driving along Lombard when he thinks he sees a caravan. He must have been coming down from a briefing, getting visions of glory and decorations. Anyway, he decides to tackle all three cars by himself. Chevy van in front, BMW in the middle with our dead guy driving, and an Olds station wagon sucking hind tit. Stevens sees the van *slow down* to make a red light and figures he's got a caravan, they want to stay together. So, he calls it in, puts on his red light and siren, and goes off in a cloud of fucking dust. You believe that guy? Next thing we know, the guy in the Beamer takes a blast at Stevens from a shotgun and blows out his window. Some flying glass nicks his ear and Stevens empties his pants and his revolver. What you see on the pavement is the result."

"Stevens talk to the news guys?"

"No way, Lieutenant," the detective says.

"Got an ID on the other cars?"

"Stolen plates probably."

Zito follows the detective to the BMW and watches while he opens the trunk. Inside is a cardboard box loaded with about three pounds of white powder. This is worth, roughly, a hundred thousand dollars on the street. Zito slits open one of the bags and takes a taste. It is stepped on, but lightly.

The detective leans over Zito's right shoulder. "You're not going to believe what's in the car."

Zito walks around the car and looks inside. Another cardboard box is filled with money, fifties and hundreds by the look of it. Some are loose bills, but most are rolls with rubber bands around them. This is the answer to somebody's prayer, Zito thinks. For an instant his head is filled with something besides snow, an idea. Zito returns to his vehicle and calls the Secret Service. He sits in his car and contemplates the caravan and its connection to his everyday life. These days he disconnects no event from his own travail. To him, each event is connected to every other event by a transference of moral energy, a dharma peculiar to John Zito. The chain—his wife, his father-in-law, two lawyers, the bank loan officer, Clemente Moreno—all are links around his neck. The chain is dragging him under. John Zito sees the cash in the Beamer as a way to break the chain. He sits in the car and wishes he had a swig of Absolut. The thought brings him back to the impairment officer.

"You *do* know what denial is, don't you?" she had asked.

"Why don't you tell me."

"It's when a person thinks he's free, but isn't."

Presumably, this equation had promise for his own life, but John Zito didn't see it. The woman smiled knowingly and Zito said nothing.

"I drink," Zito said. "Sometimes I drink a lot, but it isn't fucking me up."

"How much is a lot?"

Zito then recognized his mistake. Nothing he said would lead away from the center of this maze. There was no trail away from this impairment officer, just as there was no trail away from his wife, Lenore. The console had no Off button. In the simplest statement was an intimacy that revealed your naked self. What bullshit.

"Look," Zito said finally. "I've been doing this job for fifteen years and I'm good. You don't know shit what it's like. You sit on your ass and crap on people like me, that's all."

Zito stood up in ostensible triumph. "I'll tell you something, Lieutenant," the woman said then. "Any fucking time I like I can pull your plug. Don't forget that. I've got your balls."

Even now Zito can hear that line. Zito gets out of his car and walks up Lombard Street, then back toward the BMW. He looks at the black dude lying in the street with an arc of blood spread around his head. He is young, perhaps twenty-five years old with a shaved head and black baggy pants, a black silk shirt, and lots of gold. He is wearing pump-up tennis shoes, about two hundred dollars a pair. Zito feels respect for the guy in death. They are kinsmen. They define each other against the backdrop of the world. Zito is unaware that a Buick Regal has pulled up behind him and two Secret Service agents have gotten out and are looking at the money in the BMW.

One of the agents introduces himself to Zito as Archer. The fed is very clean-cut, wearing a seersucker suit, white shirt, and pale blue tie.

"Fucking shit is counterfeit, isn't it?" Zito says.

"I think so," Archer replies. "You've got a good eye."

"You want to talk to the guy what brought it, he's right here," Zito says, pointing at the dead man.

"Scrape his ass up, I might do it," Archer says.

"I want to keep the money for a while," Zito says. "It will help my officer just until the probable-cause hearing next week. Shove this shit and the coke and shotgun in front of the captain's face, my officer is home free."

"Be my guest," Archer says. He is happy to be of help. "Inventory it, call me up." Archer studies the black guy, probably in awe. "Besides," he says, "I've seen some of that shit before. It's made in Germany and funneled in through Montreal. I can tell you the address of the warehouse in Bremerhaven where it's printed." He smiles. "But it's truly good and remarkable shit."

Zito watches the agents get in their Regal and drive away down Lombard Street. He stands in the sunshine and talks to his men and then goes back to his own car and takes a drink of vodka from a bottle he keeps under the seat. He is loving the idea of the money now. In his head, it is the same thing as the real thing. In his fantasies, he is somewhere on a beach in Mexico with his face looking toward Christmas Island thousands of miles away. He wonders if he has the guts to cut and run. When it comes down to it, he thinks he just might. He thinks he could get on a plane and hide forever. But not with counterfeit money. Now where could he get a couple of hundred thousand American dollars?

On the way home Zito stops for a fast-food breakfast. He eats half an egg and muffin sandwich, but it makes him physically ill and he throws it out onto the street as he drives. In twenty minutes more he is across the City and parked in the basement garage of the Hall of Justice. There is a message from Elgin Lightfoot waiting for him and Zito has the man paged. When Lightfoot arrives at Zito's office, he seems upset. Zito is behind his desk, Lightfoot in front.

"How you doing?" Lightfoot asks.

Zito says OK. He has been trying to keep track of Grace Wu, but she has slipped away. How long has it been since her deal with Kyungmoon Nho? Zito gathers from Lightfoot's demeanor that she hasn't been a great success. This doesn't surprise him, for he had little faith in her. He thinks they should bust the twenty or so street dealers she knows and let her go. She could become an impairment officer, for fuck's sake.

"You still got my nine hundred thousand?" Lightfoot asks, jokingly.

"Downstairs," Zito says.

"I'm going to need it next Friday afternoon."

"You playing the stock market?"

"Grace is turning a deal," Lightfoot says.

"You got to be shitting me," Zito says. "With those fucking Koreans?"

"Surprise, huh?"

"No shit," Zito says. He didn't think this could happen. He ponders this seriously and looks at the cardboard box in the corner of his office. Right now he has a box full of counterfeit dollars, but what can it become? For a moment he loses track of himself.

"I'll be by next Friday morning to get my cash," Lightfoot says.

"Say, how did that deal go down with Nho?" Zito asks.

"I'll send you a report."

"Just send me a big bust," Zito says professionally.

Lightfoot stands to go, already thinking about Grace Wu, whom he'd like to see personally. In fact, he thinks he might leave a message on her machine and see if he can arrange dinner someplace nice. He has been thinking about her a lot. She looked nice in her pleated skirt and cashmere sweater. It doesn't matter that he is violating one rule of the DEA Handbook.

"Just imagine this little Asian bitch," Zito says before Lightfoot is gone.

Zito sits alone for a long time. His nose is runny and he has a headache. He writes up his notes and goes to a bar on Market Street for a drink.

16

at eighty-five miles an hour, things go by quickly. Spray-painted on the side of the Bank of America Building, San Pablo Avenue: "Oh boy, When your Dead you cant take nothing with you but your soul." Aside from the simple mistakes of grammar and spelling, this message is profound for its lack of profundity, the phenomenological vacuity. There are dead dogs on the road, Rastas selling falafel, patches of shattered accident glass, until Elgin finally gets out of the immediate snarl of the Bay Area and is in the grassy foothill country for about forty miles, where the condos and townhouses look like Lego Squares. Now there are truck stops, and behind them the housing developments, mid-eighties, high nineties, on up and up. It is very early in the morning and the traffic is heavy against him, but light going out. The sun is high and it is hot in the valley and Elgin is driving with all the windows down and the radio blaring oldies. Even though he is speeding, he must gun it to pass the huge tankers that hog the road, the Winnebagos, motorcycles, and vans. But right now Elgin is in a Dodge Viper, which is a high-performance automobile worth about sixty thousand dollars, maybe more, depending on the production for this year. It is low and hot and smells new, and Elgin wonders how the yuppie Contra Costa lawyer who once owned it feels now that he is in jail up in Walla Walla doing five to ten for possession, which was a pretty good plea bargain considering they caught him with eight ounces of angel dust, and five of coke, shit he would pass out at parties and sell to friends and lovers. Elgin likes the car.

It smells new and it is fire engine red with a gray leather interior. The speedometer goes up to two hundred. There are five gears, syncromesh transmission. When Lightfoot is going fifty, he can burn rubber.

Elgin Lightfoot is leaving something behind, and he thinks it may be finally gone just as he passes Davis, California. What he is leaving behind is a thought of winter on the reservation near Kalispell. He and his sister and mother lived in a trailer. The stove had seen better days and there were holes in the metal skin of the trailer where the wind would blow through and make a whistling noise. The trailer faced east and got some sun in the morning, although it was rarely enough to thaw the pipes. But mostly the sun would disappear in boiling cloud and be gone for six months and Elgin would huddle beside the stove while his mother drank. She would go out to the store in Kalispell for gin and maybe not come back all day and when she did she might be stumbling and talking to herself, or she might be with a man. The village dogs would follow her up the stairs and bark for food. By then Lightfoot and his sister knew they should be in the back bedroom where the paint had peeled off the walls, where they would listen to their mother and her friend. Right now, this is why he is driving in the central valley of California at eighty-five miles an hour—he tolerates the cold, but he thrives in the dry wind. He never wants to be cold again, even though the pull of home is strangely strong.

Lightfoot pushes it to ninety. The road tips up to Sacramento, four lanes all the way. Every mile brings him closer to the capital of California, the malls and housing developments and interconnecting freeways, truck stops, plastic condos, motels, restaurants, ten-movie complexes beside the interstate. It takes about thirty minutes to leave Sacramento behind and when it is gone completely, Lightfoot lights a small cigar and enjoys it while he goes as fast as he can without attracting the notice of the CHP. He doesn't want to be stopped and have to explain the two Mossberg twelve-gauge shotguns, the Glock, and Python, that are currently in the trunk of the Viper. This car is motionless as it speeds along. Lightfoot is a vector only. Finally, easing back to seventy, he can see the first junipers and some pinyons as he gets to the Sierra foothills, going up steeply at about a thousand feet per twenty-mile section, a one percent grade, until he eases back some more to sixty, and finally fifty-five as the trucks whiz past him, when he settles. There are railroad beds down in a canyon and abandoned mines across the gorge. The soil is red and granite-studded. When Elgin gets to a crossover on the Truckee, he takes a bridge and eases the car up an incline on an access road above the river where there is shade and quiet, some ponderosas and nobody in sight.

Elgin Lightfoot listens to the forest. Some traffic sounds escape from the interstate, but not much. It smells good here, like dust and pine needles. The river rushes past, but its sound is so natural it is nearly indiscernible. He closes his eyes and sees Grace Wu again in her pleated skirt while she ate lunch under the cottonwoods in Sonoma, California. When he opens his eyes, a gray squirrel is staring at him and eating a pine nut. It squawks and runs away.

Why does Elgin Lightfoot need to be alone? He asks himself this question over and over. Flying up to San Francisco, he could think about nothing but Grace, even though he should have been managing. What he is failing to manage, he decides, is himself, or better yet, his feelings. First thing after arriving at SFO, he went to the DEA warehouse on the Embarcadero, picked up the Viper, and drove it across the Bay Bridge to Berkeley where he was supposed to meet Grace at a place called the Bateau Ivre on Telegraph Avenue. When Lightfoot got there Grace had already come in and found a table at the back, away from the windows that fronted the street. It was midmorning and the place was nearly empty. As usual, Telegraph was a zoo. But it was quiet and aromatic in the café. Lightfoot hadn't had much of a breakfast on the plane, so he ordered some muffins and fruit, along with a cup of real coffee and cream.

"You have a good flight?" Grace asked.

"It never varies, does it?" Elgin said. His mood now was very dark. Perhaps, he thought then, his mood varied with his ability to control his environment.

"Well," Grace said, "you can get the lightly salted peanuts, the salted roasted peanuts, the honey roasted almonds, the cashews salted. You get the idea. You get the aisle, the middle, the window, the front the middle the back. You get first class, tourist."

"No way I get first class," Elgin said, interrupting. "I work for the government. I'm not elected either."

Grace's skin was damp and she smelled of soap. She had been to her dojo. She had quit her taxi job, so her days on the street were over. Mostly now she practiced shoto-kan, took long walks in Golden Gate Park, and watched the sharks swimming around and around in the aquarium where it was as dark as a green underwater planet. Elgin knew that she was having emotional problems. He felt sorry for her and he didn't like the idea that she wasn't dealing on her normal Clement Street route anymore, partly because he thought it would take her mind off things if she did, and partly because he didn't know what the future would bring. He couldn't blame her after what she'd been through. Nevertheless, as a manager, he could only conclude that it was dangerous to go out on an operation with your mind at less than optimum read-out. Still, she looked well, if a little distracted. Her eyes were clear and lustrous and she looked like she was sleeping well. She had rejected the idea of spending time in a hospital for tests, even though Elgin encouraged, even demanded that she do so.

When Elgin's muffin came, he concentrated on it instead of Grace. He wanted to ask her about the bruises on her back and the stiff neck she'd had for weeks. Instead, he ate and drank his coffee and watched the freaks on Telegraph.

Grace said, "I guess you're going to back me up on this?"

"*This,*" Elgin said. "If I knew what *this* is, I might be able to say. 'Elgin,' you tell me, 'get a couple of shotguns and some Glocks and Pythons and meet me in Berkeley next week.' Grace, I'm not cutting you slack here because I don't cut people slack. You've earned plenty of indulgence. You've earned it. But it's my ass here too."

"I go up to the El Cerrito house and take Nho's job away from him."

"Just like that," Elgin said.

"Just like that," Grace said.

"Simple."

"Simple." Grace smiled. She was having something made from yogurt and kiwi fruit, God knows what it was here in Berkeley. "The best things in life are the simple things."

"Honestly," Elgin said.

"Seriously," Grace said, cutting Elgin away from whatever it was he had in mind. "I do it this way or two years' worth of work is down the drain. You know we don't get Kim and his money man in Los Angeles unless I keep on keeping on. The government made me a drug dealer. Now you want me to quit?"

"Do you know what you're going to do when you get up there, Grace? You wanted guns and money. What the hell is on your mind?"

"We go up there and make Kim a deal. Kim comes around and we're inside the house and Nho looks like a fool. He's already cut one deal on the outside with me. I can guarantee you that wasn't part of his bargain with Kim. I don't think Nho has anyone to wholesale for him in the City, and so I offer to do it. I hand Kim nine hundred thousand as a deposit, everything I've made in two years. Is that what a real drug dealer would do?"

"A real drug dealer would probably blow Nho away and get back her hundred thousand."

"That's right," Grace said.

"But you're not a real drug dealer, Grace," Elgin said.

"I feel like a real drug dealer."

Lightfoot thought then about the rules. Where were they when you really needed them?

"So what do we tell John Zito?" Elgin asked.

"Jonn Zito is so wasted he doesn't know what time of day it is most of the time. He won't be around long. Have you seen him lately?"

"I've talked to him about the cash."

"Does he seem wasted to you, Elgin?"

"He could sell his bottled piss in Russia."

"And I think he's snorting," Grace said.

"I hope not," Elgin replied. "He's seeing an impairment officer."

"The bottom line is we can tell Zito anything we want to tell him. He doesn't read reports like mine anyway. He's got his own set of rules and they're private. So, you told him there's a deal coming down and I need the nine hundred thousand. He's probably unaware of the situation anyway. I just want to know if you can commit to this."

Lightfoot avoided the question for a few minutes. He looked around the cute-hip café with its vases of marigolds and blue plaid tablecloths.

"Are you doing this for yourself, or for me?" Elgin asked.

"Does it matter to you?"

"Grace, I can commit to this," Elgin said. "And I'll tell you why. I think you'll do something with or without me. I just have a feeling about it. And I'd rather be along if it's going to happen, you know what I mean? And second, I don't know what the rules are anymore either. You're out there on the battlefield and I make all the calls?" Elgin took a deep breath. "And I care about you," he said. "That's the only rule I know of I'm breaking."

Grace managed a weak smile. "I'm going up there tomorrow. Whatever the rules."

"All right," Elgin said. "I've done some homework. We can get behind the house on an access road to the reservoir and waterworks. It's going to be afternoon, so we can't hide. We just have to drive on in like we know what we're doing. Somebody could come along anytime and kick us out. Then we have to leave and come back some other day. Once we get up there we can get down to the house in back. Obviously, I can't get permission or clearance for this from anybody at home in Los Angeles. We're on our own. I've got the two shotguns and the Glock. We're all set."

Grace sat quietly, just listening, sipping some tea and touching her yogurt with a spoon. Elgin was disappointed but not surprised at her coolness and distance. He wanted something from her that wasn't there right now, and probably couldn't be. They made a date and place to meet.

"But I'd like to know some specifics," Elgin said.

"There's a patio with a glass door," Grace replied. "We go in that way. There's going to be four men in the house, two wholesalers, a guy named Kip, and Nho himself. Kim comes later in a taxi. We go in, sit down with them until Kim comes along."

"Maybe we could play some spades," Elgin said.

"I don't know how," Grace said.

"Mah-jongg, then," Elgin said.

"Aren't there any Blackfoot games we could play?"

"Yeah, sit around the stove and drink whiskey."

"Suppose we just go in and I deal with Nho, and then shake down Kim. He's got to be impressed with us, Batman and Robin, like."

"Shit," said Elgin. "I'm willing to forget this whole conversation ever took place. We drive up to Mount Lassen and roll boulders down the side into skiers."

The waitress came and cleaned up the table. They paid the check and went outside and walked six blocks to the People's Garden, where the University of California was trying to make a volleyball court and the street people were protesting. Two women in granny dresses were carrying machetes.

"I found your brother," Elgin said.

Grace walked away and then back.

"He's living in San José at a halfway house." He handed Grace a folded piece of paper with the address printed on it. "He's been in and out down there. He goes in a heroin addict and comes out a methadone addict."

"Is he OK?"

"Not really," Elgin said. "I'm sorry. He's had hepatitis for six months, getting better I guess."

"Good. Thank you, Elgin," Grace said.

They walked to the back of the People's Garden where there was a wall of hollyhocks. Elgin wanted out of the game right now, but he was in too deep. Here he was, personally involved with one of his people, definitely against the rules. Together they made it back to the café an hour later and Elgin got in the Viper and started to drive.

X

Now it is late afternoon and Elgin is in the mountains. It is dry and hot. He thinks about his sister, who is repeating the life of their mother. She has a trailer, a little boy, men friends. She drinks. Elgin realizes he is a long way from where he needs to be.

loria is on her stomach, half turned to see the Shark pull on a pair of violet briefs. Before he had finished with her she was wanting a cigarette, and now she is smoking one while she watches him dress—violet briefs, baggy white pants, a dirty T-shirt. She is a large-boned freckled white girl with frizzy red hair and she is only a little afraid of the Shark, able to tease him up to a point. "So," she says, "you had your ashes hauled, no?" The Shark frowns, not understanding the slang. Gloria turns on her back and blows smoke at the ceiling. It is a high blue day and the room is filled with light. Gloria is not a whore, but she takes a little something from the Shark, just for moments like this. Hers is a delicate balance, one or two steps from the street, another quarter mile from the morgue.

The Shark rolls a cigarette and stands on the small patio looking down at a vacant lot choked by thistle. Down the hill is a convenience store and some one-story apartments, then farther a circular clutch of freeway and concrete abutments which connect everything to the City, whispering its music even farther away in cloud. He has only a little English and it annoys him that he is unable to understand the nuance of Gloria's remark. When the cigarette is made, he lights it with a wooden match and stands in the sunshine admiring his many tattoos, most of which were gotten at the Oceanside pier, in between rolling drunk marines. On his palm is a pentagram, one of the sources of his reputation for clairvoyance. High on his right arm is an eagle and a snake, a small rose and thorn on his other forearm, and on his back a dagger. Even though he is very thin he thinks of himself as powerful, and makes certain to carry every bone in his body with authority. His thick black hair he skins back behind his ears, tying it with a bandanna.

Gloria turns on the clock radio and listens to the Miami Sound Machine. She is smoking in lassitude now, waiting for the Shark to leave some money and head off, to wherever he goes. The Shark looks back at the woman and thinks to himself that he should have a woman more suitable. He takes this woman from behind because he can barely manage to look her in the face. "Go make some coffee," he tells her. When she leaves he stands in the sun and listens to the sound of her boiling water, filling cups. She returns and gives him his cup and he drinks it while sitting and strumming an acoustic guitar. He sings in Spanish:

> *Someone has killed my love*
> *And now I must kill someone . . .*

The Shark drinks some coffee and admires his poetry. That's it, he thinks of himself as a poet, a Villon at least. In fact, he is a thief, and has always been a thief. He was, truly, born to be a thief, and his whole personality and intellect reflect an upbringing in which striving meant only taking, and force equaled cunning. It is he himself who has started the rumor that he killed a policeman in Mexicali, initially as part of a tactical effort to influence someone who was confronting him. After that, the story grew and became useful, until it dovetailed with the stories of his clairvoyance, sexual power, and intuition. Of course, with his Yaqui blood, he does have visions. He is good with women. But he is not a killer. Not yet, anyway.

The plain fact is that Tiburon is an orphan and was raised in a Catholic institution in Mexicali. His father was a railroad worker on the line between Los Mochis and Chihuahua who, one hot day when Tiburon was a child, lost a leg when he fell from a box car and bled to death before the train pulled into the next station, which was five hours down the line in the mountains. His mother had died at childbirth, and so this left Tiburon and his four brothers and sisters alone to be farmed out to families of uncles and aunts, except for Tiburon, who was too old. From the age of sixteen, the Shark has made a living from theft, and never once has he had to kill a man. Tomorrow, he thinks, will be Allhallows Eve, the beginning of a new life. The Yaqui in him tells him that it is a propitious sign.

Tiburon, whose real name is Arturo Cruz, stays with several women whose homes and apartments form a rough line from Santa Clara and San Jose, with its end in San Francisco. He gives them small amounts of money, and occasional presents of items he can't, or doesn't dare, sell, and of course he fucks them. Two of these women have borne him children. But Gloria looks out for herself, taking precautions against such eventualities.

"I got a message for you," Gloria says. "This guy came into El Patio last night looking for you."

"Moreno?" Tiburon says.

"Yeah, that was it," she answers. "Chubby guy looks like he jumped off a tortilla package."

Tiburon grunts knowingly. She is good, this one. He likes her style, but he wishes she weren't so fat. "So, what did he say?"

"He says he wants to see you today. He said you'd understand."

Gloria crushes out her cigarette. She is naked under the sheet and she can feel the come between her legs. After Tiburon leaves she will shower and watch TV while her sister does her nails. She is both used and user, and so long as Tiburon is willing to give her money, she can accept it. The fact that he is a thief makes no difference to Gloria. All the fine distinctions and higher forms of life have no real use for Gloria. She is a practical girl.

Tiburon looks at the clock radio, eleven. He begins to think about his meeting with Moreno and what will happen next. His whole life seems geared to this moment, and he is perfect for it. Once or twice a week Tiburon will select a neighborhood and he will steal a van or truck owned by some business. Then he will drive it around a residential street until he sees a home that looks easy and rich. He parks the van and loots the house and takes the loot away in the van. All the time he is inside, it looks like a plumber is replacing some pipes, and it's actually the Shark doing his number. If there are tools and technology in the van, he takes them away.

He has been arrested and deported to Mexico twice, but always he is able to return easily, and to blend into the life around San Jose. Even though he does not fear jail, and even though he makes a fairly good living at what he does, he has always regretted the fact that his theft profits him only about five or six hundred dollars a week. And now that he has the prospect of earning fifteen thousand dollars, he is both anxious and excited. He believes in himself, and his ability to do this thing. With the money, he thinks that he will find an apartment in Los Angeles and a good-looking woman who will go with him to the Olympic Auditorium for boxing, where she will be seen and admired by others. He looks at Gloria. No more white cows for me, he thinks.

Tiburon drives to Guerrero Street and parks outside El Patio. When he goes inside Moreno is waiting for him at the bar. It is too early for lunch, but still there are one or two gringos drinking margaritas. He orders orange juice and exchanges a greeting with Moreno, who looks fevered.

"You have the money, my friend?" Tiburon asks in Spanish.

"No problem," Moreno says. Moreno has been in Los Angeles all week making deals. He has lost some money on them, but he has enough cash for what he has to do. Later, there will be time to reestablish himself with his customers. In an envelope he has seventy hundred-dollar bills. He hands the envelope to Tiburon.

"So what happens now?" Tiburon asks.

Moreno gives Tiburon Zito's address in San Rafael. He opens a city map with the location circled in red. The house is high up on a hill above Sausalito and it is very lonely, reached by a semiprivate road. There are no children, but there is a wife. "Whatever must be done, you must do," Moreno adds with emphasis. "And it has to be tonight. I'm going to go to work on this myself."

"Hey, why not." Tiburon smiles, but he is nervous.

"Perhaps tomorrow for me, who knows? I have some business to do just now. But I don't want this man Zito coming to see me tomorrow. If he comes to see me I will know you have failed. Every Friday he comes. You make sure he doesn't come to see me tomorrow."

"The Day of the Dead inspires me," Tiburon says.

Moreno is impressed. "It is no joke," he says.

"You have a faint heart," Tiburon says. "We meet here tomorrow this time. You will have the rest of the money."

"When Zito doesn't come to the Mission, you'll get the money."

"There will be no problem at all," Tiburon concludes. He places his palm on Moreno's forehead, pentagram to brain. For a moment a silence is suspended between the two men and then Tiburon withdraws his hand, leaving Moreno shaken and impressed.

Once outside Tiburon is free to admire himself. He breathes in the fresh air which is cool on his skin. Since he has all afternoon to wait, he returns to Gloria's place and fixes himself some lunch. Watching TV with Gloria, his mind wanders, unable to concentrate on the barely understandable English spoken by the ghost creatures in soap operas, cola commercials, and a succession of cartoon features. He watches while the fat cow and her sister manicure one another like baboons. They share one another's loose enthusiasms like chickens. Gloria's sister is a cosmetician and thinks of herself as very chic, but Tiburon thinks of her as another white cow, and stupid as well. The decision to kill has given Tiburon a great well of manliness. It is a tower from which he can look down on these creatures.

At four o'clock he makes Gloria drive him to the end of Army Street where he knows there is an electrical contractor who keeps a fleet of trucks parked in a lot just off a side street. Tiburon gets out and watches Gloria drive away on her way to work. His soul is a sheet of ice now and he is impaled on his own daring. With him he is carrying a bag of burglar's tools and a .22-caliber target pistol. He watches for anyone who might see him, and goes into the lot and selects one of the smaller vehicles, a pickup style truck with tool panels and a two-way radio unit. It takes him about fifteen minutes to break in and drill out the ignition, and start the truck. He heads straight out toward Golden Gate Park, and in heavy traffic he crosses the bridge into Marin County.

The map showing Zito's street outlined in red is on the seat beside the Shark. Traffic helicopters circle overhead like hawks, relaying messages to their home bases. In traffic now, he is glad. The bustle is his disguise, and will prevent the police from following up on any report of a stolen vehicle, at least until rush hour is over, at about seven. At this time of day he has a two-hour window in which the police are immobilized by the tangle of cars and buses on the freeways. Above San Quentin, he takes a cutoff over a range of low hills where he can see the prison.

Now he's near the houses of the rich. Tiburon can barely conceive of life here, and it is speculation on speculation. Below, Sausalito appears with its rows of boutiques and coffee houses, piers where pleasure boats are moored, apartments in the hills and condos. He marvels at all the expensive cars, most of which are foreign made. He begins to see the killing he is about to do in terms of class, as rich against poor, poor against rich, and it begins to make sense. This kind of justice is brutal, but real. For those who do not believe in this way, Tiburon would offer them the example of his youth in the Catholic orphanage in Mexicali. There he would be beaten by men of God. Every day there was not enough to eat. Where is the justice in that?

Tiburon is high above San Rafael when he finally slows his thought processes. Lines of eucalyptus entomb the street, creating a thick shade. Lower down there are lemon and orange trees, shrubs with flowers. Tiburon goes by the Zito house once, then turns back and drives slowly until he stops on the shoulder of the road. A few cars pass him by, going uphill, but the drivers pay no attention to the small man sitting and smoking in the cab of an electrical contractor truck. These people are rich and tired, going home, and are too busy to attend to a peon like Tiburon. Even though he is confident of his mission, his hands

sweat. He looks at the five-pointed star on his palm. He begins
to hum:

> Someone has killed my love
> And now I must kill someone . . .

Down the hill thirty yards the house is dark. An asphalt drive
dives to a three-car garage. From where he sits in the cab of the
truck, Tiburon can see the shake-shingle roof of the house, and
beyond that more roofs, trees, other roads all the way to the bay,
about five miles away. Behind him Mount Tamalpais is already
cutting off the setting sun so that everything is bathed in a gray
glow. The wind is getting a cold bite even now. The thought enters his mind that he should take the seven thousand dollars he
already has and go to Los Angeles. This would be a simple thing
and would entail no risk. He could rent an apartment and buy
some clothes. There would be months of pleasure and nights of
fantasy before him. He sighs and thinks of the Fathers of Mercy
who beat him. He puts the gun into his pocket and walks around
the van and down a hillside on slippery ice plant.

Tiburon looks in the garage window. There are no cars in this
garage. Except for the singing of a few birds, there are few
sounds. Once he gets on the back patio, he sneaks a quick look
inside the house and confirms his belief that there is nobody
home on this night. There is expensive furniture and a fireplace
and some paintings on the wall, which likewise confirms that
this is a house where the rich live. He goes back to the side of
the garage and waits, thinking that surely this man Zito will return here soon, after work, and then he will confront the man.
The picture of what Tiburon will do at that moment is vague. In
reality, he has no specific plan, nor has he given it much thought.
Although he is in shadow beneath the leaves of a lemon tree,
Tiburon feels naked, unclothed by thought. He wishes he had
studied this matter and planned ahead. His clairvoyance, exis-
tent only in rumor, has abandoned him.

Suddenly a few deductions assault his fevered brain. For example, if this man Zito is a policeman, does it not stand to reason that he carries a gun, and is versed in its use? What if the man's wife comes home? As the minutes pass, Tiburon is near to convincing himself to flee with the money to Los Angeles. At that moment, a gray Chevrolet Caprice pulls down the asphalt driveway with its lights on and stops, thus sealing two fates.

When John Zito gets out of the car, carrying a briefcase, he leaves the motor running and the door open. Tiburon sees him exit the car and stand still as if he had forgotten something and was trying to remember it. The car is between Tiburon and Zito and prevents Tiburon from making a move freely. Besides, he is unsure of his intentions. The gun is heavy in his hand and his heart is beating wildly, frantically. But now John Zito disappears from view, walking toward the front door of the house, which is around the corner from the garage.

What Zito forgot was the crowbar. He reaches into the backseat of the car and retrieves it, then walks hurriedly up the stone walk to the front door of Lenore's house. He is very nearly delirious with his own confusion, and he spends many needless minutes thrashing with the crowbar at the jamb, the lock, pounding and howling like a crazy man. Finally, he breaks the glass panels that surround the door, reaches in and unlocks it from the inside—how simple. Tiburon has worked himself around the garage and Caprice, and is watching John Zito break into his own house.

Once inside the house, Zito goes to the master bedroom and locates his American passport, valid for two more years. He stops in the dark and laughs out loud. There is a For Sale sign in the front yard of the house and the insides smell musty, like Lenore's cunt. This is his magic moment. He can feel justice circulate in his blood. He opens the briefcase and puts the passport inside, along with the other implements of his freedom. For a brief instant, he thinks of something grandiose, truly spectacular, like setting the house afire. Instead, he marches back through the house with his briefcase and crowbar.

When Zito steps into the doorway, Tiburon emits a tiny whoosh of surprise. Two men are face to face, across an eternity.

A gun hangs between them like a black question mark, until a flame erupts like an infinitesimal star and Zito is shot in the sternum, once. A sharp, toylike pop follows in microseconds. Zito slumps passionlessly to his knees and is shot again, this time in the chest, and once again in the throat, three pops altogether, and hardly any blood to speak of.

Zito is on his back in the doorway, eyes open. Quickly, Tiburon grabs the briefcase and runs up the hillside, slipping on ice plant. When he gets to the truck, he looks up and down the road, but there is nobody there. Inside the cab, he pauses to open the briefcase. He is in an ecstasy of disbelief. Beneath an American passport are hundreds of American bills, new-looking. Tiburon tips up the pentagram and touches it to his own forehead.

18

hollowed pumpkins adorn the porch rail of the halfway house, a Victorian in San Jose. There are crepe paper skeletons of witches and black cats in the windows, reminding Grace of elementary school displays in her youth. Two young men sit in chairs and rock and watch the street as if they are looking for spies, examining every event with a minute watchfulness that is bland and correct. Grace has been staying at a Motel 8 along the freeway. Elgin is in a downtown Holiday Inn. Both of them are waiting for this day to get going, and now that it's here, it seems as if the time slipped by quickly.

In midmorning, already a brown haze has descended on San Jose. It is like a fuzz in the air that has grown in an invisible medium. The palms look worn out and the ice plant has a grayish cast. Everything is dying with hustle and bustle, like a funeral procession going nowhere. Right here it is about forty miles to the Silicon Valley, about fifty or sixty miles from Big Sur, another four thousand from Korea. But in her head, Grace Wu is still in that duplex in East Oakland where something bad is always happening to her, over and over again. Six weeks from the incident, and she still hears noises in her ears, and feels a desire to bathe ten or twelve times a day. She thinks about her rabbits, and about the Koreans, which leads her to the conclusion that she mustn't stay at her apartment. She lives in motels and motor hotels, and goes back home to dress, check the mail. Her experiences are deeply subpsychological. They are occurring against the curtain of something unrevealed that is constantly gnawing at her. There is a squalidness in her guilt.

She is driving the Viper, a cool quiet machine. In the trunk are two Mossbergs and Grace's Smith & Wesson. Elgin at the Holiday Inn is holding the Python. Grace realizes she has placed a tremendous burden on Elgin, and that he is breaking his codes, all of them, personal and professional, in order to stay behind her on this one. Right now, she only knows she must see her brother before she goes to the house in El Cerrito. She has called and arranged the visit. In fact, her brother is under no restraint. He is in the halfway house voluntarily, and can leave at any time. He has been in and out of programs, and this is another in the string. Her brother has likewise been in and out of Grace's life, and now he is out. She wants him back in.

Grace goes inside the house, which has a false cozy institutional feel. One big dining room has been cleared out and it's where there are meetings. Metal chairs are disarranged, and ashtrays are everywhere. On the walls are schedules, messages of encouragement, intonements against affliction. The director greets her, and escorts her upstairs to the dorms. In one room, she finds her brother sweeping the floor. He looks up and drops the broom and immediately sits down on a metal bed, shoulders hunched. Grace sits beside him. Greg is twenty-three years old, younger than Grace, never the apple of anyone's eye. Grace considers herself lucky to have escaped his fate of being the youngest and only male child in a Chinese family. She doesn't feel guilty about it, but she is aware of the affliction.

"Hello, rocketman," she says happily.

"Hi, sis," Greg says. He is a fine-boned youth with big black eyes and short black hair. He does not look fit to Grace, but he looks better than the last time she saw him, six months before in Chinatown when he was yellow as a lemon. "I guess you know I went back to Margaritaville," he says.

"You OK?" Grace asks.

"You tell me," he answers. He has an addict's frost. He is supercharged with suspicion. When he looks at the floor and back up he is ready to talk again. Starting over he says, "How are the folks?" This subject must always be circled.

"You know the story," Grace says. She is affecting a false cheerfulness. But it is only false in terms of its relation to her mood. She wishes to be happy with her brother, for them both to suffer and survive. "Dad answers, hands the phone to Mom five seconds later."

Greg grunts haughtily. "They ask about me?"

"No, they can't cope," Grace says. This is an implicit truth, unavoidable.

"What a bunch of shit," Greg says.

"Listen, I'm sorry I haven't been around."

"It doesn't matter. I'm hard to track."

"I'm into heavy work."

"Everybody has problems," Greg says.

"It isn't that," Grace replies. "It's my job. Things are, well, hectic."

Grace watches Greg draw himself up. He is like a pile of kindling, loosely stacked. "Why did you come down here anyway?" he asks.

Honestly, Grace isn't sure. "I thought we could live together," she says. "I've got one big job to do, then I'm free. We could try it for a while, see if it works. You can get on your feet, and we can get to know each other again."

"My big sis," Greg says.

"Give it some thought."

"Everything around me gets disgraced. Isn't that what Dad says?"

"I'm getting my priorities straight," Grace says. "You're in there, somewhere, right at the top."

"You mean you're on a guilt trip."

"Nothing like that. Don't think too much. Don't be too sensitive. You'll spoil everything."

"You sound like a sensei," Greg says, hitting home.

"I break boards," Grace says with irony. "That's all."

"Yeah, I'll think about it." Greg stands and picks up the broom. "I've got to get some work done."

"The only thing is, you can't use me as a safe house," Grace says. "No buying or selling."

Greg nods and waltzes away with his broom. He has cut Grace off now, and is alone again. The brown sun angles in the room, cutting it into diagonals of shape. There are cut-glass windows beveled into mullioned form. Grace follows Greg as he moves around the room. When she catches him she touches him. "I'm not saying forget Mom and Dad," she says. "Just drop the issue for a while. I'm not going to be a cop much longer. I give affection, you give direction."

Greg brooms away.

Grace walks outside under the watchful eyes of the spy-chasers. They are two intent young men with shaved heads and hooded eyes. She sits in the Viper and lets them look, fascinated as they are by her. Then she drives down I-880 and takes the Alum Rock exit into the hills. There has been a long drought and many sporadic forest fires, and the hills are ashen brown and bare of grass. The air pollution, of course, extends up into the hills, and is creeping into the Sierra, a color that tints everything. As she drives, it is hard for Grace to stop thinking about her brother and to put her mind on the business at hand. Two years undercover have dulled her emotions, while at the same time increasing her paranoia, psychic trends that tug her responses in differing directions. She realizes that her brother's response horizon, however, is even more limited than her own. Whatever his version of reality turns out to be, it is going to be task-specific.

Up in the hills are shopping centers which serve the housing developments hidden behind miles of stucco wall and redwood fence. California is in there somewhere, ticking past on stalks of cornflower and poppy. The construction is pink and gray or adobe brown, outlined by bright neon. This culture has already preempted individuality, long ago. It has been channeled. It is a virus spreading every which way. The road at the end of Alum Rock goes up to some vineyards and wineries, but Grace turns off to the Holiday Inn.

She parks in a lot and calls for Elgin on a phone in the lobby. In ten minutes he appears at the entrance to the coffee shop, wearing a black sweatshirt and gray chinos. There is a skull and crossbones on his Raiders cap.

They order soup and sandwiches. Elgin sips some iced tea.

"We can back out now," Elgin says.

"Not now, not ever," Grace says.

"In that case, let me bang on the patio door," Elgin offers, smiling. Long ago he abandoned the idea of dissuading Grace, so he's taking an easier tack. "Now that I think about it, this has all the advance planning features of Custer's Last Stand."

"These are Koreans," Grace says.

"You mean they're not northern Cheyenne?"

"I don't think so," Grace says.

"If they were northern Cheyenne, I wouldn't do this. For years the Cheyenne had horses and Blackfoot didn't. They regularly kicked our asses, rode in, rode out."

"OK, you've convinced me, you can bang on the patio door," Grace says.

"You know Kyungmoon Nho isn't going to stand by while you take away his well-paid job. I don't think he has a golden parachute. He's a tough little guy."

"Speaking of tough guys," Grace says, "how did John Zito look yesterday when you got our money?"

"He went to the basement and brought up the nine hundred thousand. I gave him his receipt. He didn't seem too curious what we were doing, and I didn't offer to tell him. As far as how he looked, he looked crazy."

"And your people in L.A. and D.C.?"

"One great thing about the bureaucracy," Elgin says, "is that they don't want to hear much about an operation unless it's a success. If something fails, then they don't know anything, and they're out of the loop. If this works, then they'll haul tail to the newspapers. Hell, the money is all from drug dealers anyway. So, who cares?"

"You know I appreciate this," Grace says.

"Look, Grace," Elgin says. "You can bullshit me all you want. I'm in over my head already. I shouldn't be up here with you, and I shouldn't be going into the El Cerrito house. And it isn't my ass or my job I'm worried about. How the hell do I know what the right thing to do is?"

"Then what is it, Elgin?" Grace says.

"It's you, of course," Elgin says.

They finish lunch and leave without saying another word. Elgin drives them up I-880 in the constant traffic. Both lanes are filled, both directions. In an hour, they are in Contra Costa County, going up into the hills, first off San Pablo Avenue, then through Albany on a tangle of roads lined by sycamores that are dropping their leaves. When they reach the San Pablo ridge, they are high enough to see the bay and the Golden Gate, and behind them Wildcat Canyon, a cemetery, a golf course. Wind pulls down toward the water, combing through the eucalyptus. A huge aircraft carrier is lumbering under the Golden Gate, surrounded by sailboats.

When they reach a reservoir they round its circular shape and leave the gravel road for a grassy track that winds down through a field of grass and poppies. The weather reminds Grace of the day she spent with Elgin in Sonoma. It has that dry promiseful aroma. Finally, Elgin parks in the shade from a line of eucalyptus. From here, it is about a hundred yards to Nho's property, and another sixty feet to the patio, which can barely be seen through the trees. There is no back fence and no swimming pool, just a flagstone porch and a double set of patio doors. It is a straight shot to destiny, and both of them are quiet.

Elgin gets the two Mossbergs and the Colt Python from the trunk of the Viper. He puts on a tool belt and a hard hat that belongs to California Power and Light. He wanders around to the side of the Viper and smiles at Grace.

"I wondered about you," she says.

"You didn't think I was just going to knock on the patio door and sell those Koreans some cookies?"

"I didn't know, Elgin, I really didn't."

Grace is happy now, at peace. Just before the moment of struggle is the moment of joy, and this is hers. It is cool in the shade of the eucalyptus, and there are blossoms on the oleanders. Grace breathes deeply, concentrating on her center, a point two inches below her navel. In her mind she is doing a kata. Her target is out there, and she will strike six inches beyond it.

Elgin leads, carrying his Mossberg and Colt, down through a line of trees and hedge. They are trailing dust and tiny pebbles behind them. They keep away from the patio doors, and instead move under an eave near a back wall. Pop-schlock music seeps out of the house, but it is distant. Pushing themselves along the wall, they arrive at a place only a few feet from the glass patio doors. Elgin steps out and confidently raps on the glass.

In a few moments, Kip appears in his black slacks and T-shirt, red running shoes.

"What you want?" Kip shouts angrily.

"Transformer blew out up the hill," Elgin shouts. "Got to use the telephone." Elgin puts a hand to his ear. "Telephone," he shouts again.

"Go away, no use," Kip says.

"What?"

"Go away," Kip repeats. "No use."

Elgin opens his arms in supplication. But now Kip has stood away from the glass and is holding a revolver.

Grace angles around the corner of the house and levels the Mossberg. When she pulls the trigger an arc of glass the size of a manhole cover explodes from the patio door and envelops Kip. The Korean seems to disappear in a steam of blood and noise.

19

Kyungmoon Nho likes short group encounters that are not altogether voluntary. For example, *Cock Crazy*, the strip playing while he takes a midmorning shave, features a young woman named Tina being mauled by rock stars in a hazy multi-imaged blue goggle of film that unwinds jerkily. Draped in a bath towel, Nho scrapes his beard and watches the cheap film's reflection in a mirror. Five men take after Tina in a frenzy. They poke her every orifice. Her face is seen briefly at quarter angles, beset by smiles of pain. Something in the woman's helpless joy triggers Nho's primal self, the self he knows he is most impressed by, and which he hopes he can cultivate forever and ever. In his youth, Nho enjoyed the struggles of his kidnap victims, their cries from inside the van, even their beguiling shame when he dumped them out on the verges of Seoul near dawn, at garbage dumps, industrial waste sites, and warehouse districts. Now the men cover Tina entirely, wiping her out of existence momentarily. Nho turns off the hot water and wipes his face with a towel. The VCR clicks off, and Nho inserts *Four Play*, a cheap homemade loop which has much the same theme, gang fucking, horror, the last set-to of the atomic age.

Nho brews a cup of ginseng in another part of the house while the loop plays. He takes his cup to the patio, which faces Grand Avenue below, Lake Merritt, and downtown Oakland. It is a warm day, quite beautiful, with some puffy clouds drifting overhead. Nho has decorated his home in white, shag rugs, sofas, padded chairs, and a gaudy tasteless chandelier, with black batik wall hangings and an expensive array of electronics. This is everything to Nho, his dream life, his paradise. He is beyond pride in his accomplishments, yet he harbors a secret sexual frustration, a wet deliberation on his life. His avowed creed requires abstinence and silence, but his prurience often overwhelms his vows. *Four Play* reaches a crescendo and pulls into silence, the tape ticking.

Nho goes back inside and opens his closet door. His taste is overcome by money. He owns thirty suits, maybe more, and sport coats and slacks, many pairs of shoes. Nho turns and puts on another tape. Immediately there are penises in peach light. Nho puts on a silk shirt, disappointed that the current tape is apparently "arty," devoid of sadism and voyeurism. There is no undertow of agony. This particular tape, he concludes shortly, shows people happily engaged in sex. He pushes Stop.

This big day calls for a gray silk suit that cost over one thousand dollars. The material was hand-selected by a tailor in Oakland, Nho being individually fitted and sized. This is a cut to fit his particular body form and it goes on him like a skin. Although Nho is barely five-five, the suit hangs beautifully, with no bunch at the shoulder, the cuffs neatly tipped where the thumb breaks into his wrist. He selects a gray silk tie with rose splashes. He stands in front of a full-length mirror and talks to himself in Korean.

Nho is particularly happy today. In the first place, he thinks he has found two wholesalers across the bridge who will satisfy Mr. Kim's stiff qualification requirements. Today he will present the credentials of these two men to Mr. Kim, who has already arrived at SFO and is staying in a room at the Claremont in Berkeley. It is six weeks to the day since Nho began his search, and now it is over. The men are not members of gangs or associations, but each has been involved in the drug trade before. Neither has a criminal record, although neither has immigration documents. They seem men of limited intelligence and ambition, and will present no threat to him, now or in the future. Already, these men will split their take with Nho, which will increase his percentage from fifteen to more like twenty-five.

Nho is also happy because Mr. Kim has asked him to drive over to the Claremont and pick him up. Ordinarily, of course, Kim arrives at the El Cerrito house in a taxi, alone, to be taken down the hill by Kip when their meeting is finished. This new method indicates that Nho has climbed in Kim's esteem, and even though Nho resents the deference he must show to the man, he feels that he is making progress. He welcomes the opportunity to share a few moments of privacy with Kim, which will give him time to present his new associates personally. Nho has concrete hopes that someday he will learn the details of this smuggling operation. This would increase his power, perhaps someday opening the doors to Hong Kong.

Nho drives the Lexus up College Avenue. There are students everywhere, on bicycles and mopeds, carrying books and backpacks. He is disdainful of these people, considering them soft and immoral in their idleness. It is easy, he thinks, to subvert a culture and lifestyle that tolerates this behavior, which he considers weak and directionless. Nho cuts south of the campus, then back up toward the hotel. He parks in a curved driveway in front. He can hear the soft plocks of tennis balls and the airy feather of sprinklers. Mr. Kim comes out of the shadows and walks directly to the Lexus, getting in the front seat beside Nho. Nho is thrilled. He had envisioned Kim getting in the backseat, which would have made Nho appear to be a chauffeur. Nho dons dark glasses, and pulls into traffic.

"You had a pleasant journey?" Nho says.

"As usual," Kim says.

The car glides ruthlessly. "And the hotel?"

"Adequate," Kim says.

Nho studies the man's demeanor. Because of his background and lack of education, Nho is always trying to learn how to carry himself. He looks for clues to his own behavior in that of others, especially his superiors. He likes the clipped speech of American movie actors, especially Clint Eastwood, who never betrays confusion. Nho is grooming himself with every glance and nuance. It is what separates his current self from his past self.

"I have found two wholesalers," Nho announces.

"Go ahead," Kim says dispassionately.

Nho spends five minutes on the subject. He emphasizes the toughness and reliability of the two men. He glides over their backgrounds and vouches for their truthfulness. Nho produces two photographs and gives them to Kim, who puts them in his pocket without study. Nho realizes that the syndicate will take great care with these choices. It would be a sign of disfavor if these men were rejected, but Nho thinks that unlikely at best. For a while, the men ride in silence. Nho examines Mr. Kim's dark blue suit. Kim could be a trade unionist or a diplomat. There is something in his carriage that makes Nho uneasy. It is an ambience that Nho has not perfected. But whatever it is, it is superior.

Nho drives into the El Cerrito hills and parks on the circular drive in front of the house. Unfortunately, when Nho gets out of the car, Mr. Kim stays put, which forces Nho to open the door. This kind of deference puts him in a bad mood instantly. Nho walks up the steps and opens the front door and steps inside the house.

Grace Wu is standing in the middle of the room, holding a shotgun on Nho as he comes unwarily inside. With his head down, Mr. Kim follows silently until both men stop in shock. Nho looks at the woman closely, recognizing her. Behind them someone kicks the door shut, a huge man in a black sweatshirt and gray chinos, wearing a baseball cap. He too holds a shotgun.

The surprise of the moment produces a grim falter in Mr. Kim, who is speechless.

"OK, OK," says Nho helplessly.

"Be quiet," the woman says.

The woman motions Nho away from the door. She tells the two men to sit down, lotus style. Nho's balance, always fragile at best, is completely shattered. He sees his two East Bay wholesalers lying face down on the floor with pillows secured around their heads by electrical tape. Their feet have also been bound. When he doesn't see Kip, Nho glances around frantically until, in the half light of the dining room, he sees a hole blasted through the glass doors of the patio, Kip lying in a circle of shards. Bone and blood have splattered the walls. The room is muraled with abstract patterns.

Mr. Kim says to Nho, "Who are these people?" in Korean.

"Speak only English," the woman says.

Kim is in the lotus position. Beside him, Nho has begun to think things through already. It is inconceivable to him that he didn't kill this Chinese woman when he had the chance. It would have been easy to slit her throat and leave her in East Oakland, where she would have been another statistic. Now Nho realizes that he has been unprofessional. In the eyes of the world, he has committed a silly crime to gain one hundred thousand dollars, the humiliation of the woman an afterthought. Self-love has led him to this, and away from the stature he jealously longed for.

"Do not be hasty," Mr. Kim says. "If it is money you want, there is much."

"You have no problem," the woman says to Kim. "It's Nho with the problem." Mr. Kim casts a sidelong stare at Nho, who shrugs.

"I want to tell you about my dealings with Nho," the woman says. "Better yet, perhaps Nho should tell it."

"Who is this person?" Kim asks Nho.

"Tell him," the woman says. "Or you're dead."

"We had a deal," Nho says. He avoids the stare of Kim. He does not wish to die and he does not wish to say anything to Mr. Kim. It is understood that he was to have no outside dealings while he worked for the syndicate. Nho does not understand why the woman does not just take the money in the safe and go. After all, it amounts to three times what he stole from her. "She came and I took her money," Nho says.

"Please," the woman says.

"OK, OK," Nho says. "I told her I give her some product. She brings the money but I didn't give her the product. She angry because I take her money."

Mr. Kim lets slip a Korean epithet. He is calling Nho something terrible. *Shee-pal-seki,* he mutters. Motherfucker.

"The fact is," the woman says, "I had a deal for a hundred thousand. I brought it across and three men sodomized me for fun. How do you think I should repay this dishonor?"

"She is crazy," Nho says. He is slipping away. There are sweat stains on his shirt.

Mr. Kim silences Nho with a wave of his hand. The other man with a shotgun walks to the patio door, looks out, walks back.

"I can help you," Mr. Kim says. "I will take care of this man. You will have back your money."

"That's a start," the woman says. She is standing in the middle of the room holding a shotgun, another weapon in her jeans belt. She toes forward a briefcase and tips it open. It is full of American bills. "Nine hundred thousand dollars," the woman says.

Mr. Kim hunches forward. He licks his lips and smiles, aware that something is going to happen that is entirely unexpected. "This is much money," he says.

"Everything I've earned in two years on the street," the woman says.

"I am impressed," Kim says.

"You know what a franchise is?" the woman says.

"McDonald's," Kim answers.

"I'll say this once," the woman says. "Nho isn't working for you anymore. I'm stepping into his shoes. But I don't expect you to take me in, just like that. This money is yours to invest for me, and insurance for you that I work out. I'm buying a franchise, you're getting insurance. I expect to make a lot more than this. And you'll be getting somebody you can trust."

"I think this may be OK," Kim says. Nho's head is down like a tired horse's.

"You're not just saying that because I've got a shotgun?" the woman says, smiling.

"Well," Kim admits, palms open.

Without permission, Nho rises to his feet. Nho wishes to cross the room, do something to the woman. He begins to speak in wild choruses of Korean slang.

The blast of the Mossberg hits Nho across the upper thighs.

Mr Kim ducks too late to miss the blood that whips across the room, wall to wall. A silky veil of smoke drifts upward, hovering on the ceiling.

"We have a deal," the woman says.

"I would say so," Kim replies. They discuss details.

The woman and her partner back out of the room and disappear through the patio doors. Mr. Kim sits quietly for ten minutes, not risking any movement. In a way he is satisfied with this whole matter, its violent outcome. He is rid of an unsatisfactory employee, and has gained someone strong, tough, and knowledgeable. He is no longer worried about cops, only about logistics. Beside him, Nho stirs slightly, still conscious.

The doorbell rings and Mr. Kim gets up to answer it. When he opens the door he is startled to see a tiny devil and a Batman. "Trick or treat," the children shout happily. Mr. Kim slams the door. He can hear the children outside talking.

Kyungmoon Nho feels cold. Something is stealing his breath. Across the room is a beautiful alligator shoe, his own.

az is in and out of the kitchen, preparing candy skulls for Day of the Dead. She is a reserved person, and wishes to mark this observance in a quiet and productive way. While she makes the skulls, she watches Clemente Moreno, who sits in the living room. He is in a terrible mood. For the past six weeks he has been another person from the kindly and hardworking man who picked her up off Market Street and took her to his bed. It is true that he is occasionally rough with her in a dominating sexual fashion, and that he is demanding in domestic matters as well. But this is something Paz both expects and understands, just part of the background to her utility. Only once has she been beaten severely. She is berated often and loudly, but she is never abjectly humiliated. As far as the sex is concerned, Moreno does hurt her, but probably not intentionally, and then only when he is drunk. All in all, Moreno is a decent man who now has much trouble. He does not sleep well, nor does he laugh in his usual open style. He paces the floor and speaks to himself harshly. Sexually, he has not been active. He comes home early, and stays in his chair.

But, actually, Moreno has been relatively busy. He has traveled to Crack Alley in Los Angeles, in an effort to raise immediate cash with which to pay Tiburon, and has sold a pound of cocaine for less than its street value. Right now, he is sitting on seven thousand dollars. Moreno hopes that this weekend will see the last of the policeman who has been bedeviling him, who has been taking half an ounce of his best product each Friday, and several hundred dollars in cash as well. In an hour or two, Moreno will know whose fate is sealed, his or the policeman's. Fate will smile, or fate will frown, it is all the same. In addition, Moreno purchased a .25-caliber automatic Colt and some ammunition in Los Angeles, a weapon with no pedigree, no mother and father. He sits and holds the gun, talks to it.

And much of Moreno's time has been spent trying to locate the woman narc, Grace Wu. For weeks now, he has not seen her, nor has he done any business with her, a fact which makes him worry. Nevertheless, a few days ago he did pick up her trail on Clement Street when he saw her buying groceries in a small market. Then he was able to follow her, late at night, to an apartment building on Geary Boulevard and watched as she collected her mail from a box in the front hall. She did not go inside, but when Moreno looked at the box, he found her apartment number. Another night he followed her to the same building, and watched again while she checked her mail. Only this time she went upstairs. A few minutes later a light went on in the front apartment to the east. Moreno was across the street under the awning of a tailor shop. He could not see the woman at the window. The lights went out and she came downstairs and drove away. By then, Moreno was sure that he knew where she lived. In the weeks since he began his initial vigil, Moreno has lost weight. When he sees the woman narc his life fills with meaningless pain and he knows that only her death can ease that ache. Now it doesn't matter. All the moving parts have been set in motion. The Day of the Dead approaches, when all the skeletons will dance.

Moreno sits in his living room on a beautiful warm morning while the girl Paz makes candy skulls. Moreno has delivered a message to Gloria at El Patio saying that Tiburon should meet him there at one o'clock. In this way, Moreno can go to the Mission Dolores and wait for John Zito to keep his regular Friday appointment. If the man does not come, then Moreno can pay Tiburon his seven thousand dollars. Despite his belief in fate, Moreno cannot sleep, and has been up most of the night driven by concern about this day's activities. The hours pass languidly.

He cannot speak to Paz about his problems, for she is just a woman. And besides, in what way could she be of any help? Outside, the sun is shining and the people of the street are happy. The Anglos are dressing up as witches and devils. The smell of burnt brown sugar wafts through the apartment. It is noon, and Moreno must leave to keep his appointment at the Mission Dolores.

Moreno walks to the Mission District. It is a windy day, and he wears a straw cowboy hat, a red bandanna, jeans. When he reaches the church, he sits on a wall and watches the street, the bus stop, and the two intersections a block away. There are pansies in a flower bed behind him and the wall is covered with ivy. The royal palms rustle in the breeze. Now and then a bus comes and stops and people get on and off, many Catholic schoolchildren, some older people.

On this day he does not wish to see the woman narc until much later. Right now, he does not want to see John Zito, and if he does, he will know that Tiburon is not an honest man. This will multiply his problems, and over this he is terribly concerned. But it is risks like this that must be taken in order to set in motion the fates that will decree one's liberty.

It is eleven o'clock, and then eleven-thirty, and still no John Zito. Moreno can feel the tick of the clock that is in a tower of the church. Time passes quickly at first, and then more slowly, and then, finally, it seems hardly to pass at all. Moreno scans the street, then closes his eyes and looks at the clock, which has not moved its hands. He sees a priest, a businessman, a deliveryman making a delivery to a bakery. A flower seller is selling daisies on the corner. He can smell fresh-baked bread and he watches the blue sky.

At one o'clock, Moreno rejoices. He does not believe that John Zito would be an hour late to collect his cocaine and his money. Moreno breaths deeply. He feels a great weight leave his chest in a beating of wings. The angel of his macho has delivered his soul from the clutches of this corrupt policeman. Already his mind is drifting in the wind, toward the woman narc. It will be a wonderful evening, if only fate will continue to smile.

Moreno walks up Valencia Street to El Patio. He is about twenty minutes late for his appointment. The bar is crowded with Friday drinkers. Moreno takes a stool at the end of the bar and looks for Tiburon, but he is not to be seen.

Gloria approaches Moreno, carrying a cocktail napkin. "Hey," she says. "I told him a couple of days ago."

Moreno nods. He orders a beer. "I don't see him here," he says.

"He isn't here," Gloria says. "And if you want to know the truth, he didn't come to my place last night. That doesn't mean a lot, because he's like a tomcat." She smiles and takes a deep drag from her menthol cigarette.

"You told him one o'clock today?"

"One o'clock today, Friday, yeah," she tells Moreno. Gloria uncaps a Corona and puts it in front of Moreno, with lime. "Was this something important?" Gloria asks.

"Enough," Moreno says, now distracted.

Gloria shakes her head and moves away. She is making margaritas, serving baskets of chips and sauce. Moreno sits quietly, his nerves steady. He orders another beer and sips it slowly while he watches the bar clock. When it becomes two o'clock, Moreno begins to entertain the idea that Tiburon has been arrested, and is right now telling some policeman the whole story, implicating Moreno in the crime of murder, or attempted murder. Moreno wonders if the police are already at his apartment, waiting. There is no way Tiburon will hold his tongue if he is caught.

But it is now late in the afternoon. Moreno has anxiously watched the morning news broadcasts, and has read the *Chronicle* cover to cover, and there was no mention of a policeman being shot, and no mention of an arrest. This puzzles Moreno, of course, but even more puzzling is the fact that Tiburon has not kept his appointment, one worth seven thousand dollars, American. Perhaps Tiburon ran away with the original money— no, it couldn't be, for then John Zito would have arrived at the Mission Dolores.

At three o'clock Moreno leaves El Patio and goes to his apartment. There he finds Paz asleep, and no police. Now, the moment of truth has arrived, and he takes his weapon and drives out to the Avenues to where the woman narc lives. After circling for twenty minutes, he finally finds a parking space about ten blocks from Geary Boulevard. He puts on a windbreaker with the gun in one of its pockets, and walks toward the apartment building. He is in a dream state, produced by adrenaline. In his head, he is talking to himself, making feverish arguments about his moral culpability, fate, necessity, God.

There is no denying, he tells himself, that God is a violent man. And if God is violent himself, how can he fail to understand the nature of human violence, for he creates, sustains, and participates in it. God has a will, and it overlies all human life. In this way, the woman narc has been willed to die. She has killed herself.

An alley runs behind the apartment building. It runs through from avenue to avenue, and contains dumpsters, garbage bins, parking garages. Across the alley are some small duplexes, and one or two connected houses that don't front the street. At this time of the afternoon, most of the people who live here are at work. The alley is empty of people. Around the corner of Geary, there are some bars and restaurants, but they are generally quiet. As Moreno goes down the alley, he notices the first cold of the day, and a light mist seems to be slicking in from the ocean. Later, it will probably fog over on the avenues, and become quite chilly.

Moreno has decided that he must be prepared to wait in the woman narc's apartment for hours, or even days, if necessary. He is prepared to wait all night, all day, all night again. It will do no good to become faint of heart now. If he does not kill the woman narc, Moreno knows that John Zito's death will be of no use, and his seven thousand dollars will be spent on nothing. This thought drives him, even though he is by now quite afraid. He walks down the alley, and then into a narrow passageway between two buildings.

It is dark in the passageway, which is only about five or six feet wide, and completely hidden from the sun. Above there is a fire escape with a ladder that provides access to the lower floors. The fire escape seems to be like a huge spider hulking above Moreno. He stands quietly, imagining the dark web opening, and the image of a great black spider gathering him in. He starts up the lower ladder and arrives on the landing above. He can hear no music from inside the building, nor any children playing. It is a building for working people. It carries the dust of much experience and little joy.

Moreno climbs the fire escape until he reaches the second-story landing on the east side of the building, which must be the woman narc's window. There are no bars on the window. When Moreno looks inside he sees a dark, narrow kitchen that contains a small refrigerator and stove. Moreno takes the gun and taps on the window, low down toward the sill. When the glass breaks, a large chunk falls to the floor inside the kitchen, but makes surprisingly little noise. Still, he anxiously waits, looking up at the blue sky to see the face of God watching him. He closes his eyes and catches his breath, and unlatches the window and opens it. Miraculously, the window glides open easily. There is almost no friction. It is as if someone used this window on a regular basis. This surely is a sign from God, a smile. God is to be found in details like these.

Moreno eases himself over the threshold. In the dark kitchen he expects fate to assert itself in some unexpected way, but it does not. He has not been shot and killed. No alarms have rung, there is no vicious dog. In a few minutes, Moreno eases himself down the narrow kitchen, to where there is a juncture of two rooms and a hallway. Around the corner there is an empty living room that fronts Geary Boulevard. The hallway leads in a few feet to a bedroom that likewise fronts Geary. Behind him is a small bathroom. Creeping down the hallway, Moreno sees that, indeed, this apartment is empty in the late afternoon. He can smell an accumulation of dust that says to him how little used this place is. Even in the middle of the day, he thinks, there can be little sunlight in this apartment. Moreno takes time to study the cosmetics in the bathroom, and a few photographs in the bedroom, until he is fairly certain that he has chosen the right apartment. Because there is no point in doing anything else, he decides to relax. He knows there may be hours to wait before the woman narc comes home.

Moreno sits on a metal kitchen stool. For a long time he does not move. But after half an hour he is restless and looks in the refrigerator. He finds a bottle of wine and pours himself a small glass. Then he finds some cheese, and eats a few pieces of it, along with drinking the wine. Time is passing slowly, just as it passed slowly this morning at the Mission Dolores. There are no shadows in the apartment, no way to mark the progress of the sun across the sky; thus, there is only a uniform dark gray light in all the rooms.

Moreno drinks some wine and thinks back to his childhood, another Day of the Dead long ago. He remembers his mother making candy skulls. He remembers being afraid of all the talk of skeletons and cemeteries. It is said that the dead leave their graves and dance in the flower-strewn streets. His father was drinking heavily then, and was usually quite drunk.

In the midst of this reverie, Moreno hears the sound of the front door being opened. It creaks slightly, and then hisses shut. He moves off the stool and strains to see in the half light, where, perhaps twenty or thirty feet away, a woman is at the door, her back turned. She has long hair and is wearing a lightweight coat. Moreno holds the gun on the woman's back and says a small prayer to God. He asks God to forgive him for what he is about to do. He asks God to understand that this is a killing done from necessity, and not in hate, or because of drunkenness. Moreno says to God that he is a man, and is doing what a man must do. He whispers the name of the Virgin and fires.

The noise is very arranged. It is not so large as Moreno had anticipated, and at once the woman is splayed against the door and falls precipitously. Quickly, Moreno flees back through the kitchen window and down into the passageway from where he came.

Moreno looks at the sky. There is a whorling cloud, colored pink. Can this be the face of God?

Phase Three

n a rage of anger and frustration at the beggarly betrayal performed by Kyungmoon Nho, Mr. Kim spat on the dead or dying body of his former associate. He leaned carefully over the blood-splattered corpse and carefully deposited a single glob of spittle on the forehead, drop, drop, splatter. He then untied the two dealers, and instructed them to clean the house thoroughly and dispose of the body, preferably in a dumpster at Hunter's Point, which gave Mr. Kim some momentary satisfaction for its ironical justice.

Later, numerous messages were faxed to the Far East, and a few to Hawaii. And then Mr. Kim had his dreaded confrontation by telephone with numerous businessmen in Hong Kong, during which, in a hailstorm of Korean slang and code, it was decided to do business with the crazy woman with the shotgun. Even the liaisons in Hawaii were contacted and informed of the new arrangement.

But at the heart of the matter is Mr. Kim's vision of himself as a dragon, impervious to the contemporary failures of ordinary men. Now that he has witnessed the death of Nho, and has suffered his own temporary humiliation, and now that it has been decided that Grace Wu will be a permanent part of the operation, at least for so long as she proves a valuable commodity, Mr. Kim thinks it necessary to summarize his experience.

At first, of course, the people in Hong Kong were furious and suspicious, but after a period of time they listened to reason, which consisted mainly of news about the nine hundred thousand dollars and certain logistical considerations. Hong Kong had a natural desire to take the money, and to continue to make money from a profitable venture, even though, as businessmen, their thought was tinged with skepticism. It was only after Kim explained the shotgun killing of Nho, its explosive violence, the revenge involved, and only after Kim had explained in detail the appearance of Wu and her assistant, that Hong Kong was persuaded. Mr. Kim reasoned simply that the two were drug dealers. You could see it in their faces. There was a coldness of calculation that preceded the shotgun blast, which was more potent than the act itself. At the end of the conversation Mr. Kim had mentioned the old saying—when America sneezes, Korea catches a cold. This applied, he said, with special force to Kyungmoon Nho. The Hong Kong associates, poised sixty stories above their fabled bay, mountains behind, replied more appropriately, also in Americanese, that money talks and bullshit walks.

Now it is a quiet Sunday morning. Mr. Kim paces back and forth across the patio of suite 17A, Beverly Wilshire Hotel. Now and again he pauses to gaze out at the serenity of the grounds. He can see a rectangular slice of the hotel pool, its clear azure water rippled by marbles of white light that seem to soar from the depths of some Hollywood movie version of water, and then recirculate, as if on cue. There is no direct sunlight in Los Angeles today. In the air is a damp smell of gasoline and eucalyptus bark. One or two Filipino waiters circulate among the guests below, delivering messages, offering coffee. L.A. offers only muffled sounds. Talk is hushed and far away. Traffic mixes and disappears. Even the noise of jet aircraft over Huntington Beach is smoothly distributed, filtered away. Sometimes, Mr. Kim thinks, this city is like that, differentiated from Hong Kong and Seoul, where sound is concrete.

Behind Kim, in the airy main room of suite 17A, Harry Funkhe sorts video tapes. Finally, he finds the tape he seeks and inserts it into a cassette deck, rewinds, anxiously waits for the tape to click stopped. Funkhe is corpulent, faintly unguent. He wears an expensive and tasteless suit which doesn't fit his body shape.

"You won't believe this shit," Funkhe says to Mr. Kim, whose back is turned. "This is so great, just in time. I was beginning to wonder where our next deal was coming from." The room is as cool as rare steak.

Funkhe begins to play the tape. Kim turns and stands with his arms folded. The two men have finished drinking their coffee. They have been discussing nine hundred thousand dollars.

Now, as Kim watches, coolly dispassionate, he sees on the oversize Sony television screen a professionally edited version of the Los Angeles race riots, probably compiled from news shots, documentaries, stills. Some of the tape is silent, some sound. The frames come in vibrant color and in black and white, giving the appearance, many of them, of hand-held shots made by amateurs. Funkhe turns and smiles at Kim, then turns back when Kim fails to respond. On the hued screen Kim is witnessing flame and smoke, a street scene of Korean grocers and merchants standing in front of gutted buildings, some of them old men and women, but the majority young males. Kim hears the sounds of gunshots, police sirens, ambulances, and in the foreground of one shot, a two-minute segment of automatic weapons fire. Two young Koreans fire Glocks into a crowd of looters. They create a rampage of bullet fire, guns recoiling in their hands. For a moment, pride fills Mr. Kim because he sees no fear on these young Korean faces. They remain perfectly placid, defending their property against forces arrayed against them in South Central. Pop, pop, pop, whack.

The sound of the gunfire is instantaneous and surreal. Each shot has no counterpart of echo. Each shot is a prayer, a koan, one hand clapping.

Suddenly on the video tape it is night in Los Angeles. There are random sequences now, which are the logarithms of reality. Warehouses are burning, grocery stores, supermarkets, malls, residences, cars. The sky is fogged by smoke and the streets are nearly deserted. But these scenes do not remind Mr. Kim of war. Instead, he thinks, civil unrest has an entirely different phenomenological dimension. Being a part of such events during his youth in Seoul has given Mr. Kim a healthy respect for anarchy and political disturbance, a feel for its possibility, its horizon, its profitability. From this idea, Mr. Kim begins to pay strict attention to Mr. Funkhe.

"You got to hand it to those guys," Funkhe says, referring to the Korean shopkeepers. "They have guts, no doubt about it." Funkhe fast-forwards the tape. On and on it plays, the litany of riot in color and black and white. Mr. Kim waits and ponders.

Sometimes, Mr. Kim stays at the Beverly Wilshire when he comes south from the Bay Area. At other times he stays at exclusive hotels in Bel Air and Hollywood. But always, he comes to see Harry Funkhe. Their meetings are usually brief and formal. But the matter of the nine hundred thousand dollars is an extra bother, requiring a somewhat more lengthy meeting.

Harry Funkhe is the vice president of a small savings and loan company in Los Angeles. For many years, he had occasional ties to the Korean banking establishment in Honolulu and San Francisco, and to certain Korean contractors doing business in Hawaii and southern California. Until the collapse of the savings and loan industry, Harry Funkhe was involved in serial loan transactions, beneficial to his company, and to himself, but not necessarily to the depositors and stockholders of the loan institution. The real truth is that Harry Funkhe might be in prison now, or at least might be a defendant in a suit, if not for his Korean connections. One or two Honolulu financiers saved Harry's bacon, and now Harry finds it easy to launder money for those same financiers, especially for a kickback of five to ten percent, depending on the amount.

At times, Mr. Kim is disgusted by Funkhe's informal ways, his lack of official manners. He is, in Mr. Kim's view, an entirely American specimen, open as a book, overly friendly, romantic. However, these same qualities which make him an object of loathing for Mr. Kim, make Harry a perfect go-between. He is tolerated and used.

It is obvious that Harry Funkhe is very excited when the tape clicks stopped again. "You got to listen up," he says to Mr. Kim.

"I am paying close attention," Mr. Kim says.

"What you're seeing," Funkhe says, "is money laundering in

action. What we got out there in South Central are hundreds of gutted buildings, vacant or abandoned. There's a huge push to get money in there to rebuild. Hundreds of guys like me are rushing in to make loans, half of it government insured. When I go back to the office today, I deposit your nine hundred grand in about twenty different accounts, and then we set up a few big escrow accounts, and match the money to those accounts. Hey, we could set up some charitable accounts too. Pretty soon I make construction loans to your financial friends in Hawaii, the money gets sent over there, the loans get written down by me, and hey, what do you know, the money is gone to Hawaii. The loan papers come from the Korean banks and they can mark them paid. There's so much fucking building and loaning going on in South Central that the bank examiners can't keep up with it, even if they tried." Funkhe smiles expansively, obviously pleased with himself. "And they sure ain't trying very fucking hard," he adds.

"Very ingenious," Mr. Kim says.

"Listen, don't sweat this," Funkhe says. "I'll work out the details with Hawaii."

"I'll fax my approval," Mr. Kim says.

"Great," Funkhe says. "You gotta love this shit," he says. "I mean, it was the U.S. government that pioneered this secret banking shit." Funkhe stands and smacks his lips, his rendition still pleasurable. "You heard of Iran-Contra, BCCI, Banco Nazionale del Livorno? Hey, that was the ground floor of big-time money laundering, brought to you by Bush-Reagan, Ollie North. When it comes to fake financing, importing and exporting cash, these guys pioneered getting money to the bad guys." Funkhe frowns. "Not that you're the bad guys, right?"

Mr. Kim closes the patio doors. The glass modulates, but does not insulate the city sound. It only changes direction. It is inside the room, invisible but there. It comes in as air conditioning, TV noise, carpet sweepers. It clings to the beiges and blues of the room decor. It even shudders in the gladiolas on the glass-top table.

Just then, Mr. Kim asks Funkhe to count the nine hundred thousand. While Funkhe busies himself with this task, Mr. Kim thinks about his homeland. It is being reported that religious fanatics, followers of Minister Lee Jang Rim, are celebrating the coming of the Rapture, a day on which believers will ascend into heaven, an event which will usher in decades of scourge, famine, war, and which will set the stage for the second coming of Christ himself. There are rumors of mass suicide in Seoul, of disappearances, a martyrdom of the faithful. Men and women are being transported to North Korea where they face sacrifice and dismemberment. What could this mean? And what do all the other strange sects, splinter groups, and eclectic religions signify? In addition, Mr. Kim thinks of the negotiation between Japan and Korea for the return of thousands of Korean noses presently buried in Tokyo, war trophies cut from Korean faces by Japanese soldiers in 1564. It is said the negotiations are both serious and profound. The noses will be returned. And what then?

A man happily at work, Harry Funkhe counts the bills. Kim recalls his last few moments with Grace Wu. He tries to mount a rhetorical argument against his actions. He remembers rising, calling after the woman.

"I am prepared to agree," Kim said. "Uh, tentatively."

"Good," the woman said. "You won't be disappointed. You're going to make money."

"I'm sure," Mr. Kim said.

"About our dead friends," the woman said.

"So there won't be a problem," Mr. Kim replied, "I have this place cleaned up. Nobody going to know about our troubles. It will be like nothing happened. You come back, move in next Friday, it be OK." Kim gestured to the two men on the floor, hands tied and feet bound. "You want these two around?" he asked. "I don't think they have anything to do with this other deal."

"No, they didn't," the woman said. "It's all right. I can use them. But there is another guy, a Korean. He's one of the men who—abused me. I don't want to see him around."

"Don't worry, I know who you mean. We send him to L.A., get him out of the way. I take care of him later."

The woman had cradled her shotgun. "Take good care of my nine hundred thousand too," she said.

Mr. Kim explained the drop procedure, the location of the wall safe. "In six weeks," he said, "you be set up here for good. I bring you in a shipment. I drop by every once in a while to say hello. We get to know one another better. Until then, you relax."

"I'll turn all you can get," the woman said.

Mr. Kim smiled as the woman and her associate moved back through the room and were finally gone. He looked down at Nho, and let a glob of spit fall on the man's forehead.

Harry Funkhe says, "It's all here. Nine hundred thousand."

"Invest it wisely, Mr. Funkhe," Kim says.

Harry Funkhe stands and snaps shut the briefcase which contains the money. It is a cheap black case made of fiber board and imitation leather. Harry taps the case, thinking, five years ago, when all the S&L's were failing, his life was shit. Federal regulators were all over his books. But now, things are looking up for Harry Funkhe. He imagines he is avoiding some kind of currency restrictions, or engaging in bank fraud. Really, he doesn't care. To his mind it is exciting and diverting, something that saved him from the sort of small bureaucratic life for which he was headed.

"So long," Funkhe says to Mr. Kim.

"Goodbye, Mr. Funkhe," Kim replies.

The door opens and Funkhe departs. It is time for Mr. Kim's rubdown and sauna.

22

this particular Sunday night in November hints at winter in northern California. There is a cold mist in the air as Grace Wu drives south on Telegraph Avenue away from the university. The window glass of the Viper is covered by a thin layer of water and grime, not worth wiping. Grace studies the storefronts and bookstores along the upper avenue, most of them boarded and barred, some of the merchants standing in alcoves or under awnings with their arms folded, waiting for the onset of full dark, when, once again, there may be random acts of violence, destruction, vandalism. Who can be doing this?

Well, some weeks it is simply bored teenagers on the run from television and broken homes, and other weeks it is committed politicos who break windows in the name of some idea or other. Everywhere Grace looks she can see graffiti painted on public buildings, walls, sidewalks. At times there are racial undertones to the proceedings. It is as if every crazy event has an infrastructure of some sort, a wheel within a wheel. Grace finds herself driving slowly, as if in an inverse amusement park, but she realizes all at once that the present headlines—BERKELEY: HELL AT NIGHT—nearly mirror her own inner state.

For many days she has been staying in San Jose, where she eats restaurant food, engages in long walks in the brown hills, and goes to see her brother, who remains distant and aloof, almost zombielike. Plainly Grace Wu is weighing the enormity of her own actions against all she has been taught and has learned about violence. In some ways, she sees her actions as self-involved, almost selfish, revenge on a microscale which translates to baseness. At other times she sees herself as a guerrilla fighter with objects and lessons, jungle tactics, strategies for the large-scale extermination of male violence.

For now, she has lost touch with Elgin Lightfoot, even though he is riding beside her in the Viper, silently, wrapped in a down jacket, his black eyes focused out on the street where night is rapidly falling. And as it does, the street seems to come alive, as Elgin watches. From the shadows come the scouting teams of miscreants, homeless, teenagers, and the social workers and counselors who follow them everywhere. Elgin takes it all in.

Early this morning Elgin and Grace went to the house in El Cerrito, their first visit since the last time. They drove right to the front steps in the Viper, both of them heavily armed.

Their knock at the front door was answered by a Korean. "I'm Soon Swee," the man said, nodding, bowing. "Mr. Kim, he say I take the place of Kip. I take care of the house, I drive the car, I fix the garden." Soon Swee is holding a cup of sweet tea. The house has been cleaned, it is immaculate. The broken patio glass has been replaced, and all the walls freshly painted. The carpet is brand new. There is nothing to smell in any of the rooms, no trace of the carnage. Soon Swee emptied the sweet tea into the sink as a sign of respect to the new tenants. "I stay around to make sure nobody busts inside and starts shooting." He smiled at his own joke.

Grace and Elgin inspected the two bedrooms, the one and a half baths, each closet, chest of drawers. It looked like a model home. The refrigerator and kitchen cabinets were stocked with rice, oil, raw vegetables, bean curd, yogurt, sliced pork, canned chicken and tuna. There was bottled water to drink, three varieties of tea, some ginseng, kimchi in carryout cups. Grace and Elgin decided she could move in; after all, she earned it the old-fashioned way.

Now Elgin rolls down a window of the Viper. It is cold, but he tells Grace he'd like some fresh air, if it's OK. Grace has a key to the El Cerrito house. She can come and go as she pleases. Soon Swee will be there, looking out for her interests. But there is no question who is boss. It is Grace Wu. She has the power that once belonged to Kyungmoon Nho. She has taken it from him. Grace has unlocked the safe and taken pictures of the code books and given them to Elgin. Where her power goes now is anybody's guess. Maybe it will go six inches beyond her target, right through it.

Elgin says, "I'm working on their books with some crypto guys from the FBI. I think we're going to see in detail how much money they run. The problem is finding out who launders it in the States. If we could do that, we could bust them right now."

Grace cuts over to San Pablo, heading for the Bay Bridge, and her old apartment. She has a few things left there, and she wants them moved out. As she drives, she thinks about spending her first night alone in the El Cerrito house. "Some of the books are in Korean code and slang, but we're making progress."

Grace laughs weakly, trying to participate. She is trying to lessen the distance between herself and Elgin, but events are keeping it from happening. She feels responsible for her own misdeeds, even though she was a willing participant and should eliminate her guilt. She is drawn to Elgin, but the timing is all wrong.

"I think the books are about cash," Grace says, implying that the money laundering won't be illuminated just by the code books.

"Probably so," Elgin agrees. They hit I-80 going south toward the City. Across the water the City itself glows like a ghost. It is faintly unreal, as always. Only close up can you see the real city. From way out here, it's always the City. "But maybe we can get names and dates," Elgin says. "That would get us somewhere. But hey, you've got to get Mr. Kim to tell you things. It may be the only way."

"What you're saying is that this could take a long time."

"Well, maybe," Elgin says, now looking at Grace. He tries to catch her eye, but it doesn't happen. Elgin feels the weight too, the distance as well.

"Listen," Grace says distractedly, "I know the DEA doesn't have unlimited resources. We can't pay Kim endlessly. And you don't want me turning all this heroin loose on the streets of San Francisco. Which means we have to take the drugs and give him

170

government money until we bust him. How long can we keep doing that?"

Elgin said he didn't know. He knew Grace was right, that he couldn't flood the streets with heroin. To himself he thought, these moral distinctions are so fine, especially after what we've done.

On top of the Bay Bridge, it's as if they've ascended into another climate zone. The air is raw and the mist has become cold rain. Grace activates the wipers, which move images of the City around and around, one image replacing another. It is disconcerting how the headlights distort the road. Grace feels that she is hanging in midair.

Elgin has been thinking. "Suppose you offer to do some minor-league money laundering. Maybe Kim will open up."

"You think I can come on to Kim just like that?"

"I'll have to think it over," Elgin admits. "You could have some friends in banking, that sort of crock. We could set it up."

"And suppose in a couple of weeks we bust Mr. Kim. We have a federal judge tell him he'll do thirty years at El Reno. Maybe his shell will go soft and some juice will dribble out. Maybe, huh?"

"That's a practical suggestion," Elgin says.

"But not foolproof," Grace adds.

"It's a risk."

"I don't suppose the idea of phone tapping and bugging is worth pursuing."

"Kim stays at quite a few hotels in Los Angeles. He flies in from Hong Kong, stays in one, then comes up here to the Claremont. We've checked the Claremont and he hasn't made a single long-distance call from there yet. Nothing. He's meticulous, but we'll keep trying."

"How about the pickup of the product? He has to get it in Los Angeles."

"He doesn't bring it in, we know that. He'll be followed. But even if we find him picking it up, it will already be off the boat or plane, or whatever. We'd just get some small-fry delivery boy along with Kim."

"I shouldn't count on it then," Grace murmurs to herself.

Elgin sighs audibly, by way of an answer. As they go down into the financial district, the lights of the City engulf them. The road is torn by construction projects, piles of rubble glowing in an orange light. All the way up Broadway to Van Ness they are quiet, driving and thinking. Grace is taking the long way to her apartment, partly because she wishes to delay her return, and partly because she wishes to cruise through the City on a late night when there are almost no cars and people. She likes the purity of raw air. She likes the wet streets and the orange glow. This is exactly the way she likes everything when she carries weight. She thinks of all the times she's carried another martial artist on her back, sliding along an oaken floor, back and forth, endlessly. It has been good training, after all.

She reaches Geary Boulevard from the north, behind the apartment building on one of the avenues. She asks Elgin to come inside with her, and he reluctantly agrees. He knows it is a bad idea, but he does it anyway. They go upstairs to the landing, Elgin behind, as Grace finds her keys, then unlocks the door. It is jammed shut. She looks at Elgin briefly, both of them knowing something is wrong.

"Like my mother would say," Grace jokes. "This place has bad *fung soi*. Negative *chi*." Grace gropes helplessly against the door. She opens it a crack, pushes hard, looks in, and then turns to Elgin. Together, they are able to push open the door to the apartment, and go inside.

They both stand absolutely still above the body of a dead woman in a car coat. The woman is half down on her knees, and had obviously been balanced against the door frame and the door itself, blocking it from opening. She is like a sack of bones, something found on an anthropological dig. The skin of her hands and face is grayish blue.

Grace kneels beside the body, in tears, while Elgin goes through the apartment room by room. When he returns, he tells Grace that the apartment is empty, that what he's found is a broken pane of window glass and some shards on the kitchen floor, and an empty wineglass on the kitchen counter. It is deathly quiet, except for the buses and cars hissing by on Geary Boulevard, but even that noise is distant and disembodied. Grace touches the woman's car coat, and feels dried blood behind the right shoulder. Elgin touches a wrist, but finds no pulse. But really, such inquiries are long overdue. The woman is dead, and has been dead for a long time. Decomposition is going on now.

Grace closes her eyes against the tears. She thinks of her rabbits. "It's my landlady," she says. "She comes inside and snoops around and leaves. She doesn't do any harm."

After a while, they decide to call John Zito and tell him that Mrs. Piltka has been shot dead. Grace goes to the telephone and calls the Hall of Justice and has Zito paged, but fifteen minutes go by and he doesn't answer his page. She calls in an emergency for Zito, but she is told that he doesn't answer at home. In fact, they say, they haven't seen Zito for a week now. It occurs to Grace that John Zito has gone over the hill, perhaps for the duration. She can see him in her mind's eye drunk on Market Street, standing in a hotel doorway with a crust of vodka on his lips.

Grace returns and sits down in the hallway beside Elgin, both of them on a vigil.

"I looked around," Elgin says. "I don't think anything was taken."

"I don't have anything to take."

"He came in through the kitchen window. He went out through the kitchen window. It looks like Mrs. Piltka was in the wrong place at the wrong time." Elgin looks at Grace now, gently. "Hey Grace," he says. "You have any enemies?"

Grace is so tense she has to laugh. Poor Mrs. Piltka, she thinks. She wonders what her husband must think after all these days.

"Who do you trust at SFPD, besides Zito?" Elgin asks.

"A detective named Stark," Grace replies.

"Call him, get him over here, but don't really tell him what's going down. We need a crew to photograph and print, but we don't want sirens and ambulances just yet. First we do the investigation, you get out and go to El Cerrito, then we can have ambulances and sirens."

Grace locates Stark with two telephone calls and he promises to come over without a fuss. Grace goes into the kitchen, followed by Elgin, just killing time.

"I didn't leave this here," Grace says, pointing to the wineglass. A puddle of chardonnay lies in the bottom. "Whoever it was had a shot of my wine."

"Probably not Mrs. Piltka," Elgin says.

Elgin puts his arm around Grace and they stand quietly for a few moments. "God," Grace says, "that poor woman. She was shot as soon as she came in, wasn't she? She's been there for quite a few days. Her husband must be crazy by now." Grace realizes her fatigue. She looks up at Elgin and their eyes finally meet. "It was supposed to be me," Grace says. "It was supposed to be me."

Elgin follows Grace back to the hall. "I think what you've just said is probably true." Elgin stands quietly. "We have to deal with it," he says.

Grace takes a deep breath. "Suppose this," she says, composing herself. "Suppose Mr. Kim is behind this. After our talk last week he goes back to the Claremont and calls somebody who comes over here and breaks in and waits for me to come home. Of course, I didn't go home. I stayed in San Jose. Whoever comes in here sees a woman open the door and shoots her. I know these people know where this apartment is, I know it."

"Fine, except for one thing," Elgin says. "Soon Swee didn't seem at all surprised to see you. In fact, he had everything prepared just for you. If they thought you'd been dead a week, I don't think the house would have been that well prepared."

Grace has to agree, and shrugs.

"But this does change things," Elgin says. "I can't ask you to go over to El Cerrito now. It's too dangerous. Say we bust Mr. Kim and get what we get."

"I'm going over tonight," Grace says.

"You don't have to do it."

"It isn't a question of having to," Grace says. "I don't know what it's a question of, but that isn't it."

They hear footsteps on the landing. Elgin opens the door and lets three men inside the apartment. They introduce themselves. Detective Stark takes out a pad and pencil and begins to write.

23

On All Souls' Sunday the bells of Mission Dolores can be heard throughout the barrio. Paz can hear them from the bedroom she shares with Clemente Moreno on Guerrero Street. The frosted cookies and marzipan skulls she has made are on the windowsill, and now she lies in bed hearing the stream of sounds and thinking about her mother in Agua Prieta, how she and her mother would dress for church every Sunday morning and walk the dusty and nearly deserted streets to the mud-walled sanctuary that was situated in a wash within shouting distance of the American town of Douglas, Arizona. She wishes she could go to mass again, for comfort, and in order to pray for the happiness of her mother whom she misses very much, even though she cannot imagine returning to Mexico, even though her life with Moreno has turned suddenly, and very mysteriously, hard.

She touches her damaged nose, and thinks about the crazy police officer who came into their apartment with his drawn weapon. Even now she does not understand the event. Fear pulls her back into her real life, which is one of hardship and ill use. Her injury hurts her terribly; it has gone untreated and when she bathes it sometimes bleeds, leaving the water red-tinted. Twice on Saturday morning Moreno struck her for no reason.

Even worse was his mood when he returned to the apartment on Friday night, after being out for most of the evening. Moreno had been drinking. Paz tried to hide from him by cowering like a dog in the closet, but Moreno found her and beat her, not bad, but bad enough. In Spanish he cursed her as a *puta* and *asesina*, condemning her as perfidious. Paz realized that these words were only from the wine, but she has heard enough of such talk, and now thinks about leaving this man. Finally that night he finished with her and went to sleep in a chair while Paz wandered the rooms of the apartment like a prisoner.

Since then, Moreno has remained quiet, reading newspapers in his slow, stumbling way, watching TV, drinking beer. Paz lies on her side now, listening to the bells, and to his steady snore. She can smell the burnt sugar aroma of the marzipan. She speaks her mother's name, Hortensia, under her breath and briefly sleeps again. There is nearly ten thousand American dollars in a box in the closet where Paz cowered, and she thinks about the money too.

On the Day of the Dead, Clemente Moreno wakes with a hangover from beer. He can feel Paz beside him, her body under the thin blanket. The windows are open and the room is filled with sunshine, and he can hear the church bells hammering away at his hangover and wishes they would disappear. Moreno hates the clerics, the priests, and thinks the Church is evil, even though he believes in God and the saints. But suddenly, while he lies on his side and suffers, he is struck by the terrible times with John Zito, and the uncertainty eats away at him, plays with him like a cat with a mouse it has caught. He tries to rise, but falls back and rests, then rises again and dresses quickly and, without breakfast, goes to the bakery that is just down the street and buys a newspaper and returns to the apartment. Paz has made his coffee. She brings him a cup and returns to the kitchen to cook his breakfast. Moreno can hear the woman washing herself in the sink later, and he thinks he is involved with a dreadful Yaqui who cannot use the bathroom enough.

While he drinks coffee, Moreno reads the Sunday paper for news of a murder. Although he reads poorly, he can understand the headlines, and he knows what he is looking for. His index finger guides him down the columns of dense print. On the front page is political news, local and national. There are late hurricanes off Cuba and near the Dominican Republic. Another member of the present Administration has lied to Congress. The news is everything and nothing, which is to say, it is as it always is and always will be, yet there are no police murders. No woman found dead in her apartment on Geary Boulevard. Five arrests in Berkeley for riot and vandalism. Six victims of drowning. The city of Detroit is afire from Halloween tricksters. Paz brings Moreno more coffee.

Moreno's hands tremble as he puts down the newspaper. He rolls a joint and smokes it. When he finishes the joint, he is calmed, but it is only the effect of the drug. Fifteen minutes later, the drug increases his paranoia and his mind spins off in a hundred directions at once, like a pinwheel of fireworks in the night sky over an isolated cemetery on the Day of the Dead. *Por el amor del Dio,* Moreno whispers to himself. Where is the news of John Zito? Where is El Tiburon? And where is the news of the *puta narca?*

Paz brings a plate of eggs with picante sauce and chorizo, more coffee, but Moreno declines them without an explanation. Paz has washed her hair in the sink, dried it, and has tied it back with a white ribbon. Her nose is swollen, like a lump of grayish ash. For a moment Moreno feels sorry for her but then he rushes out of the house and walks down Valencia Street to El Patio, where he finds the restaurant nearly empty, but open for business nonetheless. He sits at the end of the bar, where once he sat with the Shark. Rows of shiny glasses hang above the bar and the TV is tuned to a Spanish language broadcast of a football game from Mexico. The picture is far away and the announcers scream excitedly about nothing. The waitress, named Gloria, sees Moreno and comes to the end of the counter, counting some change and bills. Apparently, the bar is just opening, and Moreno is the first customer of the day.

"Hey *hombre,*" Gloria says to Moreno.

Moreno speaks in excited and hurried Spanish, but corrects himself when he sees that the woman cannot follow him. She looks at Moreno and tries to calm him. In controlled movements, she places a cocktail napkin in front of him, an ashtray. Gloria is much practiced at the art of traducing men. She smiles and fixes him with a distracted stare.

"It is important that I see the Shark," Moreno says.

"You mean our friend Tiburon," Gloria jokes.

"Now, as soon as possible," Moreno says, pounding on the bar with his fist.

"Relax *amigo,*" Gloria says. "You want something to drink?" Gloria leans against the bar. She thinks this *hombre* looks kind of deranged.

"Nothing to drink," Moreno says.

"Honestly," Gloria says, "I haven't seen your friend for days now. He got up Friday morning and left my place and hasn't been back. You can take it easy, though. He always shows up sooner or later when he's in the Bay Area. He's like as not to be on a drunk. He's probably down in San Jose. He's got some friends down there. But he'll come back up here, you can take that to the bank."

"Where do you live?" Moreno snaps. "I'll wait for him there."

"No way, Jose," Gloria says. She backs away from the bar and tries to look busy. "I got a sister who stays there a lot, and with a baby too." Gloria asks again if Moreno would like something to drink, and this time he orders Tecate and lime. Gloria brings the beer, and she watches while he drinks off half of it at once. "Listen," she says, still calming, "you know the guy. Hang around Valencia Street long enough and you're sure to see him."

While Moreno drinks more of the beer, Gloria secretly wonders what has brought these two men together, and what has gone wrong, or right. At the same time, Moreno thinks about the seven thousand dollars he has paid Tiburon, and he thinks about all the cash he has hidden in a box in the closet of his apartment. There is some cocaine there too, and some basuco, all of it worth maybe forty thousand dollars. He wonders if he could make a new beginning in Denver or El Paso. It is conceivable to start again. There is cocaine everywhere you look in this country. He pays for his beer and leaves El Patio without another word to Gloria.

Moreno decides to give himself one more chance. After all, he has a beautiful apartment and many clients and contacts on the street. He goes to Los Angeles for his supply, and it has become a nice routine. If he began again in another city, he would have to cultivate an entirely new chain of supply, something that is dangerous. It would also cost him money to buy trust from the people he dealt with. Instead, he thinks he will risk everything and drive over to the *puta narca*'s apartment on Geary Boulevard.

Moreno owns an Impala, which he stores in a rented garage behind his apartment. It is midafternoon and the sky is hazy and blue and cold. The beige and pale greens of the buildings along Geary are subdued. As Moreno cruises back and forth in front of the narca's apartment, he can see that the windows are dark. He decides to find a spot to park and to wait, for he has nothing better to do. On Fifteenth Street he finally finds a place where he can see the apartment building. He stays in the car for a time, then walks around the block, and gets back inside the car. It is a pattern he will follow for hours, until the day begins to darken and night begins to fall. He sits in the Impala and listens to music. He leaves and walks down Geary Boulevard across the street from the apartment building, pauses directly across from it, then moves on, waits twenty minutes at the end of the block, once or twice ordering doughnuts from a shop, then walks back to his Impala. He listens to radio news, but there is none. Nothing eases his torment. Waiting this way only increases his anxiety.

Now that it is nearly dark, Moreno thinks that he should be at home, having a bath while Paz brings him shots of tequila and washes his back. But instead here he is, sitting in his automobile, waiting for something to change his life. Even now mist hangs over the apartment building, just as in real life a fog hangs over Moreno. In his imagination, cadavers are dancing in a windswept cemetery, fireworks bursting over tombstones.

Yet, in this instant of reverie, Moreno sees a red Dodge Viper pull to a stop around the corner from the entrance to the building. Moreno strains to see. To his horror, the puta narca gets out, followed by another person, someone large with long hair tied back behind his head. Moreno shuts his eyes in disbelief. On the

Day of the Dead, Moreno is seeing a cadaver on the street. He shudders, then feels some relief to know the truth. Now there is no mystery about Grace Wu, because she is alive. This is terrible, but it is also liberating. Where once he had conceived of himself being haunted for life, now he knows that he is only the victim of fate.

And now fate guides the actions of Clemente Moreno again. He decides to wait where he is, for what else can he do? Once in the grip of fate, one can only allow it to take over and make the most of its opportunities. Right now, fate offers Moreno the opportunity to understand this puta. Perhaps he will have to kill this woman again? Would this not be fate in its strangest dress? Moreno turns off the car radio. It can be of no more use to him.

Moreno watches the building for an hour. Three more people enter the apartment and go upstairs. These men are not like the woman, for they carry valises and cameras. They walk like cops, Moreno thinks. And now Moreno begins to wonder who it is that he shot, there in the apartment. Perhaps she was a friend or a housekeeper, perhaps a sister, a lover. He releases his breath slowly, his mind now under icy control. Fate is indeed a mysterious thing.

But then Moreno realizes that he has no weapon, neither the tiny .22 automatic, nor the .25 Colt. He watches as the woman comes out of the building and goes to the Dodge Viper and sits in it without moving or starting the engine. She is just down Fifteenth Street, not a minute away, not twenty meters separated from her second fate. How easy it would be, Moreno thinks, to drive alongside the car and fire into it and end the puta's life a second time. But then the woman starts her engine, and Moreno starts his, and something else begins to happen.

The Viper goes north on Fifteenth Street with Moreno following. It is lucky for Moreno that on Sunday night the streets are not dense with traffic. Moreno feels compelled to follow the woman narca, down Clement Street where the Chinese restaurants are busy and well lighted, all the way to Gough Street, back south, onto the Central Freeway, and then to I-80 and the Bay Bridge. Nearer the water the mist becomes a steady drizzle, which is good for Moreno, because it smears images, makes him invisible behind the woman. His windshield wipers click slowly against the glass, just twenty inches in front of his face. It is good that he is following this Viper, because it is unique, easy to see, shaped like a red lizard. Moreno changes lanes often, slows, then speeds up, changing lanes again. Finally, they reach the Bay Bridge, then the toll plaza, then go north toward Berkeley, past the racetrack, the Bart stations, where the Viper suddenly leaves the freeway and turns inland at Potrero and goes to El Cerrito.

They climb into hills behind the suburban city. Now, Moreno must exercise extreme caution because there are so few cars on the street, and almost no people. He hurries to make traffic signals, until finally they are into oaks and sycamore-shrouded lanes where it is dark. There is a Private Drive sign, a dead end, and Moreno goes partway up it and stops. He can see the Viper far away, red taillights. There is wind in the eucalyptus and things are very still. At the top of the hill is a house, outlined. The woman parks in front of the house and goes inside it.

Moreno waits and waits, until nearly midnight. At last he leaves and returns home to Guerrero Street. On the way he does not listen to the radio. He is no longer interested in the news. It is another fate he is living now, not one that speaks in public and discernible ways.

24

after he leaves the Golden Gate, and maneuvers around San Quentin, it takes Elgin Lightfoot half an hour to find the right road up into San Rafael. He goes up a private drive that dead ends at a cliff, then does it again, again.

He's using a government LTD. The upholstery stinks of cigar smoke and human sweat, and even though it's a cool day and the windows are open he can still smell the odor. It reminds him of his mother's trailer on the reservation, the closed-in aromas. Every time his mother would bring a man back with her from a night on the town, the two of them would drink and smoke cheap cigars and turn up the heat. Then when Elgin would go into the main room early in the morning he would see them passed out together and he would smell the cigar smoke. Ever since he has associated cigar smoke with his mother and her men, and with his own youth spent in a cramped trailer where it was always cold. Now he is trying to put it out of his mind, but he can't, because it isn't in his mind, it's in his past, which is the same as saying it's in his blood.

He goes up a road and looks in the rearview mirror. The City recedes, sprinkled blue and gold, a city of fable that makes him sad. Below him the lights of Sausalito twinkle. There are trendy waterfront boutiques and spiffy California restaurants, olive tableclothes and Perrier to drink. Now he goes up and up along switchbacks through glades of white spruce and gum trees, houses hidden inauspiciously away from the road. There are a few high gates and electric fences, but most of the homes are screened by nature, by hedges of oleander, trellis roses, lemon trees.

Elgin has been in Los Angeles for a week, doing paperwork. His district supervisor demands clear and complete reports for every work schedule. Elgin writes them with regularity. Right now he needs to explain how he is going to spend all the money the DEA is giving him, which has already amounted to more than a million dollars on the Korean operation. Being back in L.A. is something of a shock. But being home is nice. It means being alone.

Elgin spent all his first day home cleaning and puttering around with his plants. He sat on his small balcony and spent an hour looking at the smog over Lincoln Boulevard. He cleaned the refrigerator and bought some beer and sipped it while the Lakers played a regular season game on the road at Portland. He checked in with the office, and found that the man following Mr. Kim had watched him all the way in and out of the Beverly Wilshire Hotel where Kim spent a day, then flew to Hawaii, spent another day, then on to Hong Kong. Even now, other men are surveilling the El Cerrito house and watching the activities of Soon Swee. Elgin is excited that things have come this far this fast, but he is also concerned that he has no good way to uncover Mr. Kim's money laundering operation, unless Mr. Kim tells Grace what is going on, or until he gets a break from the surveillance. Right now, it's a matter of time, and Elgin worries about Grace's safety, especially after what happened to Mrs. Piltka. On his second day at home, Elgin wrote a glowing report about Grace and the operation. Elgin needs space, which in beaureaucratic language translates to *latitude*. Yeah, he thinks, he needs latitude.

How can Elgin explain Grace to his superiors? He uses the word *daring* in his reports. He decides he will simulate everything that has happened in San Rafael, except for the killings of Kip and Kyungmoon Nho. Of course, the word *daring* has both denotation and connotation. He realizes that the word denotes courage and skill, but he also realizes that it connotes recklessness. Thus, he represents Grace Wu to his superiors as a daring agent, one whose skill should be rewarded with both time and money, or, in a word, latitude. He is satisfied that recklessness will remain only a hint. He files his report, checks all the cases he is handling, and has numerous meetings with other agents, detectives, police officers, and snitches.

At times it seems to Elgin that the West Coast will sink from the weight of all the illegal drugs coming in and going out. There are times when he must fight through the hopelessness of folly. And of course he worries about Grace Wu on a personal level. She is way out there, he thinks to himself. Her posture reminds Elgin of the famous Japanese woodcut, a fisherman in a tiny boat, poised beneath a massive wave, the tsunami in everybody's life.

Then, on a Friday in early November, after lunch and after several meetings, Elgin Lightfoot takes the afternoon flight to SFO. Somehow he feels he must maintain direct contact with Grace. He has prepared annotated photographs of Mr. Kim's account books, and he wishes to review these with her. Perhaps he is doing something else, something entirely off the ledger. He keeps seeing her in her blue skirt, dust on her shoes, as they had their picnic under the cottonwoods in Sonoma. But when he gets to the local DEA office in San Francisco, there is an urgent message. He checks out a tan Ford LTD and heads into the San Rafael hills.

Once Elgin finds the right street, it takes him a while to find the right address. It's way up at the top, and there are three or four cars parked on the shoulder of the road, and an ambulance halfway down the driveway. Elgin parks the Ford, and walks down the driveway where his ID is checked by a uniformed officer. Elgin is standing in the driveway when he sees Stark about fifteen yards away. There are five or six SFPD types, some county sheriff's officers, and a coroner in a confab near the front door of this expensive home. Elgin can see a tiny car parked nose-up to the garage with its driver door open. Standing here in the shadows of the large sycamores, the lemon trees, it is cold, and Elgin wishes he had brought along a sweater. As it is, he is just wearing a dress shirt and slacks. He has some time, so he walks over and takes a look inside the car. In the backseat there is a suitcase, and beside the suitcase some loose socks, underwear, towels, a razor and shave kit. He sees a bottle of Absolut vodka on the back floorboard, a package of cigarettes on the dash. Elgin walks around the car, just looking. Some EMS types are sitting on the back lift of the ambulance, playing cards. The wind kicks up and drops mist from a gray sky.

Elgin walks down a flagstone path, skirts the garage, and stands by while Stark finishes with the coroner. Elgin notices the body, down behind Stark, half in and half out of the front door. Elgin nods to Stark; he nods back.

Elgin kneels over John Zito. One of Zito's eyes is open, the other closed. His face looks bruised, but Elgin guesses that this is just bloating and decomposition. There are no facial cuts or lacerations of any kind. Actually, the skin looks as if it has the texture of clay, or would if touched. Otherwise, Zito appears to have fallen asleep in the front doorway of his wife's home, his home. One of his arms is inside the house, touching the white shag carpeting. The other arm is beside the torso, posed naturally. Elgin leans over, trying to see the wounds, one of which is a small blue hole in the throat, which looks as if somebody has glued it closed. Except for crusts of dried blood, there is no evidence of another wound. As it is, Elgin can't tell how often Zito was hit. Two, three?

"Well," Stark says, leaning above Elgin, "we know why Zito didn't show up for work all this week." Stark darts his froglike face into the picture. "And here I thought he was drunk again."

"Who found him?" Elgin asks.

Stark explains that a Marin County judge had ordered the house put up for sale as part of the divorce proceedings. Zito didn't oppose the sale, in fact, he didn't even show up for the hearing on the motion. A real estate agent came to the house over the weekend to show it to a couple and found Zito in the doorway. "Imagine their surprise," Stark says.

"Has the ME got anything so far?" Elgin asks.

"John Zito was shot three times." Stark fumbles for his notes, but goes on without them. "Throat, upper chest, abdomen. It was like a stepladder. He got zipped up tight. The holes aren't very big, and there aren't any exit wounds, so we figure small caliber from close range. He just fell down backward into the door entrance and stayed that way for a whole week. Hell, nobody could see him from the road and the house has been vacant. Zito's wife never came around. I guess she was afraid he'd come back. He still had a few things inside, and she didn't want to meet up with him. I can't blame her, yeah. It's no secret he's been drinking like a son of a bitch lately."

"There's a bottle of vodka in his Caprice."

"It's funny about that," Stark says. They move aside while the EMS technicians prepare Zito for shipment to the morgue. Elgin becomes aware that there are other men inside the house. "The door to the car is wide open, you can see that yourself. And the key is in the ignition, and the ignition switch is turned to the On position. The goddamn motor was running."

The EMS technicians wrap Zito in sheeting and put his body in a black rubber bag. He is tagged, then covered by an orange blanket. The corpse is strapped to a stretcher and then taken to the ambulance. Elgin watches while the ambulance rolls up and out of the driveway.

"So," Elgin says, "Zito came by his house for a few minutes. What did he have in mind?"

"Picking up some stuff from the house, who knows?" Stark says. "But I can tell you a few things right now. We checked with his new landlord over on Turk Street where Zito rented a walkup dive down by the YMCA. The landlord says John would just sit inside and drink. But the guy hadn't seen John for a week, and it was the first of the month and John hadn't paid the rent. The landlord went up there last week and John wasn't around, and most of his stuff was gone, so the guy gave up and rented it to someone else. Easy come, easy go. My men have been over to the place and they talked to the new tenant. He says there were booze bottles all over the place, even some skin-popping equipment. But he didn't find any of John's clothes, because they're all in the suitcase in the car, or in the trunk. And another thing, a lot of John's clothes are still in closets in this house. I'd say he was splitting town and came by to get *something*, but what it is I don't know. It's too late for John to tell me."

"Suppose he just got here and surprised a burglar. After all, the house was vacant."

"No way," Stark says. He gestures at the broken glass, most of it inside the house on the carpet. He shows Elgin crowbar marks on the door panels, higher on the wooden frame as well. "I can give you a dozen reasons why that isn't what happened here." Elgin shrugs and smiles. "For one thing, you'd have to assume it was the burglar who pried on the door and finally broke the glass to get inside. So, John could have seen that when he came up to the door. John had a gun on his hip, his police issue. Wouldn't you think he could have drawn his gun when he was coming up the walk with the front door open and glass everywhere? And for another thing, how did he get spread-eagled on the ground with his feet outside the house as if he were *leaving?* And finally, I have to tell you there is absolutely nothing valuable missing in the house so far as we can tell, and there is some good shit in there, electronics, silver, a coin collection, booze. Right now, I'd say it was John who tried to pry the door open, got pissed off when it wouldn't come, broke the glass, went inside, got whatever it was he wanted, then came outside and got killed by somebody who was waiting for him."

"You say he's been here a week?"

"Yeah, ain't that funny. Around the same time as that old lady got dusted in Grace Wu's apartment."

"You think it's one of our cases."

"Don't you?" Stark says.

"Well, I didn't think they wanted to kill the landlady."

"By the way," Stark says, "I got the report done on that one. We got a set of damn good fingerprints off the wineglass, but they don't match anything in the computer. Whoever killed the landlady is clean so far."

Stark is interrupted by other officers and techs. Elgin listens to them, and then goes inside the Zito house where he inspects every room—plush white shag carpet, expensive oils on the walls, a view of the bay. Elgin wanders around in the den and the bedrooms, trying to imagine what it might have been like here. Only in the kitchen does he begin to get a picture. There are two cases of empty beer bottles stacked in one corner. Bottles of Absolut and Stoli line the kitchen counter. Late afternoon sun streams inside and wraps around the scene. The porcelain surfaces seem to whisper to Elgin and he thinks he can detect the subtle aroma of cigar smoke. Elgin feels haunted by the kitchen, trapped in a silken envelope of time. He hears Stark behind him, breathing deeply.

"Quite a mess," Stark says.

"What about the weapons in our two killings?" Elgin asks.

"The landlady got it with a twenty-five. Here I'd say John took a twenty-two. If we can find the guy who drank some wine in Grace's house, I think we got something. We've been over this house and there are lots of prints, but I'd say our killer never came inside. We've been up and down the hills too, and we can't find a gun. If we can find the one person who wanted both Grace Wu and John Zito dead, then we've got something. Otherwise, *nada*. You know what I mean, Elgin?"

Elgin follows Stark out into the front yard of the Zito house. They stand side by side in the shadows.

"Let me tell you something else," Stark says. "John had himself a bag packed, I told you that. When we looked inside it was all lightweight stuff, slacks, short-sleeve shirts, swimming trunks, white cotton socks, sneakers. There's some sunglasses and suntan lotion too. The fucker even packed that zinc ointment for your nose, so it won't get sunburned, you know? Pal John was on his way out. And I don't think he was headed to Greenland."

"Mexico, Brazil," Elgin says.

"And we scrubbed the trunk. There's about an ounce of residue from our white mother in there. John was doing major toot, right up there with the heavyweight champs."

Stark walks Elgin all the way to the LTD. Stark lights a cigar, and Elgin realizes where the aroma came from inside the house. From here, Elgin can see Mount Tamalpais webbed in sunshine. Elgin is thinking, but he can't fit all the pieces of this puzzle together. He agrees to work with Stark, to stay in touch, and then he drives away, across the San Rafael Bridge. He uses a pay phone to call Grace on her cellular at the El Cerrito house.

"Hello," Grace answers, far away.

"Is this the boat works?" Elgin asks.

"You've got the wrong number," Grace says.

"This isn't 883-7645?"

Grace politely says no, and hangs up. This means that she will meet Elgin at the Bateau Ivre at six forty-five tonight. Elgin hangs up. He has an hour and a half to kill and no idea how to do it.

25

oday is part of the ration plan for the Valley, an official No-Watering Wednesday in Sherman Oaks. By early morning there is a dull haze over the ocean and everyone can smell ozone as it settles into the suburbs where Harry Funkhe is getting out of bed, drinking coffee, and checking the *Wall Street Journal*. He kisses his daughter Sarah off to school. His boy Leonard is already at basketball practice and won't be home until seven or eight at night—that is, if he stays at the mall and plays video games as he usually does, or roams the numberless drives and cul-de-sacs that define this part of L.A., just over the mountains from Westwood Village, where Harry Funkhe is vice president at a savings and loan, and where he is making a killing with these Korean dudes he knows. Good wife Faith is at her tennis lesson, out of the house already, so Harry sits at the kitchen table and drinks coffee, then takes his cup to the back patio and looks around at his demesne, surveying the good life as he knows it, the quarter acre of green, well-fertilized lawn, the tawny buckskin-colored fence that separates him from the estate of his neighbor and the thousands of square acres of desert turned city.

Harry thinks he is doing pretty well. He used to flatter himself that he'd fallen into a kind of instinctual luck situation that could change at any moment, so that he needed to take out all he could before the well went dry. In that regard, he was like millions of others in the eighties, on the moral record as looking out for number one.

Harry walks across the lawn in his bare feet. At this time of year, the tree roses are in bloom, and Harry smiles at Faith's natural horticultural ability. This year there has been a little rain, and so there are some fruit on the avocado. Harry drinks the last of his coffee and notices the sky.

It hasn't always been this good for Harry. He thinks back ten years, and then five, when the family moved up to Downey. He shudders to think of the two-bedroom box they called home, and the house that faced due west so that the sun blazed away on its pink stucco all afternoon. Back then he would go to the branch savings and loan and put in his ten hours and come back home and wonder how long it would take the federal examiners to come in and shut down the business because of all the bad loans, the self-dealing of the directors, the commercial flops. Back then he thought of himself as unlucky, and noninstinctual. But that was before he met some Korean businessmen in Hawaii, and was off to the races.

Now Harry dares to dream about getting rich, really well off. Everything he makes off the Koreans is going into a Minneapolis bank, certain mutual financial operations, and a tax shelter in the Caymans. Harry is drinking Kona coffee, in honor of his Hawaiian friends.

Harry goes inside and puts on a suit and tie. The house has ten rooms, twenty-one hundred square feet, four bedrooms, three baths, rec room. There is an electronic garage door opener, a Ping-Pong table out back. There is a window seat in the master bedroom that looks out on the backyard. Someday Harry thinks he will put in a Jacuzzi. When Harry sits down now to put on his shoes and socks, he wonders if he should install a ground pool for the kids. Perhaps they could have school parties and everybody in the family could get to know one another better. He's heard about this Generation-X shit, and he doesn't want it near him. The necessity of these decisions reminds Harry that he's come a long way from Bakersfield High, from Encino Savings, and from the debacle of the eighties, when everybody was raking in the cash, but getting indicted too.

Right now Harry Funkhe is sitting on more than three million Korean dollars. Mr. Kim has been showing up every six weeks for two years with three hundred thousand dollars a week. In his head, Harry calculates his percentage. This is really, really good money, and tax free. Harry decides that six weeks from now he will hold up Mr. Kim for another two points because of the added work. For a moment, Harry feels godlike and serene, his house an Olympus from which he looks down on the mortals below. There they are down there, scurrying around, carrying loads fifty and sixty times their individual body weights, and here is Harry Funkhe way up here, observing, making notes, socking away the cake.

Sure, he says to himself, I've got problems. He's had to work night and day for a week setting up accounts to handle the recent cash influx from the Koreans. All totaled, he's created twenty-four accounts to handle the flow, and now he's created another six charitable ones as well. In time he will forge loan documents, escrow papers. He will create false lines of credit, all connected to a series of imaginary construction projects and charitable trusts, and some holding companies. Now he can pay nonexistent construction companies on fake construction loans. He can switch money from one account to another. He can make cash sit up and dance, just so long as it winds up in a Korean bank in Honolulu. After all these years in the loan business, Harry thinks he knows which buttons to push, and he is pushing them for all he's worth. As head of the branch, a guy with fifteen years in the business, he has seen some rough times. But that isn't now. Now is lush. Now is happening to Harry.

Harry is ready to go to work, and takes one last look at himself in the mirror. Faint reddish hair, paunch, washed-out blue eyes. He thinks he looks a little like Van Johnson, or better, Rod Taylor in *The Birds*. Just before he leaves the mirror for the day, Harry thinks he'd like to have a mistress, something juicy and young on the side, like a fried egg with your pancakes.

The drive to Westwood Village, over the mountains, takes a standard forty minutes. Harry can see Mulholland Drive on the way, its brow of Hollywood Hill, and below him the whole of the Los Angeles basin spread out beneath a choking haze. Harry likes this city, because it is greedy and shallow. Just the thought of being close to something this dirty gives Harry sexual chills. It thrills him and enters his mind. In a way, it's the juicy mistress Harry wishes he had.

Harry parks in his space behind the building at ten o'clock. He noses in the small Mercedes and sets the burglar alarm and goes inside the savings and loan. Harry has an office on the mezzanine of the brick and stucco structure, a teak desk in front of smoky windows that release onto Wilshire Boulevard, the Los Angeles Country Club just down the block. Someday, Harry thinks, *he* will join the club. It is cool and hushed inside the building when he enters it. He feels himself relax, his cruise control on, the sweat already evaporating.

A worried clerk meets Harry immediately, a mouse named Jane that Harry wouldn't fuck if his ass was on fire. She tells him, anxiously it seems, that two people are waiting for Harry in his office, and that they're from the government. Harry blinks and goes blank for a second. A stab of pain enters his heart, just where the ribs attach to the breastbone. Harry is back ten, five years, but then he jump-starts and forgets about Encino, when the savings and loan closed and the whole place was crawling with government types. Back then, Harry had plenty of loans out himself, and he was sure he was going to come in light once the auditors were finished rummaging in his files. But shit happens, and savings and loans all over town started going down, and the job got too big, and then came the Koreans to the rescue. Harry wonders if some of this old news is coming back to haunt him. He thanks Jane, and goes up the stairs to the mezzanine, then walks down the hall, and into his office.

Sure enough, two people are waiting for Harry Funkhe. They stand in front of the wall-to-wall window, looking down at Wilshire Boulevard. It's natural, it's what people do who haven't been in the office before. They hear Harry open the door and turn around.

"I'm Harry Funkhe," Harry says, trying to sound dignified.

Harry scopes: White man, tall, well groomed, short crew-cut hair, lightweight wool suit, a runner, jogger, lifts weights. Harry is intimidated by this man immediately. Black woman, short, severe blue suit, briefcase. Harry smiles as if he were biting his knuckles.

"You've got a great view here," the man says.

Bullshit, Harry thinks. "Yeah, not bad," Harry says.

Harry crosses the room and sits down behind his desk. He doesn't know what to say. The man and woman study Harry. Harry places his hands palms down on the desk, but removes them quickly when he sees that they are leaving slick sweat spots on the wood. Harry's legs are like jelly. His blood pressure shoots sky high. Harry thinks that now that he is sitting, he won't have to shake hands with these people when they're introduced. They won't touch his sweating hands, and realize how scared Harry is.

"Dick Archer," the man says. "United States Secret Service."

"Secret Service," Harry says, noticeably relieved. Piece of cake, he thinks. "Whaddaya know," he says.

The black woman says, "Verna Bayless. Federal Bureau of Investigation. We'd like to ask you some questions."

Harry is back to being himself. He had expected bank examiners, or people from the Office of Thrift Supervision.

"Uh, actually," the man says, "Verna is an accountant. She specializes in bank fraud."

"All right," Harry says. "I'm kind of astounded."

"Beg your pardon," Archer says.

"I mean, I thought that old savings and loan business was over. We're quite well managed here."

"Oh, you mean the failures," Archer says.

"Yeah." Harry smiles. "We're on solid ground here. We've had our bad years. They're behind us now. I don't approve commercial bullshit and I don't make any correspondent deals. This is strictly construction loans and residential. But if you want to do an audit, hey, be my guest." Harry leans back. He thinks he can handle an audit, especially one that's looking for real estate loans from years before.

"Well, that isn't it, Mr. Funkhe," Archer says.

Harry leans forward again. "I don't understand," he says.

"Actually, there's another problem," Archer says. Archer has his arms folded now. It isn't a nice look he's giving Harry and Harry knows it. It is making Harry uncomfortable again. "Two days ago," Archer continues, "the local Federal Reserve reported to the Secret Service here in Los Angeles that it came across two hundred thousand dollars in counterfeit bills. The counterfeit money came from here, Mr. Funkhe."

"You must be joking," Harry says.

"It's not a joke," Archer says.

"Frankly, I'm amazed," Harry says. "I'm sure none of my big customers is doing anything illegal."

"Yeah, well," Archer says. "Imagine my surprise when I realized that the last time I saw this particular batch of counterfeit money was during a drug bust in San Francisco about two months ago." Archer is motionless. "On Bay Street to be exact," he says.

Harry's panic comes and goes. "I'm not following you," he says truthfully. Harry begins to tap a fingernail on the top of his desk, a nervous reaction. "I mean, I don't have anything to do with counterfeit money."

"Maybe I can help you, Mr. Funkhe," the black woman says. "Last night I served a search warrant on your institution. In fact, I spent all night working in here." Harry's eyes glaze when the woman passes him an official document. "The money we're talking about came from accounts maintained and handled by you."

"But counterfeit money," Harry says.

The black woman says, "That's only part of the problem." She opens her briefcase and takes out some notes. Harry is trying to stay calm and weather whatever this is. "Even though I've only just begun my audit, I've found maybe twenty-five accounts that show unusual activity. Frankly, I'm having trouble with them, their business purpose. Of course, I'm sure everything can be explained. It's just going to be necessary for you to explain them in detail. For example, the Dragon Construction account." She simulates a smile. "For a start."

"But I don't understand what crime it is to do business with your depositors?" Harry says.

"Oh, that's not a crime," Archer says. "But, hey, your records show that the two hundred thousand came in as part of a deposit on a South Central charitable building trust. You couldn't blame me if I was curious who brought that money in here, could you?"

"Well, I guess not," Harry says. In his wildest dreams, Harry can't think of an explanation right now. "I'm sure we can get to the bottom of this."

"Gosh, I'm glad you feel that way," Archer says. "Let's go down to my office and talk it over."

"What did you say?" Harry stammers.

"We'd like you to come along with us," the woman says.

"I've got some work to do," Harry says. He is trying to draw on some inner strength now, but it isn't there. "Look, I'm not under arrest, am I?" he asks.

"Forbid the thought," Archer says.

"Please," the woman adds. "I know you'd like to cooperate, wouldn't you, Mr. Funkhe?"

Harry telephones his home and leaves a message for Faith that he won't be meeting her for lunch. In front of Bayless and Archer, he walks down the mezzanine steps, watched by four bank employees. They stare at Harry, as if he was going to be executed on the street outside. Harry averts his gaze and keeps walking. The traffic on Wilshire is bumper to bumper and moving.

olor John Zito dead. Page five, Los Angeles *Times*, Sunday Metro Section: SLAIN COP DISCOVERED. Small box, page one, late Saturday edition, San Francisco *Chronicle*, and then page 2, main edition, Sunday *Chronicle*: OFFICER MURDERED IN MARIN.

Elgin pauses in his newspaper reading and thinks about the weekend, his late night flight to San Francisco, his attempts to get some sleep, the long walk he took on Venice beach when he got back. It is almost beautiful to be so tired. You can feel your body then. It's like being on some drug, the exhaustion is so exhilarating. Elgin thinks about Grace, there in the big house all alone, or with Soon Swee. Now that it's midweek she must be settling in, if you can say that about a safe house used by Korean drug dealers.

Over the weekend, after meeting with Detective Stark at the Zito house, Elgin drove over the San Rafael Bridge and killed time at the arboretum in Strawberry Canyon before his coded date with Grace at the Bateau Ivre. Then he went to the café and waited for about twenty minutes, drinking a cup of too sweet cappuccino with oat bran muffins. He knew he was going to catch an evening flight and he knew he was going to go home and take a long walk on Venice beach just to come down. When Grace came in finally, about five minutes late, he was glad to see her, giving her a big smile. When she sat down she looked as if she really needed to talk.

They chatted for about five minutes. All at once Elgin said,

"John Zito is dead. A real estate agent found him today up at his house in San Rafael. He'd been shot three times. Zipped up from stomach to neck."

Grace looked away. The waitress came and she ordered some herbal tea. Elgin thought she looked pale and undernourished, thinner than he remembered her, but maybe that was the effect of the black leather pants and dark sweater, her hair slicked back and tied behind her head. He wondered if she'd been working out at the dojo, because karate was something he knew she needed. Grace trembled as if she were cold.

"I'm sorry, Elgin," Grace said. "You're going to have to tie this up for me."

"Zito's wife had kicked him out of the house. He was living in a dive over on Turk, you know that. The real estate agent found him dead in the doorway, like he was on his way out. He had broken in to get something, but we know it wasn't clothes or money. He had his clothes all packed, swimming trunks, suntan lotion. His car was left running, and the trunk had coke residue."

"My landlady, and now Zito," Grace said quietly.

"Things are hairy, Grace," Elgin said. "I'd be shitting you if I said otherwise."

"And you wouldn't shit me, Elgin," Grace said.

"No, I wouldn't," Elgin said.

"Which means drug dealers killed them both," Grace said.

"It's possible," Elgin replied.

"Somebody's after me," Grace said. "They wanted to do me and John Zito, all at once."

Out on Telegraph the crowds were heating up. The street was thick with traffic, and you could hear shouting. Aimlessness was in motion all over Berkeley, bad vibes on the move.

"We don't know that," Elgin said. "How are things up in El Cerrito?"

"Everything is fine up in El Cerrito," Grace said. "My major-domo Soon Swee takes care of everything. He's armed to the teeth. There's a motion detector that's been installed in the back-yard and Soon takes a bead on everything that rustles out back.

He also mows the grass, washes my Lexus and my Viper and eats kimchi by the bucketful. His breath stinks and I think he wants to come on to me."

"I'm still worried about you, Grace," Elgin said.

"I know you are, Elgin," Grace replied. "I don't know what to do about that."

"We could pull the plug right now. We'd have Kim and four or five wholesalers. It wouldn't be a bad bust at all. We'd put a real dent in them, Grace. Whatever you want to do, Los Angeles is behind you, you know that."

"Let me think about it," Grace said. "Somebody tried to kill me last week. There's got to be a connection between Mrs. Piltka and Zito. Maybe it's something else entirely. Maybe it has nothing to do with the Koreans."

"That's all I'm going to be thinking about for a while," Elgin said. "Maybe we're lucky Soon Swee is taking such good care of you. Somebody stumbles around in that backyard they are going to eat a semiautomatic sandwich."

"Suppose I sit tight," Grace said. "In a few weeks Mr. Kim comes back with some product and I pretend to sell it. In six weeks after that, I'm going to ask him to bring in several pounds. If we don't pay for it and bust him, then we've really hurt them in Hong Kong."

"You really are braced for this, huh?" Elgin asked.

The tea came and Grace drank some slowly. She thought about her brother in San Jose who was losing interest, who looked like he might be getting ready to go back to heroin. She wished she'd kept her mouth shut about getting together so soon, because now with the events at the El Cerrito house, she was going to have to break her promise. On top of that, she had stopped going to the dojo, and was feeling her body going downhill. During her long weekend at the El Cerrito house, she had listened to music and tried to sleep. But instead of sleeping, she found herself restless and coming down with a cold. Her mind, which was the thing she had trained the hardest, was no longer supple and compliant. It was thinking by itself and without discipline. She would think about Elgin and then she would think about Greg and then she would think about Mrs. Piltka, and then she would begin to weep. Her discipline was focus, and without focus, Grace couldn't act.

"OK, Grace," Elgin said. "Sitting tight for six weeks is fine with me. But Kim is coming back to town and he's going to bring plenty of product. The department can't keep paying for that much product week after week, because we don't want the money getting out of the country. Unless I find the money laundering funnel, then we'll have to press Kim and then bust him if it doesn't work. I'll give you plenty of cash when you need it. But press Kim whenever you can. Wave money in his face. It worked once, it'll work again. I need to find out how they launder that money."

"Well, Elgin, this is what you wanted, isn't it?" Grace said. "It's your dream come true, your historic bust."

"It isn't that way," Elgin said.

"Oh God," Grace said. "Don't make this any harder than it already is."

Elgin tried to touch Grace's hand. She accepted the gesture, but then looked away again. "I've got to get going back to L.A.," Elgin said. "I've got reports to write and work to catch up on. But I'll come back next week or whenever you need me. Right now we're going through Zito's files, every last scrap of paper, and Stark is working his ass off on the murders. We've got to get a break on this soon, but right now, no gun, no eye witnesses, nothing. But I do know that Kyungmoon Nho and his boys were across the bridge when Mrs. Piltka got it. They could have hired it done, but it's a stretch. The question isn't so much why somebody tried to kill you—hell you're out on the street selling and dealing, and all that shit. But the question is why somebody killed Zito, what he was doing at his house, everything like that."

Grace smiled gently. "My mother was very old-fashioned," Grace said. "She taught me everything about *fung soi.* It's a Chinese mystical belief in power. If you're into the thing, it's supposed to give you an ability to predict and understand the environment, a kind of horoscope of place. Anyway, you buy a house, but only after checking out the way it faces the sun, the winds and how they blow, the soil. Once you put all that to-gether, you know whether your house is going to be happy if you buy it. So, I've been sitting on my hill in El Cerrito think-ing about the *chi* of my old apartment, its power. I'm afraid it had all bad signs. But hey, the house in El Cerrito has great chi. The front door faces west, there's a grove of eucalyptus on the south, the winds blow up and down, very good chi. I'm up there now, soaking up all this hot chi."

"It's birds for the Blackfeet," Elgin said. "Crows, eagles, hawks, especially crows. And elk, fox, and bears. Different chi, same idea."

"And how are the signs?" Grace asked.

"I'm just like you," Elgin said. "I'm out of practice and a long way from home."

Elgin looks up from his newspaper. He realizes that he has been fantasizing about Grace. The words SLAIN COP DISCOVERED jump off the page at Elgin. He hears traffic humming out on the Hol-lywood freeway. His office is a wall of compressed computer noise, walls gray, pink wainscoting, tones and hues soaking up conversation. Pretty soon, Elgin finishes his coffee and tries to stop thinking, hoping that something will come to him that way, but it doesn't. Nothing about the death of John Zito makes sense. Elgin wonders if he himself would have the guts to go away for a long time, to leave everything behind, get on the run, the way John Zito was doing. Australia? Alberta? Maybe Alaska, where it's dark for six months at a time.

Elgin takes out a pocketknife and slits around the articles in the newspapers and places them in his file. He goes out into the hallway and takes an elevator up to the tenth floor and walks down another long hallway of anonymous gray to the local of-fices of the Secret Service. He encounters men wearing suits and ties, and women in stiff, smart skirts and jackets. Elgin goes in-side the Secret Service office and tells the receptionist who he is. She smiles and buzzes him through a glass partition, metal de-tector. She leaves and comes back and tells Elgin he can go back.

Elgin makes his way through a warren of doorways and enters an office where he recognizes Tom O'Brien, the local Secret Service agent, and another man. He doesn't know the other man, but there's a woman in a suit with them. The unknown man has a funny crew cut, like a USC running back in the 1950s.

"Thanks for coming up, Elgin," O'Brien says. They all shake hands as Elgin is introduced around, Archer, Verna Bayless—Archer, Secret Service from San Francisco. Everybody seems happy to see Elgin. O'Brien adjusts the blinds so that only a dusting of sunshine filters through. Elgin thinks that it's the same up here on ten, same computer noise, same gray walls with pink wainscoting.

"Archer," O'Brien says.

"Can I call you Elgin?" Archer says.

Elgin nods pleasantly.

"I have a problem," Archer says. "It's a problem I hope you can help me with."

"Your problems are mine," Elgin says.

"Fair enough," Archer says. "Then I wonder if you could help me figure out how the fuck two hundred thousand in counterfeit American dollars shows up being laundered through a Westwood Village savings and loan. The counterfeit was being held by a San Francisco drug cop named John Zito, who I understand is your principal at SFPD."

Elgin sits down, stunned. "Could you run this all by me?" he asks.

"So you're interested?"

"Definitely," Elgin says. "Very interested."

"It goes something like this. A couple of months ago SFPD busted a caravan on Bay Street. The middle car was carrying the counterfeit in the trunk. One of the dealers got killed and Zito asked me if he could hold the money while they made a case on the dealers, and while the cop who killed the dealer went through his admin hearings. Hey, no problem, I tell Zito. Besides, I've seen this stuff before and we're deep into making a case on it. Zito gives me a receipt for the money and I go on my way. So, two days ago the Federal Reserve calls and says they've got two hundred thousand in counterfeit. I get a call from O'Brien, I come down, I recognize the money, which I last saw in the hands of John Zito. Now it's being laundered down here. I think, What the fuck? Can you blame me?"

"You know Zito got shot last week?" Elgin says.

"I was told this morning."

"Somebody shot him three times. By the look of it John Zito was heading upcountry, someplace warm."

"Which makes him a dirty cop."

Elgin explains the Korean operation, just to tell Archer the biggest thing he has going with Zito.

Verna Bayless says, "I've been over the books of a savings and loan like Archer told you. I'd say we've got a classic money laundering operation going there. We've got a vice president creating accounts and escrows, deposits which disappear. If you were interested in money laundering, then you'd be interested in this."

"Amazing," Elgin says. "Who's the vice president?"

"A geek named Harry Funkhe," Archer says.

"I always did like geeks," Elgin says. "How big a geek?"

"I was about to make him lay an egg so we can see," Archer says. "You want in?"

"Oh I want in, yeah," Elgin says.

"Fair enough."

Verna Bayless says, "Funkhe sprinkles his deposits like around two million. It will take me a couple of weeks to backtrack, but I'll tell you where it goes and who gets it. But it would be simpler if he just told us now."

Elgin walks to the window and lifts the blinds, letting in the outside light. Smog is convecting up the gullies above Hollywood, and everything is turning yellow as it goes. By noon, he thinks, we'll have stage two at least, and we'll all be breathing carbon monoxide and getting happy. Elgin turns around and says, "John Zito handled a fund of nine hundred thousand dollars for me. Two weeks ago he turned it over to me and I used it to impress some Korean heroin dealers who took it away and laundered it, but I don't know where or how. All I know is that my main Korean flies down to Los Angeles, and when he leaves the country for Hong Kong, he doesn't have the money anymore. Maybe he gives it to Harry Funkhe, the great geek."

"Let's go," Archer says.

Verna Bayless and Archer start out the door in tandem. "Harry Funkhe is two floors down," Archer says, turning. He smiles at Elgin. "And the asshole looks a little green."

Elgin says, "I like it," and follows.

Two floors down is a bare room, except for a long metal table and chairs. There are no windows. Ashtrays are scattered on the table, but no water carafes or glasses. Harry Funkhe sits at one of the places around the table, his hands folded on the table, as if in prayer. Elgin follows the agents inside the room and takes a good look at Funkhe. He is about forty, pudgy, soft-looking and meek. He has sandy-colored hair and some freckles and he looks scared as hell.

Archer says, "Harry, this is Agent Lightfoot of the Drug Enforcement Agency. You don't mind if he sits in on our little chat, do you?" All smiles.

Harry Funkhe shakes his head.

"Fine then," Archer says. "Let's tee it up."

27

harry Funkhe is at the bottom of the food chain. He can swim but he cannot hide.

The air around Harry is flat and unmodulated. It has a stale coolness that comes from being forced from floor vents, recirculated, cleaned, then forced again, again and again. It has, with bottled water, nothing in common with the elements that compose it. The light inside the room is, likewise, manufactured. As Harry sits by himself, he feels naked, glued to his seat by unseen forces, but he has no evidence that anything of the sort is happening to him. On the contrary, this feeling of helpless servitude comes from nowhere and goes nowhere, echoing off his slavery, crawling on his skin. It is the physical concomitant of pain, but there is no sensation to speak of. Harry would like to get up and walk around, but if anything, he feels embarrassed, too embarrassed to move. He thinks it would be absurd to walk around and around the rectangular metal table, chart its contours, hover nowhere in its simple shape. Perhaps, he decides, he could go and stand in a corner and try to stop hyperventilating. Instead, he sits quietly inside a cube of his own making, its detentive power everywhere around him in the silent rush of composite air, the manufactured light, the awesome suffocation of arrest.

And then Harry invents a mind game. Perhaps this idea proceeds from the brilliance of his despair. It has rules, perimeters. In a word, it is real: Harry imagines the best day of his adult life. He conjures a time about ten years ago when his wife, Faith, was pregnant with their child, and when they were living in a shit-hole in Culver City, a slab of concrete somewhere in the wilderness. Harry had just graduated from Pepperdine and he felt that he was on his way up a ladder of success, despite the shitty house in Culver City and the fat, pregnant wife. He could smell the eighties coming. Making money was in the air, you could sense its vague contours taking shape before your very eyes, and Harry knew he was, somehow, going to partake. If nothing else, he thought it would trickle down to him, that it was his due—that, like Reaganomics and the defense buildup, it was inevitable. You just had to stand at the trough with your mouth open and something would tumble in. Harry remembers, sitting in the cold rush of manufactured light, that one single shining day he closed the largest commercial deal of his young business life, a real head-on ripoff deal that would net him five points, a personal readjustment of income to six figures. Harry smelled ink as it hit paper. Now he can sense himself hitting the door and its tactile reflections, the heat outside on the street, and his joy when he pierced the wall of realization.

At a bar on Chandler Boulevard in Van Nuys he began to drink very dry gin gimlets, made with Rose's and a twist. In an hour, he must have had six or seven of them, straight up with just a blush of ice in the shaker. Harry sipped them down, feeling better and better, stronger and stronger in the faint red atmosphere of the suburban Los Angeles bar. During Happy Hour, Harry began a conversation with a blonde who sat at the next table, small round spaces you could share from far away, if you could hear. He remembers talking, talking and hitting it off big in a bar-sort-of-way, which means shouting, moving over, buying drinks. When he got tight, all Harry could think about was Faith's misshapen body and the big deal he had turned and the hard-looking blonde sitting next to him, how she smoked Kool after Kool and blew the smoke out sideways where it would hover and spin, then disappear. Harry went home to her apartment later and fucked her maybe two or three times, fucked her good, on the floor, in the bath, then once on the bed. Yet he managed to drive home around midnight and go straight into the shower without waking Faith.

Right now Harry thinks that was the best day of his life, certainly close.

The door behind Harry opens. Archer says to his back, "Harry, this is Agent Lightfoot of the Drug Enforcement Agency. You don't mind if he sits in on our little chat, do you?"

Harry shakes his head.

"Fine then," Archer says. "Let's tee it up."

The FBI agent sits across from Harry. Archer and Lightfoot flank him, two seats away. There are ashtrays on the table, but nobody smokes.

"Look now," Harry stammers. "Can you just tell me what this is all about?" Harry takes heart. He decides to portray himself as a victim, so long as that camouflage works. He will feign confusion, fatigue, lack of knowledge, which to his mind are the indicia of innocence. Surely, he thinks, these government agents will see him as a normal human being, someone above suspicion, vice president of a savings and loan in Westwood Village, a homeowner, father, husband. "I don't think it makes sense for me to stay around here very long. I've got a lot of work to do."

"You can go anytime," Archer says.

"Well, OK," Harry says. But he doesn't move. The moment passes, and Harry is surprised, but he feels, more than ever, immobilized. What is it that's holding him here?

"I mean you aren't under arrest," Archer says. "You aren't a suspect or the target of an investigation. As far as I'm concerned you can go anytime. You said you wanted to cooperate, that's all." Archer smiles and looks across the table at Agent Bayless, who holds a Sony tape recorder, hand-size, which runs and clicks, recording everything. Bayless nods her head. Archer looks at Harry, who says nothing. Harry shrugs, plays dead.

"Well, I want to get to the bottom of this, sure," Harry says finally. The silence is killing him. The thought that he can leave whenever he wishes unnerves and paralyzes him. It is the idea of becoming a specimen that holds Harry in place. "I suppose I could answer a few questions."

"Hey, I'm happy about your attitude," Archer says. Bayless puts the recorder on the table. Its tiny whir seizes Harry. It is like his own voice at the bottom of a bottle. "Suppose we start with the two-hundred-thousand-dollar deposit to the Southland trust. Your initials are on the deposit slips. You tell us who brought in the cash and you go home. That's really the nut here, Harry. The two hundred thousand in counterfeit you took in on deposit."

"I'd have to check my records," Harry says.

"It was a cash deposit?" Archer says.

Harry thinks to himself. He thinks, then he slows down and stops.

"It's recorded as cash," Bayless says. She opens her briefcase and looks inside, just so that Harry can't see what she's doing. The woman reads deposit entries for Harry, right into the microphone of the tape recorder. For every deposit and receipt, she pauses and looks up, over the briefcase, at Harry, who says nothing as the woman continues to read. "These deposits total over two million in the last two years. Around three hundred thousand at a time. The money stays six months, then disappears. All I want to know is where the money goes." The woman is wearing glasses. She takes them off and folds them on the table, looks up.

Suddenly, Harry remembers the name of the hard-looking blonde he fucked three times in that drunken encounter. It was Lilith, or maybe Eileen. He remembers her down on the floor with her legs up on the sofa, Harry between them on his knees. Lilith? She had pointy breasts, and acne on her face. Harry recalls he could hear her vomiting into the toilet bowl as he left, late at night.

Harry is confused. There are two questions, and he can't think of answers for either.

"Look," Harry says, "I'm not in control of everything that goes on day to day."

"Your initials are on the deposit slips," Bayless says. "Your initials are on the withdrawals."

"The OTS has been over our books," Harry says.

"We're not OTS," Archer interrupts. "I don't want to shit your ass, Harry, but this is about money laundering."

"Money laundering," Harry says.

"You know what that is, don't you?"

"There must be some mistake," Harry says. It comes out funny, like a recording with lint in the grooves.

"You're right there, Harry," Archer says.

Harry looks over at the man named Lightfoot. He thinks that if he looks around the room he'll find an ally. Somebody will take pity on him. Lightfoot remains impassive. "If it's about counterfeit money," Harry says, still looking at Lightfoot, "I didn't know anything about it. I don't pass counterfeit money. I'm just a vice president."

Archer moves one chair nearer Harry. The food chain shrinks, drawing Harry near its mouth. "Listen, asshole," Archer hisses in a whisper. "We know about Mr. Kim. We know about the Beverly Wilshire. We have a good idea where the money goes. I'm trying to give you a break here."

During this exchange, Bayless has turned off the tape recorder. She flips it on again when Archer is finished. Harry feels his life becoming abstract now. "Look, I think maybe I should see a lawyer. Something like that," Harry says, smiling.

Bayless flips off the tape recorder.

"A FUCKING LAWYER!" Archer screams, pounding the table with his fist. The table jumps. "You goddamn asshole prick," Archer continues, still shouting. "Now Harry wants a lawyer, Bayless, you hear that? Harry wants a fucking lawyer." Archer stands up, looms over Harry. Bayless plays back what Harry has said, then erases that portion while Archer watches. "Jesus H. Christ," Archer says. "This is fucking drug money, Harry. I want you to have a lawyer, Harry, I really do. I want you to have a lawyer to explain to you the thirty years you're going to do. I'm walking out of here and you're going to get your lawyer. But I'm now taking a hard attitude with you, Harry. Bank on it." Archer twirls away, nearly knocking over one of the metal chairs. Out the door he goes, breathing smoke.

"I'm sorry about him," Bayless says. She closes her briefcase.

The silent recorder stands across from Harry like an Easter Island carving. "But you know he isn't kidding about the thirty years."

Harry pleads, "I didn't know, really."

Lightfoot says, "We just want the higher ups. We know you're not a bad guy. I guess this can be a good experience or a bad experience for you. I mean, you can learn something or you can do thirty years for nothing, just because some Korean drug dealers got their claws into you. Believe me, I know how it is."

"You were saying, Harry?" Bayless asks.

Harry is hapless now. "I didn't know about drugs," he says. Maybe, he thinks, he has already been eaten, and is being shit out. "I didn't, I really didn't."

"Hey, I believe you," Lightfoot says. "I've been in the business ten years. You don't look like a real drug dealer to me."

Harry is relieved that he's found a friend. He wants to pour himself out to Lightfoot. He wishes for a cross to bear, vinegar to drink, a crown of thorns. "What am I going to do?" he asks nobody in particular.

"Suppose we go back on the record," Bayless says.

"I'll go get Archer," Lightfoot adds.

"We'll make a real record of all this. You can tell your side of it, make a voluntary statement. That's always a good start. Archer isn't such a terrible guy. I think he just lost his temper a little. He'll calm down."

Harry nods his assent to something he doesn't understand. He no longer feels like a victim, but he doesn't feel guilty either. He feels dirtied and in need of salvation. Harry is playing with the idea of his own complicity, but he isn't yet ready to confess. Yet somehow he feels better. The pain is transforming itself to pleasure.

"Would you go out and get Archer?" Bayless asks Lightfoot. "Tell him Mr. Funkhe is really going to cooperate. Try to calm him down, will you?" Funkhe smiles and Lightfoot smiles back at Funkhe. Everybody is getting to be friends. It is going to be a mutual effort.

Lightfoot steps into the hallway and closes the door. The

hallway is empty, except for Archer, who stands with his back to the wall, one foot up on the pink wainscoting.

"Congratulations," Lightfoot says.

"He broke down?"

"Worse than that. He's a fucking martyr."

"Well, he isn't a pro," Archer says. "He's just a greedy little wipe from Sherman Oaks. He never did have the stomach for this kind of deal."

"Still, he's an answer to my prayers," Lightfoot says. "I've got an agent in the East Bay trying to nail down these Koreans. Now that I know where their money goes, I can bust them quick. I bleed them dry of product and money, then take them away from mommy."

"Hey, I'm still confused about the counterfeit stuff. No Korean drug dealer is going to deposit two hundred thousand in counterfeit in a savings and loan. What the shit?"

"I think I can tell you about that," Lightfoot says.

"John Zito?" Archer says.

"Yeah, I think so. We know Zito is holding two hundred thousand counterfeit for you. He was holding nine hundred thousand real for me. He gives me the nine hundred thousand light two hundred thousand. The two hundred thousand he makes up for by substituting it in the nine hundred thousand he gives to me, out of your stash. That way, he winds up with two hundred thousand in real American, and the Korean drug dealers end up with nine hundred thousand, only with two hundred thousand in counterfeit. Then John Zito takes a powder to Mexico or Brazil and gets a nice tan. The only trouble is he got dusted on his way out of town."

"Yeah, what about that."

"I don't know."

"And where's the two hundred thousand he owes you?"

"Yeah, I don't know that either."

"But we know about this geek Harry, right?"

Lightfoot smiles, and follows Archer back into the interrogation room. Archer sits back down in a metal chair, two away from Harry, who is brooding. "I'm sorry I went off half-cocked," Archer says.

"No, I understand. It's OK," Harry admits.

"It's just a job," Archer says.

Harry has his head in his hands. He talks as Bayless records every word. "A man named Mr. Kim comes down to L.A. every six weeks. He brings cash and I make deposits for him. I didn't really know what I was doing was wrong. I just make deposits."

"Don't shit a shitter," Archer says.

Harry smiles grimly. "There are some Korean bankers who, like, take the money. I can fill you in on the whole thing."

"Good," Bayless says. "Let's get a stenographer down here."

"One more thing," Archer says. "Harry, you're under arrest."

Harry feels like crying.

Bayless takes a card out of her briefcase. "You have the right to remain silent. You have the right to an attorney. If you can't afford an attorney . . ."

Harry gropes for his past with Lilith, or Eileen, the great raw rush of power as he sucked her down to the floor.

he oak is cool and smooth against the soles of her feet. She glides across its surface, an experience both familiar and comforting. She recalls the many late nights she has spent working it with an oily rag, alone in the many-windowed night. She glides and glides, thinking of herself on an ice-bound lake with the wind whispering in pines, circles of light haloed down from a perfect pearl gray sky. On and on she whirls, performing kata after kata, one rhythmic transition after another, coming from some region of her mind and body that is deeper even than memory, a blood-and-sinew region beyond reaction or temper. Gradually, she feels her arms and hands grow warm, then her chest and legs, her ankles. She fits inside the room. She is lodged inside a huge rectangle of space with narrow windows high up toward the ceiling. It is empty space, punctuated only by the tatami strike mat, by a heavy punching bag in a corner, by a Japanese flag. As she dances, she proceeds beyond her own fears, rendering herself invisible to them, not even aware of the sensei who stands behind a glass partition in his office, silently watching, his hands folded inside the white cuffs of his gi. Time strands Grace here. She seems a witness to her own extinction, her hands and knuckles like ineloquent beasts. Numb, she is beyond pain too. And in this state, there is nothing save the approach of exhaustion and joy. An hour passes, perhaps more. Grace kicks and kicks, striking air, six inches beyond air, through to some target that seems impossible to strike. She is so fatigued that she forgets herself. She meditates, which means that she thinks of nothing. When she is ready to leave she backs away from the space, out the door, uttering Ussss! The sensei bows, Grace returns the bow. Outside, on

Telegraph, the day has grown dark and rainy. Grace is so light she thinks she can fly.

X

When Clemente Moreno examines his soul, he finds fear. As is the case with many men, he is afraid of what he cannot control. He is afraid of mistaking the things he can control for those things he cannot, and so he bandages his motives as if they were wounds. It has been weeks since he has seen the Shark, Arturo Cruz, and even though Moreno knows that John Zito is dead, he has no idea what caused the disappearance of Tiburon, who should be in the streets, seeking more of Moreno's money. This aspect of things, the uncontrollability of life, what might happen, frightens Moreno most of all. He fears being busted by the narca. As he thinks about that Friday afternoon when he went inside her apartment, through the window above the fire escape landing, and how dark the rooms were, how dusty, Moreno grows cold inside. He cannot imagine doing such a thing twice. He remembers the weight of the gun in his hand, the smell of smoke as it closets itself in the apartment. He believes he can hear the dull thud of the bullet as it entered the woman, whoever she was. Moreno realizes that luck was with him, and he knows that he cannot control luck, any more than he can control fate, even though they are different aspects of reality. This is, in fact, the very problem of life, and with selling drugs. The variables are everywhere, on every face, so many personalities.

Moreno sits in his apartment. He yells for the woman Paz to bring him a shot of tequila, which she does without question. Moreno sits in his chair with the Colt on his lap where he can, again, feel its weight, the heaviness of its purpose, the inevitability of its cause. Moreno curses the woman narca, hexing her perhaps. The longer she lives, the more certain it becomes that he will be arrested and put into prison, that his present comfortable and enviable life will be destroyed forever, and that he will be sent back to Mexico. If this happens, he will never be the master of all he sees, a wealthy and respected man, someone to be reckoned with, feared even. And so it is the equation of fear that Moreno balances in his mind, that motivates him to sip tequila and chew his anxiety, feel the burning in his mouth and stomach. Fear will motivate him to kill the narca again. This time, he reasons, there will be no mistake. Fate, unlike luck, arrives when it is needed.

Paz begins to rub Moreno's back and shoulders. Standing behind the chair, she touches him courteously, massaging the muscles in his neck and upper arms. In Spanish, again, she asks if she may see a doctor. Moreno growls a no, but encourages her to keep touching him. After a while, he grows weary and pushes her away, then dresses in jeans and white guayabara, a light jacket to keep off the rain. From an open bottle of tequila he takes a long drink and tells the woman he will return in two hours, to prepare him a meal and hot bath. Paz lowers her eyes, which is a sign of recognition and duty, her way of combining resignation and agreement. To Paz, these reactions are one and the same. For years, she has been unable to differentiate between them. Moreno understands this too, and leaves the room without comment.

Moreno drives the Impala out of his rented garage and heads down Guerrero Street to Army, and then hits the James Lick freeway just as afternoon traffic begins to clog the approaches to the Bay Bridge. A light rain falls, which slows traffic. Moreno tunes into a Spanish language station in San Jose and listens to music as he crawls along with all the commuters, bumper to bumper and moving. In his mind, Moreno has already committed murder. Over and over he has rehearsed the event, so that he knows it, has become its friend. It no longer terrifies him. He sees himself driving to the private road, parking the Impala. He sees himself walking in the rainy half dark through eucalyptus groves and clumps of lemon and orange trees where there are caverns of shadow. As if he were hiding in a painted cloud above the proceedings, Moreno envisions himself at the narca's house, peering at her through a yellow skylight, firing a fatal shot. He is nerveless like God. He is safe, flying away.

Moreno crosses the bridge in traffic and goes north to Albany where he exits. It is nearly full dark and clouds roll in off the ocean, covering the hills in mist. In the short uphill stretch that is Albany itself, Moreno sees people in the streets, coming and going from shops and bars. The restaurants are crowded. Beyond the two blocks of city, there is a maze of oak-shrouded streets, more hills, then shaded side lanes where there are oleander hedges and tree roses. Moreno locates the private drive, parks, and starts up the sidewalk, keeping to the shaded side. From just below the narca's house, he can see a Dodge Viper parked in the circular drive, the house above the drive, some lighted windows. Another car is parked inside a garage. He passes to the side of the house. Inside the pocket of his jacket, the Colt rests.

Moreno finds a hill sloping up behind the house. It proceeds sharply to a fenced reservoir. The hill is an open space hedged by eucalyptus, several lemons. Moreno moves, keeping to the trees. There are other houses, but far away and screened from view. No dogs bark, and this surprises Moreno. He stops, catching his breath. He is sweating inside the cotton jacket and his hands are wet. He goes to his haunches, and then his knees, trying to see inside the house. There is a flagstone porch, a patio and glass doors, someone moving inside the house. Moreno readies and moves downhill, expecting fate to act.

When he is close, he recognizes the woman. She is bent over the sink, washing fruit. Moreno stands beside a covered table, beneath an umbrella which partially shelters him from the rain which drips, strikes metal, drips. The sound counts seconds away, in much the same way a metronome casts a piano its notes. "Fucking *puta*," Moreno hisses. His heart beats wildly.

Moreno does not hear the shot which sends a bullet deep into his neck, just below the right ear. Something bright and intangible mediates the event and rushes into Moreno's brain, just before he falls. He is full of light and sound, but it is not of his own making. He falls against the table, shoving aside a chair. The Colt clatters to the flagstone porch where it glistens in the rain. Moreno watches a ribbon of blood descend his right arm. He tries to catch the liquid in his fingers and then he feels himself stumble on numb legs which no longer support his weight. He lies now, drinking in the rain, exposed to the light. In time, he recognizes the narca, who looks down at him, and a man, an Asian whose face he does not know.

The Asian man aims a weapon at Moreno's face.

"No, not now," the narca says.

"How do you like the motion detector now?" the Asian man says. He lowers the weapon to his side.

Moreno tries to think. He does not understand the silence that has struck him down. The cold rain mixes with the warm blood and steams up. He is burning. For a brief moment, Moreno is somewhere else in time, watching a *vaquero* die in the dusty moonlight. The woman kneels above him. "Moreno," she says. "What are you doing here?"

Moreno smiles. He wishes to accommodate her. He tires of thinking and tries to swallow, but cannot. In Spanish he says, "It's true then, you're a narca?"

The woman shakes her head. "Speak English, Moreno," she asks. "In English, quick."

"I am unlucky," Moreno whispers. "I don't know."

"Don't know what?" the woman asks.

"One of us must live, the other must die," Moreno says, choking. "That is the face of fate, no?"

"But why?" the woman asks, still incredulous. The Asian man moves off, then back. Moreno does not understand the game. For a moment, he wishes to laugh.

"I am dying, yes?" he asks.

The woman nods. This is mysterious, Moreno thinks. How can a man die without pain? He cannot feel his legs. It cannot be so easy to enter . . . well, can it? "God help me," Moreno groans.

"Tell me why you're here, quick," the woman says.

"Zito," says Moreno. "Zito."

"He was bleeding you?"

"Yes, very much," Moreno says. Moreno is cold now. He wishes for a priest, but says nothing.

"Zito told you about me?" the woman asks.

"He was a bad man," Moreno says. "He said you were a narca."

"Narca?" the Asian man says. He moves close. "You mean a narc?"

Sound is a coiled shell in Moreno's ear. The rain falls steadily, filling his eyes.

"Go inside," the woman says to the Asian man.

"A narc," the Asian man says. "You knew Zito?"

The Asian woman has a Glock upturned and with it she shoots the Asian man. Again, the sound has no meaning for Moreno. He sees the man fall, beside him, only face down and motionless. Together, they lie just outside the reach of the umbrella. Moreno wishes he could crawl beneath the table, so as to be out of the rain.

"Did you kill the old lady on Geary?" the woman asks. She is breathing heavily.

"Help me," Moreno says, and closes his eyes again.

"*Vaya con Dios,*" the woman says.

✕

Paz is washing her long black hair. She will dry it with a towel, and shake it before the radiator until it is soft. Then she brushes it while sitting in front of the window that looks down on Guerrero Street and the gathering night. Rain falls steadily from a dark sky, and the streets are crowded. She eats a candy skull, and thinks of the many hours she spent preparing for the Day of the Dead and how little appreciated were her acts. Although she is uneducated, she often contemplates the violence that men do to themselves and others, particularly the small acts which seem insignificant, but which loom large in the inventory of human wrong. Her nose bleeds slightly, and she halts the flow with a cotton plug. She wonders why Moreno will not allow her to see a doctor. She wonders why he is unwilling to go to church. To Paz, God is present, and in everything, even in the candy skulls she eats. She believes in ritual and rite. When she looks out at the street, she begins to wish that she could see her mother again, even though that would mean returning to the streets of Agua Prieta. She watches and watches, until she sees two police cars funnel through, their red lights dancing. The cars stop right outside, and four police officers get out. Paz panics then, for what is happening is something she fears most, especially since the crazy police invaded her home. Her fear rises to action, and she goes to the closet where Moreno keeps his money and his drugs. Paz puts on a light coat. She gathers all of Moreno's money, which he keeps in a shoe box, puts the shoe box, along with some scarves and socks, in a wicker shoulder bag. Hurriedly, she leaves the apartment and walks slowly down the hall, just as two officers burst up the stairwell at the other end. "Hey," one of them says to her. "A guy named Moreno live up here?" Paz smiles. "Moreno, sí," she says, pointing. The officers go by, heedless, as Paz goes down the stairs and outside. Paz feels light enough to fly. She thinks of her mother and clutches the wicker basket to her side, keeps right on walking.

29

Mr. Kim affects a disdain for *fung soi*. Nonetheless, he comes to Po Fook Hill where the wind and water are favorable. The sun plunges and the air is sweet with mimosa. Jagged valleys and pyramidal hills jut down toward Hong Kong Harbor, which is, in Mr. Kim's mind, primordial. Mr. Kim is protected here, with one side of Po Fook like the rounded flank of a white tiger, another ragged as a green dragon. Yet, it is here, high above the city, that investors and developers have built a columbarium, part temple, part crematory, a vast dreamlike project with turtle ponds and marble tombs to house the dead of Hong Kong's devoted Buddhists, who worship their ancestors in the old way, whose ideas of wind and water operate to give Po Fook Hill a unique hold on the people's minds.

Mr. Kim has come here to celebrate his American success. It gives him pride and satisfaction to be responsible for the syndicate's largest single delivery of raw heroin to the United States since beginning business only four years before. Now, in the deepening reds and golds of the sunset, Mr. Kim touches the cool metal of his Lincoln Town Car, speaks to the driver, and breathes in the silky air of evening. He smells sea and air. He stands, arms folded, like a Shan overlord, like General Khun Sa himself, whose bandit armies provide the raw chandu, which becomes opium, which becomes heroin, its long trail leading east from Burma to Laos to Hong Kong and onto fishing vessels and thereafter to Los Angeles, a jungle trail, like the road up Po Fook Hill, winding, winding, winding. Mr. Kim looks across the hills to where a Chinese family are burning their paper imitations of money, jewelry, video cameras, gifts to a dead ancestor. Smoke trickles up and erodes. Mr. Kim says to his driver, "Take me to the airport." He slides into the plush interior of his American car, already anticipating the whores of San Francisco.

Grace steps outside the El Cerrito house where she lives alone. The whole bay is backlit by an enormous sun. Behind her, inside the door, is Elgin Lightfoot, dressed in jeans and sweater, with his long hair tied back by a red bandanna.

"I can't wait to see Mr. Kim's face," Elgin says.

Grace turns slightly. "I'm worried about my brother," she says. "He's been gone from the halfway house for weeks now. My parents haven't heard from him, and he hasn't tried to call me at the department. He does his disappearing act all the time, but he usually shows, wanting a loan or a place to crash. It worries me, Elgin."

"When this is over, we'll go looking for him," Elgin says. "We'll overwhelm him with concern. He's probably down in Santa Clara having a good time."

Grace shudders, as if cold. "Do we have all this figured out, Elgin?" she asks. Her voice is small and far away. She hasn't seen Elgin for weeks either. Both of them have been waiting for time to pass. "Is this really over?"

"Everything is tied up tight," Elgin says. He wants to put his hand on Grace's shoulder, but he doesn't do it. The moment passes, and the urge as well. He understands the fleetingness of opportunity and emotion, their unfathomable dovetailing. It seems to him another age when he sat with Grace beneath the leathery limbs of a cottonwood tree in Sonoma. "For one thing," Elgin says, "our friend Harry Funkhe has given us everything and everybody in the money laundering operation. Right now Harry is sitting quietly in Westwood Village waiting for the bottom to fall out, the boot to drop. We're looking for Mr. Kim to fly in and when he sets foot in the airport, my guys are going to serve arrest warrants in Honolulu and Los Angeles, some subpoenas.

We've got about two or three million tied up in Los Angeles right now, and another three million in Honolulu. When the syndicate can't get that money out, they'll be seriously bruised. If Kim brings in the three pounds you asked him to, they'll lose that too, and that's a goddamn lot. I'd like to tell you we know how they smuggle it, but we don't. We'll arrest a dozen guys, and hope somebody cracks. The bottom line is the syndicate is finished. We let Kim walk up here, say hello, and then, boom, he's gone."

"And we know Zito's story?" Grace asks.

"Yeah, I think so," Elgin says.

"He really turned me over to Moreno?" Grace asks. "I mean, handed him the whole story?"

"It looks that way," Elgin says.

Grace is busy remembering. "We're sure?" she says.

"For what it's worth, I had a long talk with Zito's impairment officer. She's pretty sure Zito had a coke habit, probably supported it for a couple of years on what he could steal from the property department downstairs at the Hall of Justice, and here and there from busts, scruffing the shit from suspects. You know, bust a guy with an ounce, steal a gram, scrape some onto your cuff and snort it, run the gun in, and keep two grams to do later in your room. She thinks it just got to be too big a habit to support that way and Zito turned over and went after a source, big time. I think that source turned out to be Clemente Moreno, only Moreno wasn't enjoying having bites taken out of him by John Zito." Elgin goes out the front door and stands beside Grace to watch the sunset. It is a long, delirious glide of ocean and color. "Moreno probably knew that Zito would sit on him and sit on him. Zito gives Moreno your name to back up his claim on Moreno's shit, and bingo, Moreno knows he has to kill you both."

"And so poor Mrs. Piltka had to die."

"And Zito sprinted out of town with two hundred thousand in DEA money, only he blew a fuse in San Rafael."

Grace sits down, Elgin beside her. Inside the house are six heavily armed DEA agents, two men from SFPD with their dogs, a Contra Costa County sheriff's officer, and one observer from the U.S. Attorney's office, special drug task force detail.

Grace says, "I guess we should have checked the money we gave to Zito."

"It would have helped, only who knew? I guess Zito got to the point where he needed money and took it from the DEA fund I gave him. He had a bunch of counterfeit he was holding for the Secret Service, and so he took two hundred thousand of that and put it in with ours. He probably figured we wouldn't check it out, why should we? And so, we give counterfeit to Mr. Kim who gives it to Harry Funkhe, who gives it to the local Federal Reserve. Bingo, it all falls into place, except for Mr. Kim, who is going to think it fell apart."

"I just don't get it," Grace says. "Did Zito hate himself that much?"

Elgin shrugs. "He lived in a cold world. When you get around to vodka and coke, nothing looks right anymore except more vodka and coke. The impairment officer had a word for it, denial. To me, it's more complicated even than that. I used to watch my mother go out for booze, and come back with booze and men who would beat her. That's cold too, cold as hell. I think about her all the time, and wonder what made her do it. And I don't know. With Zito, I haven't given it as much thought, so I have no idea. Sometimes a guy wants to say, quick, let me go to sleep, this shit is too awful. Sometimes he thinks it isn't worth it staying awake for the next sick scene. Too much self-involvement, which is the same as saying too much self-pity."

"What are we going to do about Kyungmoon Nho and Kip?"

"Not a fucking thing," Elgin says.

"You mean, you aren't going to do anything. I guess I mean what am I going to do?"

Elgin watches the clouds. They are puffy pink and ragged. The gulls circle gracefully.

When Elgin says nothing, Grace says, "Are you staying in?"

"The DEA?" Elgin says, surprised. "I guess. I think about Montana a lot, like it's my home. But when I really think about it, I don't suppose I have a home. Indian boarding school, the army, the DEA, it's all the same thing. When I go back to Montana, I play hoops with the kids and I see them acting out the same frustrations I acted out as a kid and I realize I can't tell them a thing about growing up, which is about the only thing I can think of worth doing—that would be worthwhile if it were possible. But it isn't. Shit happens fast now. I ask myself if John Zito wasn't partly right when he decided to fly away."

"I could really care about you, Elgin," Grace says.

"But," Elgin says.

"But I'm not ready," Grace says, laughing. "I don't know what that means, but it's the truth."

Elgin looks around pointedly. "You're right about one thing, Grace. This house has great *sung foi.*" They share another laugh as Elgin puts his arm around Grace. "So, you staying in, or what?"

"I need some time to sort out my brother's problems. It would do me good to focus on him for a while. Then I'd like to travel. Go away somewhere, maybe Asia. I think I've done some awful things I need to understand."

"Be easy," Elgin says. "Me, I'm going back to L.A. and watch the Lakers and count the homeless in Santa Monica. It's like bird-watching now, counting the homeless."

"You're a good man, Elgin," Grace says quietly.

"No, no," Elgin says. "I wanted Kyungmoon Nho myself. I'd have done him too. All that shit, I could taste it. I'm so tired of these drug cowboys, you know. Well, I could have blown him away too."

"But you didn't," Grace says. "It was me out there, breaking boards like an asshole."

Elgin struggles with something. "Oh, all this is so much bullshit I can't believe it," he says. It is a relief to laugh again.

Grace looks down at the Bayshore freeway. Traffic streams like fluid neon. "Did we ever figure out who killed Zito?" she asks.

"If it wasn't Moreno, then we didn't. And I don't think it was Moreno. The ME did a serious autopsy, and the time of John's death was a Friday afternoon. That puts it around the same time somebody was up trying to kill you. We know that was Moreno. So it doesn't seem likely he could have stalked Zito over in San Rafael too."

"And what happened to the money Zito was carrying?"

"The guy who killed Zito got a windfall, how do I know?

Don't get me wrong. Stark did a good job at the scene. His people scoured those hills for miles around looking for a gun, a bill, a footprint, anything. They went door to door interviewing everybody. They turned over every rock and knocked on every door, and didn't find a damn thing. But I tell you, the same gun didn't kill your landlady and John Zito. So, unless we get lucky, we aren't going to find out who killed John Zito."

"Maybe it doesn't matter," Grace says.

"Maybe," Elgin says. "Can we see Mr. Kim coming from here?" he asks.

"I think so, he's due anytime. You'd better go inside. You might scare him off, even though he's seen your face before."

"OK," Elgin says. "I do have a scary face."

"I'm just going to sit out here," Grace says. "Maybe if I sit here Mr. Kim won't think about Soon Swee not being around."

Elgin stands. "About your brother," he says. "How about if I give you a hand with him?"

"I don't think so," Grace says. "We grew up and grew apart. There's not much connecting us, really. I think it would just confuse things to have another person around, especially a cop. I'm not using that as an excuse, it's just the way it is."

"I guess it wouldn't work to ask you to come visit me in Los Angeles? We didn't see much of Disneyland the first time, you know."

Grace smiles. She thinks she sees a taxi coming up the Albany hill. It is just a slash of orange and black, but it is coming nonetheless. Elgin goes inside and closes the door. He makes the rounds of all the rooms, touching bases.

The taxi approaches uphill, then turns into the circular drive. Grace can see Mr. Kim in the backseat, counting his money, speaking to the driver, getting out of the cab, the cab pulling away. Mr. Kim comes partway up the steps, and then turns to watch the taxi disappear. Grace stands now, and smiles a greeting to Mr. Kim. She is clear in her head. The target is six inches behind Mr. Kim.

Mr. Kim is carrying a small suitcase. He puts the bag down and buttons his suit coat. He is wearing an expensive and shiny sharkskin suit, white shirt, pale blue tie with white stripes. His black hair shines. He walks purposefully up the stairs to where Grace waits.

"I hope you had a good journey," Grace says.

"Same thing, same thing," Mr. Kim jokes. He is self-assured. Glossy-eyed, frisky. "They show an Eddie Murphy movie. Do you like Eddie Murphy?"

"Not much," Grace admits.

"I don't know why they show that movie," Mr. Kim says. "Next time I take a Japanese airline and see what they gonna show on the movie."

"But otherwise," Grace says.

"Everything very satisfactory," Mr. Kim says.

"You have the product?"

"Of course," Mr. Kim snaps, displeased. He is used to giving orders, asking questions. He senses an impertinence which is particularly displeasing as it comes from the mouth of a woman. "You the real question here," he says.

"Don't worry," Grace answers.

Mr. Kim steps to the door. He looks down at Grace, emphasizing the difference in their height. "I have to tell you," Mr. Kim says. "Not everybody in Hong Kong happy about working with a girl. Maybe I stick up for you. But for now, you have to prove our trust has not been misplaced. And you have to prove yourself to me, as well." He smiles. "But this product the finest."

"The product is already spoken for," Grace says.

"I am impressed," Mr. Kim says.

Grace opens the door so that Mr. Kim can step inside in front of her. It is warmly dark inside, the shades drawn. It is decorated much as the Koreans had decorated it before, white shag carpet, black furniture, vases, lithographs, a look of modern shiny steel and chrome.

Sitting down, Mr. Kim opens his suitcase to reveal a black plastic sack. "More than a kilo," he says. Already Elgin has appeared in one doorway, more agents in another.

"I want you to be very quiet, you shitbag," Grace says.

Mr. Kim arches an eyebrow. He cannot believe what he just heard.

30

On Potrero Hill there are no metaphors, no hidden meanings. These women's lives symbolize nothing. Each shimmering moment is the truth.

"Oh honey, hold still," Paula says.

Her sister Gloria says, "I'm just wanting to change the channel."

They smoke and watch TV together, one of their unspoken bonds. The room smells of a boxed permanent solution. Gloria taps through the remote. Electrons shift through their changes, smoke gods on the screen, a range of colors and hues and garbled sound, music. Paula puffs her menthol brand. She has switched twice this month, maybe changing to generic soon to counteract all the price hikes. While she smokes, she continues to dab solution on Gloria's pink cocoon of tiny buttons and bows that are hair curlers. Behind them, the bed is unmade, the dishes unwashed.

"There *ain't* nothing on, honey," Paula says.

"Then what am I paying thirty dollars a month for, anyway?" Gloria says in a stylized whine.

"Well, I don't know," Paula says. "But there ain't nothing on, so there." Paula rolls another curl, dabs at it. "Isn't there a talk show on? There's always a talk show."

"On Saturday morning?" Gloria asks.

"Crap, this stuff burns," Paula says. "Give me that *TV Guide* over there." Paula pauses to read through the guide, messing the pages with her wet fingers. *"Bonanza,"* she announces. *"Fly Fish-*

ing Video Magazine, Hey Vern, It's Ernest, and *Paid Programming.*"
Paula puts down the guide and crushes her cigarette in an ashtray overflowing with butts. The gray day stirs inside the room.
Standing there in the smoke with the gray day stirring is like
wearing wet clothes to bed. The evidence of a delivered pizza
turns green on the kitchen counter in the next room. For breakfast, there are store-bought doughnuts. "Something called *Rug-
rats* on Nickelodeon, get that!"

"That's what I need," Gloria says. "A rugrat!"

"I thought you was going to have a little Mexican rugrat
once," Paula says.

"Don't remind me," Gloria says. "Besides, you did worse
yourself if you ask me."

"Don't remind me!" Paula exclaims. Now she must shout
over the noise of a World Vision commercial. "Hey," Paula says,
"you want to watch MTV? You want to watch videos?"

Gloria taps the remote. A band called Nose Candy performs
heavy metal in black and white. The two women are poised in
front of the tube, hearing the music, immersed in its nothingness. Gloria taps the remote again.

"What'd you do that for?" Paula asks.

"I'll switch it back," her sister says.

"Well?" Paula asks in five minutes.

"Don't get in a hurry," Gloria says. "I just don't like metal,
you know that. It's too damn busy."

A feminine deodorant pad commercial, then the sound of a
crash outside the apartment, both sounds incongruous. The
noise outside reaches up to the two women on the second floor
of the apartment building. Paula stops working on her sister's
hair, and goes to the window.

"Well, shit," Paula says. "Somebody in a powder blue Cadillac just knocked over all them trash cans."

Gloria taps the remote, off goes the TV. Now that it is quiet,
she can hear a car engine running high and hot. A horn beeps
once long, then once short, and stops. For a while there is nothing, and Gloria taps the remote again. It is cable channel 2, the
one that shows the time, temperature, and schedules.

"Well, double shit," Paula says. "I think it's that asshole Arturo Cruz."

Gloria hurries to the window, trailing permanent solution. She is wearing a flowered dressing gown, slippers. She stands at the window with her sister and watches Arturo Cruz emerge from a brand-new Cadillac, stagger against the door he has just opened. The door slams shut, nearly catching the man's hand as it does. Cruz wheels once and nearly falls, but regains his balance. There are four trash cans in various states of destruction under the wheel wells of the car. Two have been sent rolling into the open field. The car itself is nosed to the edge of the building's wall. Luckily, there are no windows until the second story, because the hill slants so sharply down. As always, the City is far away and gray, like a pile of boulders or rubble.

"Crap, crap," Gloria says. "He's drunk as hell."

"What are we going to do?" Paula asks her older sister.

The man fumbles for something and reaches air. He leans inside the open window of the Cadillac and comes up with a blue gym bag which he clutches like a woman he is dancing with, hearing strange silent music. Minutes pass as the man struggles for direction.

"I need this like a hole in the head," Gloria says. She is angry and frightened. Paula beside her, in her white cosmetician's uniform, blinks.

"You want me to stay?" Paula asks.

"Would you?" Gloria says.

"Jesus, he's drunk as hell."

"Don't worry, honey, he's pretty good most of the time."

"Like when he blackened your eye."

Gloria puts on a pair of glasses. Cruz hunches as if he were about to vomit, but doesn't.

"Where'd that little shit get a brand-new Cadillac?" Gloria wonders out loud.

"How long's he been gone, anyway?" Paula asks.

"Two months and something," Gloria answers.

"Shit, he's coming up here."

The women watch Cruz weave toward the back entrance to

the complex. He takes a step, stops, another step, lunges, falls back, then moves on. He is making slow progress. Cruz seems to look up but the women are out of his view.

"Let's not answer the door," Paula suggests.

"He'll probably pass out."

"You suppose he stole that car?"

"I don't doubt it," Gloria says.

Now they hear Cruz in the hallway. His body hits the walls and pings away, but here he comes. The women are still beside the window when Cruz pounds on the door. Gloria goes over and opens it.

Cruz falls inside the room. He is wearing a gray leather jacket, black T-shirt, and jeans. Something has stained the T-shirt, probably beer. The stink of him fills the room. Cruz tries to focus and speak, but nothing happens for him. His eyes are blazing red, moused closed. He holds the blue gym bag under his right arm like an animal he's found on the street.

"Well," Gloria sings, "come on in."

Immediately, Cruz falls to his knees and gets back up slowly. Gloria returns to the center of the room where the sisters have set up a table and chair for the permanent. She lights a cigarette and smokes it for a minute or two, watching Cruz get to his feet. He's been in the room for three minutes, and he hasn't said one sentence, much less a single word. He is in one of those deep drunks that is an automatic pilot of the brain. The only thing that could help is more booze, but he doesn't seem to have any. Gloria exchanges a knowing look with her sister. This isn't going to be as bad as either of them thought.

Cruz staggers forward, upsetting a pan of permanent solution. The liquid drips from the table to the floor. Cruz falls straight down to the floor like a bomb.

"Smooth move Ex-Lax," Gloria whispers.

Cruz snores.

Paula moves over to where she can get a good look at the passed-out drunk lying in a puddle of permanent solution.

"Now what?" Paula says sarcastically.

Gloria leans over the prone drunk. One of his hands is upturned, revealing a pentagram tattoo. She sees something curious, and opens the unzipped gym bag. She sees cash, nothing but hundred-dollar bills, some in bundles wrapped by rubber bands, some crumpled and wet. There is nothing else inside the bag, just cash. Her sister looks inside. Gloria walks over to the window and stares down at the blue Cadillac nosed up to the building.

Paula follows her over. "Where'd he get it?" she says.

"He stole it likely," Gloria says. "Or it's drug money."

"That much?"

"I don't know. How would I know?"

"How much you think it is?"

"I didn't count it, did I?"

"Well, don't get mad at me. What are you getting mad at me for?"

"I'm not mad at you," Gloria says.

"That's thousands of dollars, honey," Paula says.

"I bet it's more than that."

Paula goes over to the gym bag and looks inside again. Cruz makes a noise, but not the waking-up kind.

"Well," Paula says.

"Let's take it," Gloria says.

"And do what?"

"Just take it."

"Just take it, just like that?"

"What's stopping us?"

"Nothing," Paula says, pouting.

"You like how you're living?" Gloria asks her sister.

"NO."

"Neither do I."

Gloria begins plucking curlers out of her hair. She takes them out quickly, one by one.

"We'd have to leave here," Paula says.

Gloria shrugs, takes out more curlers. "I'm going," she says. "You're welcome to come along."

"Where to?"

"Florida."

"Florida," Paula says. "We could go to France."

They giggle quietly. "I'm going," Gloria says.

"Florida's OK, though," Paula says.

"I didn't say we couldn't go to France," Gloria says.

Gloria pulls on a pair of corduroy pants and a sweater. She dries her hair with a towel. Under the influence of the permanent solution, her hair has gone orange.

"Can we take your car?" Paula asks.

Gloria picks up the gym bag full of money. The women, one white-uniformed cosmetician and one orange-haired barmaid, are ready to leave. Together, they ease around the prone man and close the door.